THE MINER'S MYTH

THE MINER'S MYTH
BY RUSSELL W. JOHNSON

ADDITIONAL
PRAISE

"Russell Johnson has done it again! Leaping effortlessly between excitement, adventure, and good ol' fashioned fun, *The Miner's Myth* cements Sheriff Mary Beth Cain as one of fiercest characters in any mystery today. When a Detroit heavyweight invades her small town, Mary Beth doesn't hesitate to go toe-to-toe with his thugs. After all, big city gangsters are no match for a woman born and bred in the state of West—by God—Virginia!"

—**J.G. Hetherton**, author of *Last Girl Gone* and *What Lies Beneath*

"With The Miner's Myth, Russell W. Johnson brings to a close one of the finest mystery trilogies in recent memory. Over the course of this series, which started with the explosive The Moonshine Messiah, Sheriff Mary Beth Cain has evolved into such a complex and compelling protagonist. This third book is definitely the most personal for the main character and employs a unique structure that keeps the reader guessing, as well as turning pages. The finale is so damn satisfying, even though I am personally sad to say goodbye to all these wonderful characters. The Miner's Myth—which is equal parts Elmore Leonard and John Grisham—is one of the year's most entertaining reads that stands on its own, but is all the more satisfying for readers of the entire Mountaineer trilogy. I cannot recommend this novel enough."

—**Casey Stegman**, writer of *"Murder in the First"* column
for *Mystery Tribune*.

RUSSELL W. JOHNSON

THE MINER'S MYTH

A MOUNTAINEER MYSTERY

Published by **Shotgun Honey Books**

1808 Huber Road
Charleston, WV 25314
www.ShotgunHoney.com

Cover Design by Bad Fido.

Trade Paperback ISBN: 978-1-956957-84-6
Digital eBook ISBN: 978-1-956957-85-3

10 9 8 7 6 5 4 3 2 1   25 24 23 22 21 20

*This book is about endings and new beginnings.
It is dedicated to Dylan and Gabi
who are my new beginnings.*

THE MINER'S MYTH

SHERIFF MARY BETH CAIN had made a lot of enemies since succeeding her dearly departed husband, Bill, to become Jasper County's first-ever female sheriff, but none who pissed her off more than Alexander Pomfried. The smug, rotund attorney, in his overstuffed seersucker suits and pretentious bow ties, had first crossed swords with her during his days as a shitbag criminal defense attorney, during which he'd been infuriatingly successful, winning more dismissals and acquittals than the rest of the local bar combined. He'd also been Mary Beth's most vocal critic, waxing eloquent, in his faux genteel, grandstanding way, about her "extralegal" methods for serving up a headbanging, hillbilly version of justice. And while all that was bad, the thing that had riled Mary Beth most about her legal nemesis was Pomfried's belligerent insistence upon calling her "Sugar."

There she'd be on the witness stand, armed with weapons of lethal force and all the imprimaturs of the State of West— *by God*—Virginia, and still Pomfried would address her like a little girl.

"Wouldn't you agree, Sugar …"

"Isn't it fair to say, Sugar … "

"Hypothetically, Sugar … "

"So what I hear you saying is, Sugar . . ." And on, and on, and on. Back then it had been all Mary Beth could do not to leap down off the stand and pistol-whip the son of a bitch.

Things only got worse when longtime district attorney Royce Parker retired, and the geniuses in the county commissioners' office recommended Pomfried as his interim replacement, giving him prosecutorial authority over every case Mary Beth put together. It was a move that flipped Mary Beth's world upside down. She knew there was no way she and Pomfried could coexist on the same side of the law for long. But the sheriff never dreamed she'd find herself in her current position, once again in the witness chair being questioned by her biggest enemy, only this time as the target of a grand jury investigation.

"Please state your name for the record, Sugar," Pomfried said, looking awfully satisfied with himself as he leaned against the jury box. He was running his thumbs up and down the insides of his suspenders while the full heft of his girth spilled over his seersucker slacks.

"Mary Beth Cain."

Pomfried put a hand to his ear as though he must not have heard her right. "You mean *Sheriff* Mary Beth Cain, don't you?"

"No," Mary Beth said through gritted teeth. "As you are well aware, I've been placed on administrative leave from my position. Chief Deputy Izzy Baker is currently the acting sheriff."

Mary Beth studied the jury for any reaction. She knew naming Izzy, who'd been her best friend since high school, as acting sheriff was bound to be controversial. Not only was Izzy the only Black deputy in an overwhelmingly white county, but he was routinely underestimated due to his short stature, standing just four foot eleven, even with his boots on.

The jurors all looked back at her impassively, but Pomfried was smiling wide beneath his bushy Mark Twain mustache.

"Well then, *Miss* Cain," he said—emphasizing the "Miss" in a way that somehow sounded worse than Sugar ever had—"you are aware that you are a target of this grand jury's investigation, correct?"

"Yeah," Mary Beth said, "I got your shit-ass letter." She waved the paper she'd received in front of her.

Pomfried retrieved it and had it marked as State's Exhibit 73 before reading it into the record.

This correspondence is to inform you that you are the target of an investigation by a Jasper County Grand Jury. You are hereby invited to testify.

If you choose to appear, any such testimony shall be private; the only permitted participants are you, the Grand Jury's members, attorneys from the district attorney's office, and a stenographer.

Please be advised that the Grand Jury investigation regards potential criminal violations including, but not be limited to:

Pomfried paused for dramatic effect before reading the suspected charge: "Murder in the first degree."

Judy Nelson, a local librarian who'd been selected as the grand jury foreperson, shook her head, giving Mary Beth the same scolding look she leveled on noisemakers in her quiet sanctuary.

"That's what it says," Mary Beth agreed.

"And as a *former* sheriff, you are aware of your constitutional rights against self-incrimination and the fact that you could have chosen not to appear and testify here today?"

"I've got nothing to hide," Mary Beth said proudly.

"We'll see about that." Pomfried straightened from where he'd been slouched against the rail of the jury box and took two steps in her direction. "Have you had the opportunity to consult with a lawyer about your appearance here today?"

"I don't think much of lawyers," Mary Beth said, drawing a couple smiles from the jury.

"Not my question, *Miss* Cain. What I asked was, have you in fact consulted with an attorney about your appearance here today?"

"I met with a lawyer who told me what I already knew. That these grand jury proceedings are mostly a formality. They always result in whatever indictment the prosecutor wants. The old joke is that a grand jury would even indict a ham sandwich if the prosecutors wanted them to. My attorney thought it would be extremely foolish of me to appear and testify."

Mary Beth knew that her discussions with her attorney were privileged, but it was her privilege to waive, and she wanted the jury to know that she knew full well what she was up against.

"And yet, you've chosen to come and tell this jury, face-to face, that you're not guilty, is that it?"

"No," Mary Beth said. "I've come to tell them that I am guilty."

A stunned silence fell over the courtroom until Mary Beth explained. "I am guilty of many things. Just not of the charge you're targeting me for."

"Okay, Sugar." Pomfried smiled as he stroked his chin. He was going to enjoy this game of cat and mouse. "How about we get on with it, then. I'd like to start out asking you about your investigation of Leonard Velino. Do you recall that?"

"Of course."

"Can you tell the jury who Leonard Velino is? Or … I guess I should say, *was*?"

Mary Beth still bristled at the mention of Velino, a man she considered lower than whatever was worse than pond scum. She did her best not to reveal her emotion but knew her fair skin was turning red as a teacher's apple as she tried to dispassionately explain, "Lenny Velino was a drug trafficker. Leader of the crew that moved in to fill the void from where we ran off the McCray County Mafia."

"And when you say McCray County Mafia, you are referring to a well-known crime syndicate that was led by your mother, Mamie, correct?"

Mary Beth felt an urge to obfuscate but reminded herself that she was there to tell the truth—at least up to a point. There was no use denying the things everyone already knew. And the Charleston newspapers had done a big exposé on Mary Beth years back called "Rough Justice," exposing her family connection to coal country's criminal element, as well as her borderline-vigilante methods for enforcing justice within her jurisdiction.

"That's right," Mary Beth said. "I can't change who my parents were or control the things they did. But I can tell you that I went to great lengths to keep law and order in this county. When I first took over as sheriff, we made it our number-one priority to clear it of all the illegal drug operations, the meth dens, the street-corner hustlers, and all the crooked pill pushers. The McCray County Mafia never operated in Jasper County under my watch. Then, when McCray's population dwindled to the point that the two counties were combined, I forced my mother clear out of the state."

What Mary Beth had said was true. Much to her shame, she'd been born into a criminal family, her daddy having turned to dealing after losing his job in the mines. He'd combined his muscle with Mamie's menacing strategery and long list of criminal kin to build the McCray County Mafia. When Mary Beth was a teenager, her father was shot and killed in a DEA raid, leaving Mamie in charge of the family racket and giving Mary Beth an excuse to leave home and live with her paternal, law-abiding grandparents in Jasper Creek. Mary Beth and Mamie maintained only the loosest of ties from that point on, which became even more strained when the always rebellious

Mary Beth stuck it to her mama good by marrying Bill Cain, the latest in a long line of lawmen, who followed his grandfather and father to become Jasper County sheriff. It was a few short years later when Bill went and got himself shot and killed in another drug bust, just like Mary Beth's daddy—although Bill had been the bust-*er* rather than the bust-*ee*. Mary Beth stepped in to finish out her husband's term as the county's top cop, much the way Mamie had succeeded her murdered groom to head the family crime business, and the two women brokered an armistice whereby Mary Beth helped take out Mamie's competition in exchange for the old lady keeping the hard drugs outside of Jasper. The arrangement worked well enough until the counties consolidated and Mary Beth forced her mother out of the state all together.

"For those of us who aren't as familiar with the drug trade, could you explain to the grand jury the primary sources of drug trafficking in West Virginia?"

"Well, I guess you could say the largest cartel at play in this state is Big Pharma. We've mostly got them to thank for the opioid epidemic. I think they saw a perfect target in Appalachia. A lot of people working heavy labor jobs, getting injured and prescribed pain pills, combined with poor economics and the sparsity of rural health care making routine follow-ups more difficult. It was kind of the perfect storm for—"

"Yes, yes," Pomfried said, cutting her off. "I'm referring to illegal drugs."

Mary Beth wasn't quite ready to get down off her opioid soapbox but decided it was best to play nice as long as she could stomach it. "We get some crystal meth and weed from the Mexican cartels," she said with a sigh. "But not a lot, to be honest, because there's a decent amount of local production of those. Historically, most of the illegal drugs in West Virginia—cocaine, heroin, fentanyl, black market pills—have actually been sourced by organized crime out of Detroit. We get some from Pittsburgh and Ohio, too, but Detroit is the biggest player. By the 1990s or so, their conglomerate had pretty successfully infiltrated the whole state. Everywhere except for McCray County, that is."

"Why is that?" Pomfried asked.

Mary Beth gave the jury a knowing smile, suspecting they'd all heard stories about Bloody McCray.

"Well the McCray County Mafia didn't take too kindly to outside competition and gave the Detroit boys more resistance than they were used to, backed by pretty much the whole community. Big heavies from the Motor City would go down there throwing their weight around, making fun of the way people talk, thinking they were intimidating everyone. And folks would act real passive. Meek and polite. Then when the mobsters would catch some shuteye in a local boarding house at night, they'd wake up with their throats slit. And the local cops were happy to look the other way. One guy got stabbed in the back seventeen times and still had it ruled a suicide."

As an OG McCray girl herself, Mary Beth had always felt a sense of pride in the no-nonsense way the law in that county had historically operated in what was a rough and tumble part of the world.

"Is that what you did as sheriff, Ms. Cain? Turn a blind eye to the McCray County Mafia's efforts to drive their Detroit-based competitors out of Jasper County?"

Mary Beth's hackles went up over the implication. "What I did was enforce the laws to the best of my ability. Going after anybody who pushed drugs in my county. No matter who they were. Now, did I get tips from the McCray County Mafia that sometimes aided me in that endeavor?" Mary Beth gave the jury an earnest look. "Yes, sir, I did. And I'm damn glad. 'Cause we managed a span of the lowest crime rate this county has ever seen."

A male juror in the back row gave Mary Beth a little fist pump that buoyed her soul. *The people know what I've done*, she told herself. Despite the mixed press she'd received over the years, being called out for unconstitutional methods and suspected corruption only to be later hailed as the hero of the Old Wengo Affair when she headed off a bloody standoff between the Feds and her late brother Sawyer's anti-government militia, not to mention her incredible arrest and case closure rates, Mary Beth had to believe that most in Jasper knew she'd poured her heart and soul into protecting them.

"Let's talk about that crime rate," Pomfried said. "It's kind of gone through the roof as of late, wouldn't you say?"

Mary Beth turned her attention back to the prosecutor. "As I said before, we've had people moving in, trying to fill the void. Detroit is back. And . . ."

"And?" Pomfried asked after she trailed off.

"And, in retrospect, I've been forced to accept a hard truth." Mary Beth took a quiet moment with her thoughts before saying, "Look, I came here to tell y'all the truth, so I'm gonna go ahead and admit something I refused to acknowledge for a long time but have ultimately come to accept."

"Which is?" Pomfried prompted.

Mary Beth glanced down the row, looking each juror in the eye as she gave her answer. "Sometimes the devil you know is better than the one you don't."

02

IT HAD BEEN WELL OVER A YEAR since McCray County was annexed into Jasper, but Chief Deputy Izzy Baker didn't think he'd ever get used to driving the steep, winding roads through coal country. He was in his highly modified Chevy Blazer, with its monster-truck-sized tires and extended pedals to accommodate Izzy's exceedingly short legs, leading a convoy of deputies toward what promised to be the biggest drug bust in southern West Virginia's history.

Sheriff Cain was riding shotgun, pensively staring out the windows at the kudzu-covered rock formations, as Izzy maneuvered his massive vehicle through the switchbacks down the south side of the Old River Mountains. She had a habit of getting quiet whenever they rode through that area. Izzy knew Mary Beth had grown up in McCray, a former coal mecca that had become a hollowed, burnt-out shell of its former self.

"You thinking about your family?" Izzy asked. Not mentioning the ungodly mess law enforcement had gotten themselves into by running off their organization. The McCray County Mafia, headed by Mary Beth's mother, Mamie, may have been sinister, but at least it was homegrown and thus infused with a begrudging respect for the community. The hillbilly racket kept their vices to the seedier sectors, careful not to "overshear the sheep" as Izzy once heard Mountain Mamie explain. They'd never have allowed the kind of open street-corner violence that had erupted in recent months or the mass overdoses from fentanyl-laced heroin. All that had become the way of life under the carpetbagger cartel from Detroit. Now the drugs were everywhere and more lethal, and civilians were no longer shielded from the criminal violence and turf wars. Witnesses weren't simply intimidated or disappeared; they were mutilated, tortured, flayed, and displayed. It was terrorism plain and simple.

"I know what you want me to say," Mary Beth said. "And I'm not going to. So just drop it, okay?"

"I don't want you to say anything," Izzy responded.

"Sure you do. You want me to say that I should have left well enough alone and let my mom operate in our county to keep the peace."

"I didn't say that."

"No, but you were thinking it."

"I wasn't thinking anything, woman. Damn. I just asked what you were thinking. Sitting there all quiet, staring off into space."

Mary Beth gave Izzy a probing look like she was assessing his earnestness. "I don't want to talk about it," she said, finally.

"Good," Izzy said. "I don't want to talk to your grouchy ass anyway."

Mary Beth huffed and turned her attention back out the window.

It worried Izzy to see her so irritable. Mary Beth had always been irascible, but ever since the Old Wengo Affair and the death of her crazy brother, Sawyer, Izzy was pretty sure she was suffering from a serious case of PTSD that made her dangerously volatile. That kind of unpredictability often worked to her advantage in bullying local thugs, but in going up against a cold-blooded killer like Leonard Velino, it was like dropping a lit match into a bag of fireworks. You didn't know what all was going to explode or which way it would blow.

Some quiet moments passed before Mary Beth muttered the word "Excuses."

"What?" Izzy asked, not sure if he'd heard her right.

Mary Beth turned back to Izzy in time to point out an upcoming hairpin turn where a rusty guardrail was all that protected against a precipitous drop down the mountainside. Izzy pressed the extended brake pedal and slowly eased Beulah, his behemoth SUV, around the sharp curve.

He was thinking maybe Mary Beth was engaged in a rare bit of self-reflection, but once they survived the dangerous curve she explained that the excuses she was talking about were the ones her father used to justify his turn to a life of crime after he lost his job in the mines.

"'What else can a man with nothing but a strong back do around here and still provide for his family?' That's the kind of shit he used to try and sell," Mary Beth said. "Well, I ain't buying. Look at Mr. Percy. He and my dad grew up together, buddies since sixth grade, worked the same mines, dug the same coal, and Mr. Percy even got tore up in a cave-in and nearly killed, and could have laid out on disability the rest of his life if he wanted to. But he didn't. And he sure as hell didn't start slinging dope with his in-laws. He took his one good leg and his one good eye and found another honest way to make a living."

Mr. "Lem" Lemuel Percy was the man whose intel had precipitated that morning's raid. After his mining career ended, he had moved to Jasper Creek and turned to railroading. It was from that vantage point as a conductor for Norfolk Southern that he learned how the Detroit outfit was bringing in their product, packed into mining equipment delivered by rail. Lem Percy shared that info with Mary Beth, at great personal risk to himself.

"When I moved in with my grandparents in Jasper Creek, after my dad died, Mr. Percy would always check up on me," Mary Beth explained. "He'd take that glass eye out of his head and put it on my shoulder and say, 'You better be good, little girl. Remember, I've got my eye on you.'"

Izzy didn't find the joke quite as funny as Mary Beth. But he could tell it was a memory that touched her. There'd been so few positive male influences in Mary Beth's life, save her for her now-deceased grandfather, that she tended to savor what little she'd received. All of which made Mr. Percy a very special person to her.

The road was finally leveling out, down through Honeysuckle Pass, where Mary Beth pointed out how the railroad tracks cut a relatively straight, level path through the mountains. "Quite a contrast to these windy-ass roads, huh? They made everything nice and smooth for the trains because they had to cart off the precious coal. The barons couldn't have cared less about the people they sent underground to dig the stuff. We got to travel these roller-coaster country highways and live in houses that barely clung to the sides of the mountain."

As they pulled into the remnants of the first little town inside old McCray, Mary Beth checked her watch and said, "We're just a bit ahead of schedule. Pull into the Grant's parking lot up here."

Izzy wrangled his vehicle into the triangular parking lot of a corner grocery store across from a one-room red brick post office for the unincorporated town of Gray Stone. It was just a mile and a half from Hoot Owl Hollow and the Loretta #4 mine—that morning's destination. Four cruisers full of deputies followed and parked beside them.

The timing of the bust was important. Show up too early and the police presence was likely to be noticed by someone who might tip off the bad guys. Show up too late, and you might miss your chance. The train carrying the drug-stuffed mining equipment was set to arrive at Loretta #4 any minute.

Mary Beth radioed Deputy Goforth, who was already stationed in Hoot Owl Hollow, playing the part of lookout, with a mountainside view of the intended ambush.

"How we doing?" Mary Beth asked.

"Train's pulling in now," Goforth said.

"Good. You're recording, right?"

"Oh, yeah," Goforth said. "Getting it all on camera. Nice clear day."

"How many shitheads are there?"

"Not sure yet. They're still in their vehicles. Got one pickup truck and two sedans. One's a Mercedes with a big, God-awful Penn State sticker on the back."

Mary Beth and Izzy looked at each other, both knowing what that meant. Velino. Along with his many negative qualities as a career killer and drug trafficker, Lenny Velino was also a known Nittany Lion fan. They hadn't been expecting him to be there personally. His presence upped the ante big-time.

"Well, shit my britches," Mary Beth said.

"They're getting out now, sheriff. Looks like two, four, six … eight, no, nine guys total. Velino's here, sheriff. He's hanging back, watching the others go to work. They've got a lot of equipment up there. It'll take them a bit to unload."

Izzy started up the engine, but Mary Beth motioned for him to wait. "I don't want to move until they've got the last piece of equipment down off that train. I'd like to let the train—and more importantly, Mr. Percy—get on their way before we spring the trap."

The staging area for Loretta #4 was in a little alcove cut into the mountainside, where the train entered out of one tunnel and exited into another a few hundred yards away. It sounded like Mary Beth wanted Mr. Percy to be safely out of sight and into the far side of the mountain tunnel before any potential shooting started.

"You let me know the instant the final piece of machinery touches the ground, and we'll swoop in," she said to Goforth.

"Roger, sheriff."

Goforth signed off, and Mary Beth looked over at Izzy, apprising what he knew had to be a sour expression on his face.

"Something else you want to say?" she asked.

"Oh, now you want to listen to me? It's a little late for that."

The whole time she'd been putting this operation together, Izzy had been trying to convince her to involve the federal government and let them take the lead on this thing. But Mary Beth had her reasons for not trusting the Feds. One was that it was a twitchy DEA sniper who'd killed her father, thinking the old man was making a move when he was actually trying to surrender. Then there was the ATF and FBI, which had both been ready to lay siege to her brother Sawyer's compound and slaughter everyone inside before Mary Beth intervened to defuse the situation. Not to mention the fact that the US Attorney's Office had previously investigated her for bogus corruption charges and brought a failed prosecution against her in the aftermath of the Old Wengo Affair.

Izzy got all of that, but still, the Velino business was too big for them in his opinion. It called for the Beltway's big guns.

"This is my mess," Mary Beth said. "I'll clean it up myself."

Izzy closed his eyes and sighed. "There it is."

"There's what?"

"There's your excuse. Always telling yourself it's all on you. When it's not."

"I don't see anybody else here."

"Only 'cause you haven't called them."

"Called who?"

"State police. DEA, FBI. Neighboring jurisdictions. Shit, call the Ghostbusters. I don't know. There's got to be twenty different agencies out there with a hard-on for Velino who'd be willing to help."

Mary Beth shook her head defiantly. "You're scared," she said.

"Goddamn right I am. And you should be, too," Izzy said. "Any sane person would be. We've got no idea what we're about to roll up on."

He was interrupted by Goforth, who broke through over the walkie. "Getting close, sheriff. Be any second now."

Mary Beth held up a finger for Izzy to hold his thought while she radioed her response. "We're ready. Just say when." Then, to Izzy, she said. "Don't worry. The second these guys hear sirens, they're going to scatter. That's why our first move is to seal off the exits and keep them pinned up against the mountainside. They won't have anywhere to go, or anything to do, other than surrender."

"Or just open fire on us with machine guns. You ever see the movie *Heat*? What happens when the cops roll up on a serious crew they aren't equipped to handle."

Mary Beth waved Izzy off. "We've got the element of surprise. Shock and awe."

Before Izzy could respond, Goforth came across the airwaves again to announce that it was time.

Despite his trepidation, Izzy didn't hesitate. He had his vehicle in gear and rolling before Mary Beth could instruct him to do so. "No sirens until we get close enough to see them," she reminded. "Then—"

"I know," Izzy groaned, "Shock and awe."

03

MARY BETH WAS GETTING NERVOUS. This was taking too long. She knew from Mr. Percy that Velino was smuggling the drugs inside mining equipment. If he was able to get the equipment inside the mines before they could intercept him, then Velino's men might be able to hide the contraband and the bust would be ruined.

"Come on, Izzy. Move your ass."

The chief deputy was taking his sweet time, maneuvering Beulah through a turn. "I go through these switchbacks any faster and we'll roll."

"You go any slower and we'll miss our shot."

Izzy stepped hard on the gas, going hand over hand, turning the wheel so sharp through a turn that the right side of the massive vehicle momentarily lifted off the ground. When it crashed back down, Izzy said, "Remind me again why we couldn't take your car."

The road straightened out, and the entrance to the mine was in sight. A thin metal gate was all that separated them from the gravel parking lot between the mine entrance, machine shop, and the railroad tracks that entered and exited the parking area through tunnels cut into the mountains.

"That's why," Mary Beth said pointing to the locked gate.

"You didn't say anything about—"

"Quit being a little bitch," Mary Beth said. "Hit it."

"Fine," Izzy groaned, "but you're paying for any damage."

Izzy mashed the accelerator to the floor, and his nitrous-boosted engine roared like a jet plane as they busted through the metal gate.

"Now," Mary Beth said into her walkie.

Instantly, Izzy and the four squad cars following them engaged their sirens as more deputies descended from where they'd been taking cover on the wooded mountainside. The squad cars fanned out, blocking the entrances to the mine and train tunnels. Velino's crew started to scatter but quickly realized there was nowhere to go. They were all close to the tracks, where the mining equipment had just been unloaded. All except for Velino, who was standing outside his vehicle about twenty yards away. Izzy headed straight for him but had gathered so much speed to ram through the gate, he had to pump the brakes hard to avoid running Velino over.

"Woah, woah, woah!" Mary Beth yelled. Izzy yanked the wheel to avoid a collision and the big vehicle's inertia took it up on two wheels again. It hovered in that precarious position for what seemed like forever, as though Beulah was debating whether to right herself or roll on over. Finally she teetered back toward equilibrium, and her ten thousand pounds slammed down on all four tires, kicking up a mushroom cloud of black dust.

"Jesus, Izzy!" Mary Beth shouted.

"Hey," he said. "You wanted shock and awe."

Despite the demolition derby entrance, the trap Mary Beth had laid was sprung more or less perfectly. Velino's crew had huddled together near their boss and were encircled by Mary

Beth's deputies who closed in unison, guns drawn, tightening around them like a dog's choke collar. By the time Mary Beth dropped down from the monster truck into the remnants of the dust cloud they'd created, Velino's guys had surrendered without a shot being fired.

Izzy was taking forever to descend his vehicle via a rope ladder, so Mary Beth didn't wait on him before getting a status update of what her guys were uncovering in their cuff-and-frisk. Velino himself was unarmed, other than a silver lighter and a pack of Newport cigarettes—which could kill you, though it would take a while. Four men with Detroit accents and names that ended in a vowel turned out to be packing, though along with their firearms they had concealed carry permits.

"Licensed private security," Velino said, in his gravelly voice. "We work for the coal company."

Mary Beth told Velino to shut it while she got a report on the rest of the assembled detainees, who turned out to be local boys—genuine coal miners—though the only one Mary Beth recognized was Wormy Robinson, whom she hadn't seen since elementary school when he used to eat his boogers in science class.

Izzy finally got his boots on the ground and drew his .44 Magnum pistol, which had an extended revolver as long as his forearm. He took position next to Mary Beth as she was turning her attention to Velino.

God, he's a hideous-looking man, Mary Beth thought. She'd often used the expression "uglier than sin" but had never truly witnessed it before. He was a lean and lanky six foot two, accentuated by a long neck, thin nose, bald head, and gaunt, clean-shaven face with high cheekbones. He reminded her of Eden's talking snake, squinting behind dark, almond-shaped sunglasses with a smile that revealed sharp yellow teeth. Velino was wearing a pinstripe shirt, unbuttoned at the collar, exposing a thick scar across his throat from where he'd survived a garrote attack in his early twenties. It had left him with a raspy voice that sounded like a slithery hiss now that Velino was in his fifties.

According to legend, he had more than twenty hits under his belt, including two cops and one prison guard, though none of the murder beefs had ever stuck, due to the witnesses becoming unavailable. Despite all that, or maybe because of it, Mary Beth wanted to make sure Velino knew she wasn't intimidated.

"Okay, dickhead," she said, rubbing a hand across Velino's shiny dome. "You were trying to run some line about being private security?"

"It's not a line, sheriff. I don't know what you think we're up to. But Mr. Velino was hired by the mine."

Mary Beth recognized the voice of her old classmate and said, "Shut up, Wormy," without taking her eyes off Velino. "I want to hear from Mr. Clean."

Velino hissed, then smiled a thin, contemptuous smile. He gestured with his head toward the mining equipment. "Like the man said, we're here for protection. This is valuable equipment."

"Oh, I bet it is valuable." Mary Beth hesitated to say any more, afraid that if she expounded on her knowledge of their drug smuggling operation, she might let something slip that would identify her source, and the last thing she wanted to do was put Mr. Percy at risk. She loved that one-eyed old man.

Wormy Robinson tried again to intercede. "Sheriff, you're making a big mistake. Really, I—" He was silenced by Mary Beth's vicious glare.

"Wormy, if I want you to speak, I'll point at you, okay?"

The miner kept quiet, and Mary Beth was feeling pretty good about herself. She felt in control. She ordered Velino and the others to all take a seat, with hands cuffed behind their backs. She, Izzy, and Deputy Goforth kept watch over them while the other deputies conducted a thorough search of the mining equipment.

The detainees' demeanor was surprising. She'd been expecting to hear a lot of lip, but they stayed mostly quiet, like experienced cons who knew they'd been caught and saw no point in wasting their breath or energy.

It was Mary Beth who broke the silence. "Private security for the mining company. That's nothing new around here. I bet you boys from Detroit never heard of the Baldwin-Felts Detective Agency have you?"

Velino turned his sinister gaze her way but said nothing.

"They were basically a bunch of gun-thug mercenaries sent in to bust the union. Tried to evict them all from their company-owned homes until the local sheriff, a guy by the name of Sid Hatfield—you know, like the Hatfields and McCoys—he stood up to them. Old Sid deputized a bunch of striking miners, sent them home to get their guns, and they had themselves a little shootout. It was called the Battle of Matewan. Happened not too far from here, over in Mingo County."

Velino's dark sunglasses had slipped down his nose. He glared over them. "Is there a point to this story?"

"Yeah," Mary Beth said. "I just wanted you to know how we handle things down here. When a bunch of city slickers come in thinking they're gonna push people around. We don't take too kindly to it."

Velino chuckled.

"Something funny?" Mary Beth asked.

"Hilarious."

"Oh, yeah. What's that?"

"You left out the best part of the story," Velino said. "See, I've heard about your Sid Hatfield. And what I heard was, after that little shoot-'em-up in Matewan, the Baldwin-Felts men caught up to that hayseed sheriff and killed him. Shot the man in broad daylight, right on the courthouse steps, in fact. And not a single one of them was ever even charged, much less convicted."

Shit, Mary Beth thought. She walked right into that one.

Velino said, "You see, sheriff, in my experience, when local shitkickers go up against big money with all its resources and political power, it never turns out too well for them. You of all people should know that."

The two locked eyes, and Mary Beth realized she was being threatened. She struggled for a good comeback. Not thinking of one, she decided instead to make sure Velino's handcuffs weren't too tight, so she could take the opportunity to chicken-wing his arm behind his back until he cried uncle. But she was interrupted by Deputy Skipwith, who, after thirty minutes of searching, had drawn the short straw and was tasked with telling Mary Beth the bad news.

"We didn't find anything, sheriff."

Mary Beth's initial reaction was one of disbelief. The drugs were there. Old Mr. Percy assured her he'd seen them loading them into the mining equipment carted in by train. If her guys hadn't found anything, she assumed it was due to their usual dipshittery. But Velino's vicious snickering soon got her feeling otherwise.

"What do you mean you didn't find anything?"

Skipwith shrugged. "It's clean, sheriff."

Velino's snicker rose to a cackle.

"Bull butter," Mary Beth said. "There's drugs in there. Go find them."

Skipwith cowered. "Sheriff, we've been all through it. There's nothing there."

Mary Beth wasn't ready to accept that. "I'll find it myself," she said, pushing past him.

Velino called after her. "You're going to pay for any damage to that equipment, sheriff."

Mary Beth gave Velino the finger as she stormed off toward the mining equipment, until Velino said something that stopped her in her tracks.

"I'm going have to keep my eye on you, sheriff."

Mary Beth stopped dead.

"What did you say?" she asked, turning back to Velino.

He winked at her and smiled. "I said, I'm going to have to keep my eye on you."

Mary Beth felt an ice-cold fist seize hold of her heart and begin to squeeze. Velino's line was the exact same one Mr. Percy used to say to her when he'd joke about his glass eye. And it had been uttered with a tone of such evil delight that Mary Beth immediately knew in her bones that Velino had discovered her source of information. Instantly she knew that Skipwith was right. They would find no drugs on that train. Velino had known about the raid, which was why they'd surrendered so easily. He'd allowed it to go forward just to embarrass her. And Mary Beth would have been dangerously embarrassed under most circumstances. But at that moment all she could feel was fear. Fear for the sweet old man who'd been like a father to her for so many years. Fear for Mr. Percy.

04

ALEXANDER POMFRIED STOOD next to the jury so that Mary Beth was forced to look their way. She knew the prosecutor hoped they'd see the fury in her eyes as she answered his next set of questions.

"After the failed drug bust, did you discover what had happened to your old family friend, Mr. Lem Percy?"

"No," Mary Beth said, trying to keep her emotions under control and her voice flat and even.

"He disappeared?"

"Yes. We presume he's dead but can't be certain."

"Dead," Pomfried said. "Murdered? Murdered by Mr. Velino? Is that what you believe?"

"Most likely," Mary Beth answered, knowing for damn sure it was the God's honest truth.

"But Mr. Percy's body was never discovered?"

"No. Well, not really."

"What do you mean?"

"A few days after the failed drug bust, I received a package that contained an eyeball."

The jurors gasped.

"Mr. Percy's glass eyeball?" Pomfried asked.

"No," Mary Beth said, "the other one."

A woman in the front row of the jury clapped her hand to her mouth.

Pomfried slowly approached Mary Beth and asked in a gentle tone, "Sheriff, would it be fair to say that after all of this went down, with the embarrassment over the failed drug bust and the apparent murder and likely torture of an old man who was dear to you, that you wanted to get revenge against Leonard Velino?"

Mary Beth knew Pomfried was trying to bait her. "I wanted justice," she said.

"Justice?"

"That's right."

"An eye for an eye?"

"Is that supposed to be funny?" Mary Beth said, not appreciating the pun.

Pomfried raised a hand of apology. "Forgive the poor choice of words. I guess what I'm asking is: What in your mind would have been justice for Mr. Velino?"

"That's up to the legal system."

"Yes, of course. But I'm asking about your state of mind. What do you believe would have been justice?"

Mary Beth started to deflect the question, but Pomfried headed her off. "Shoot straight with these folks," he said, gesturing to the jury.

"Fine," she said, wanting to demonstrate her earnestness. "If you ask me, killing Mr. Percy and sending me his eyeball should have got Velino the death penalty, if we're talking about justice."

Mary Beth could feel the color rising in her face. She hated that she was so easily excitable. It was one of the many reasons her lawyer told her it would be far too dangerous to go before the grand jury.

"Ms. Cain, you do realize that West Virginia banned the death penalty back in 1965, right?"

"Yes."

Pomfried had his thumbs hooked inside his suspenders and snapped them against his chest to emphasize the importance of the answer she'd just given.

"So, when it comes to Mr. Velino, you were willing to go further than the law allows?"

Mary Beth should have immediately denied the accusation, but instead, she took her time before answering, selecting her words very carefully. "I didn't kill Lenny Velino," she said.

Pomfried looked back at the jury to make sure they were with him. "We'll come back to that, but first I want to ask you, right now, under oath, isn't it true that there have been times you've gone beyond the law to carry out your own form of vigilante justice?"

Mary Beth wasn't sure exactly what Pomfried was getting at. There were so many things he could be suggesting. She'd bent the rules plenty when justice required but had never really broken them. Not totally. That was Mary Beth's special magic. She'd been raised by criminals, so she knew how they thought and had learned their skills; she'd inherited her mama's mad-genius moxie. But Mary Beth had chosen to use her powers for good. Unlike Mamie, Mary Beth actually had a conscience. Her moral compass might be a little suspect at times, but at least she had one, dammit. That was the difference between her and her mother that Mary Beth prided herself on. There were some lines Mary Beth wouldn't cross.

"Mr. Pomfried," she said, "I have no idea what you're talking about."

"Let's take your brother, Sawyer, for instance."

Speaking of sociopaths, Mary Beth thought. Her deceased brother had been just as devoid of empathy as Mamie and was much more hateful.

"What about Sawyer?"

"A few years ago he was responsible for what's been termed the Old Wengo Affair, when your brother's militia blew up a federal courthouse, provoking a siege of their mountain compound, correct?"

More smear tactics, Mary Beth assumed. Just like he'd discussed her parents' drug dealing, Pomfried would now go through her brother's greatest criminal hits to further suggest to the jury she was one more bad apple from the same rotten tree.

"I'm ashamed to admit that what you've said is true. But again, that was my family, Mr. Pomfried, not me. I got away from my family. Was mostly raised by my paternal grandparents, who were good, God-fearing citizens right here in Jasper Creek. My brother, Sawyer, stayed behind in McCray and was raised by our mother and brought up to be just as much of a menace as she is."

"You and Sawyer were not close, then—is that what you're saying?"

That's an understatement, Mary Beth thought, though despite their massive differences, she had always harbored a begrudging love and sense of responsibility for Sawyer and still mourned his death. "We weren't exactly on each other's Christmas card list," she said.

"It must have been quite embarrassing for you to have your own brother provoke this big standoff that became such a spectacle, with lots of national media coverage."

"I suppose," Mary Beth said, not sure what Pomfried was leading up to.

"Sawyer's plan was to wait until the Feds breached the walls of his compound, and then he was going to blow them up, along with his own followers, all from the safety of an underground mineshaft, isn't that right?"

"Until I stopped him," Mary Beth said.

Pomfried smiled. "Oh, yes, you stopped him. No one here

will deny you've gone to great lengths to protect your constituents. Heroic lengths. But even with the Old Wengo Affair, where you prevented a bloody massacre, instead of following protocols and turning your brother over to the Feds, you exercised your own version of justice and snuck him out of there through an underground mineshaft. Isn't that right?"

"He *was* under arrest," Mary Beth insisted. "He was in my custody. But with the heightened tensions, I was afraid to turn him over right then. Some federal agents had been killed, and they were angry. You have to understand, Mr. Pomfried, that our father was killed by a DEA sniper while he was trying to surrender. I didn't want the same thing to happen again."

"You preferred to handle it on your own."

"Perfectly within my discretion as sheriff. A point that you yourself argued, Mr. Pomfried, when you defended me against the federal charges that were later dismissed."

Mary Beth thought she'd scored a serious point there, but Pomfried didn't flinch.

"Oh, what you've said is true. The jury was informed before your arrival that back in my defense days I temporarily represented you, which is why I've been sure to limit myself on this subject to matters squarely within the public record. And that public record establishes that after you so thoughtfully secreted your brother out of harm's way, he thanked you by having his men ambush you and leave you facing those federal charges while he absconded. Correct?"

Mary Beth hated how all of this was sounding. "Mr. Pomfried, you of all people should know how unfair it was of people to suggest that I wanted my brother to escape. A point I disproved quite thoroughly by ..." Mary Beth hesitated, which gave Pomfried a chance to complete her sentence.

"Killing him?"

Mary Beth saw too late what Pomfried was doing. He wanted to establish a pattern. Criminals do something to piss Mary

Beth off, and they end up dead. She'd like to tell Pomfried where he was wrong, at least when it came to Sawyer, but couldn't. Everyone knew that Sawyer was shot and killed after breaking into Mary Beth's home and holding her and her son, Sam, hostage. But what they didn't know was that it was actually Sam who shot him. Mary Beth arranged the scene to make it look like she had, to protect Sam from any possible repercussions. One of those examples of her bending the rules for a greater good.

"Sawyer was killed in self-defense," she said. "He broke into my home and attacked both me and my son. The shooting was ultimately cleared—deemed justified."

Pomfried chuckled sarcastically as he said, "Oh, I'm sure it was. I have no doubt that *your* department made that ruling."

Mary Beth wanted to point out that the state police did their own independent review that concluded the same thing, but Pomfried didn't give her a chance before moving to his next question.

"Let's talk now about Mr. Randy Law. You remember him, don't you?"

Mary Beth groaned. She knew where this was headed.

"Yes," she said through gritted teeth.

"Another gentleman you crossed paths with who is no longer with us. Why don't you tell the jury who he was."

"A murderer," Mary Beth shot back. "He was the man who hired a hitman to kill a beautiful young woman named Maria Ruiz in order to cover up their affair and the fact that Maria was pregnant with his child."

Pomfried shook his head like a disappointed schoolteacher. He had a short neck and extremely chubby cheeks that drooped like a bulldog's and contorted against his shoulder as he turned his head from side to side. "Now, Ms. Cain, you are assuming facts not in evidence."

"I don't understand what you're—"

"Mr. Law was never convicted of any of the crimes you've just accused him of, was he?"

"Well he …" Again Mary Beth hesitated, searching for the right way of explaining how Randy Law died before he could be prosecuted.

"Ms. Cain, it's a yes or no question. Mr. Law was never convicted of any crimes, was he?"

"No, but—"

"In fact, Mr. Law was never even charged with any crimes, was he?"

"Well, not—"

"Not ever, right?"

"He—"

"Died, right?"

This was not fair at all. Randy Law had killed himself rather than be apprehended. Mary Beth had tried to prevent it. Yet Pomfried was making it sound like he was another of her vigilante victims.

"Randy Law killed himself after being confronted with his crimes."

"Confronted with his crimes? Is that what you call it when you show up at his place of business with a death squad of deputies."

"Death squad? We were there to arrest him."

"Ms. Cain, at the time of Mr. Law's death, he was not the subject of any active investigations, was he?"

Only because there wasn't time, Mary Beth thought. They had been in the middle of the trigger man's prosecution when he made a deal and identified Randy Law as the one who'd instructed him to kill Maria Ruiz.

Mary Beth had been so hot to trot she hadn't waited for an arrest warrant before going to confront Randy, who immediately started shooting and ultimately turned his gun on himself.

After that there'd been no reason to go through the motions of charging him.

Pomfried didn't give Mary Beth a chance to explain all of that before saying, "In fact, this man you have called a murderer was a former law enforcement officer with no criminal record, who was running to unseat you as sheriff, correct?"

"That had nothing to—"

"His death occurred shortly before Election Day, right? Remind us, Ms. Cain, who was ahead in the polls at that time?"

Dammit. Randy had maintained a pretty sizable lead over Mary Beth throughout much of the campaign, though she'd narrowed things considerably.

"It was close," she said, "But Randy may have had a slight lead in the polls at that time."

Pomfried turned and nodded to the jury, as if taking a bow. With no attorney of her own to protect her or judge to intervene when things got unfair, Mary Beth had underestimated just how much she would be at Pomfried's mercy during her grand jury testimony. Regardless, she was determined to soldier on, even as Pomfried turned back to her, smiling, and said, "Now, that we've covered that background, let's return to the Leonard Velino investigation."

05

RETURNING TO THE LEONARD VELINO investigation was all Mary Beth could do in the weeks following the failed drug bust. She became obsessed with nailing the Motor City mafioso and worked day and night, pressing every possible angle, tailing and surveilling Velino and his men way past the point of harassment and investigating every possible business front for smuggling or money laundering—car dealerships, construction companies, waste disposal, even Walmart. There'd been some near misses, particularly with Braun Automotive, who Mary Beth strongly suspected was bringing drugs in for Velino hidden in their new fleet of Chevy trucks, but every time she got close, Velino managed to stay one step ahead. And every time Mary Beth put the screws to a witness or accomplice who under normal circumstances could be flipped, they either clammed up out of fear or disappeared.

All of this meant Mary Beth's typically crotchety moods became especially volatile. Izzy had been on her ass about the need to take a break, which was a suggestion Mary Beth wasn't trying to hear until the request was made by her son, Sam, to take a day off and accompany him to church that Sunday.

Mary Beth rolled her eyes at first. She was too cynical to be religious, and Bill was a lapsed Catholic, so Sam grew up mostly unchurched. Mary Beth had pushed him to attend the local Bible college only as a way to keep him close to home but had left unimpressed from the few services she'd attended there during Sam's freshman year.

"Sammy, baby, every time I've been there it's the same schtick. The preacher tells a bullshit story about some mysterious person who had a deadly tumor until the congregation prayed and miraculously cured him. Then the ladies gasp and everybody applauds, and they pass the offering plate around." The last time Mary Beth attended a service at King's Chapel, she'd made a scene afterward by asking the pastor for the name and address of the cancer patient he'd described so she could send flowers. The pastor had turned red-faced and flustered before ducking the questions by citing privacy concerns.

"Mom, it's—"

"I'm wondering what in the hell kind of cancer cluster they've got going on at that church, with all of these tumors they're praying away."

"Mom, if you—"

"And don't get me started on the whole—"

"Mom!" Sam yelled.

"What?"

"I'm not talking about that church. I want you to go with me to Granddad's church. You know, St. Michaels."

That surprised Mary Beth, though it shouldn't have. She'd encouraged Sam to maintain contact with his grandfather, Sid Cain, after Bill died, and she knew he had occasionally gone to church with him there.

"Oh. Yeah, I don't know, Sammy. I'm not into the whole

Catholic thing. Your dad didn't care about it, and I was raised more on real religion."

Sam huffed. He really was the spitting image of his mother, slender and wiry with red hair and fair skin that easily pinked up with emotion, the way it was right then.

"Whatever, Mom. You never even went to church."

"Not true," Mary Beth said. "My Uncle Ot used to run a traveling tent revival where he'd get the folks all riled up, talking in tongues and handling snakes. Of course he secretly defanged the vipers he worked with, but it was always a crowd pleaser, regardless. Sometimes he'd get Sawyer to pretend to be crippled and would heal him on stage."

"Great."

"Hey, Uncle Ot may not have had genuine fruits of the spirit, but he brought in a pretty nice take."

"It's called tithes, Mom."

"Not the way Uncle Ot did it."

Sam sighed. "Would you just come with me on Sunday?"

Mary Beth didn't know what the big deal was. If Sam wanted to go with his grandfather, fine, but what did that have to do with her?

"I mean, I guess. If you really want me to," she said.

"Thank you," Sam said, exasperated. Then added, "Guadalupe is going to be there too. It will be nice. Granddad said he'll take us all out to lunch at Cracker Barrel after."

The mention of Guadalupe helped Mary Beth piece together what this was all about. Bill had died when Sam was young, after which Mary Beth largely abandoned her son to become sheriff, entrusting a lot of his daily child-rearing to Guadalupe Angeles, their housekeeper, who got a battlefield promotion to nanny. And since Mary Beth had always done her best to limit Sam's exposure to her side of the family, Bill's dad, Sid, was the primary grandparent in his life. This was the little family Sam had cobbled together, and he wanted them all together in one place. It was the ritual of attending a service followed by a nice family meal that Sam craved, Mary Beth assured herself. The Catholic church was just the setting.

Thank God for that, Mary Beth thought, halfway through that Sunday's service, because she found her first experience in a Catholic church to be utterly bizarre. Half of it was in Latin, the priest wore funny clothes like he'd gotten dressed in medieval times, and was tossing incense around. Meanwhile, the congregation would respond in unison at various points without any prompting or written program telling them what to say. And it seemed like every other minute they were kneeling down or standing back up.

After it was all over and Sam asked her what she thought, the nicest thing Mary Beth could say was, "It weren't no Baptist thing, that's for sure."

Sam looked put out, but Sid Cain guffawed in his overbearing way and slapped Mary Beth on the back. "You always had a way of putting things."

Sid Cain looked an awful lot like Mary Beth's dead husband. A man's man, big and burly, who still had tree-trunk-sized arms despite a sagging midsection. Sid's hair was mostly gone now, and what was left was powdery white, including the Cain mustache that he, Bill, and Bill's grandfather, Sheriff Gus Cain, had all sported.

Visual similarities aside, though, Sid had a very different demeanor than his dead son. Bill had been quiet, dutiful, and fiercely loyal. As sheriff, he'd relished the day-to-day police work. Whereas Sid, with his big laugh and easy, backslapping personality, had excelled in the position's more political aspects.

After an early heart attack sidelined Sid from serving as sheriff, he had turned his talents toward religion by fund-raising to build the stone castle they'd worshiped in that morning. And he'd led a considerable consolidation effort he proudly described while giving Mary Beth a tour of the facility.

"When I was growing up, the Irish, Italians, Polish, we all had our separate little churches. And there aren't all that many Catholics in these parts to begin with, so it just made sense to band together. And now that we've got all of these fine Spanish-speaking folks moving to this area," Sid said, wrapping his big arm around Guadalupe's tiny shoulders, "we've started a Spanish-language service in the evening."

Guadalupe, who at eighty looked like a child next to Sid, seemed uncomfortable in his embrace. "Where is Father Gonzalez this morning?" she asked.

Sid raised an eyebrow. "I'm not sure. Haven't seen him. But I'm sure he's around here somewhere."

"It's all quite impressive," Mary Beth said, just being polite and hoping they could get on to the lunch part of the outing so she could get back to work.

Sid caught her looking at her watch.

"You know, sheriff, if you have a few minutes, I was hoping maybe we could have a private word."

"Oh?" Mary Beth had no idea what that could be about. She was pretty sure Sid had never really liked her much, though he'd always been cordial, to maintain his relationship with Sam.

"Yeah, with all that's been going on of late, I thought you might indulge this old cop's curiosity and maybe catch me up on where your office is with things. Who knows, I might even have some insights to offer. You know we were dealing with the Detroit stuff all the time back in my day."

Mary Beth did her best not to roll her eyes. The last thing she needed was her know-it-all father-in-law playing Monday morning quarterback with her Velino investigation.

"Maybe another time," she said. "But if we don't get a move on soon, you know the Cracker Barrel's going to be crazy busy."

Sid stared at her quietly for a moment, clearly disappointed, like he was waiting for her to capitulate. Mary Beth didn't.

Sam interrupted the silence. "So, Mom. There actually was a reason I asked you here today."

He positioned himself between Sid and Guadalupe, giving Mary Beth the impression that with whatever Sam was about to say, it would be three against one.

"What's that?" she asked.

"This," Sam said, gesturing around the mostly empty sanctuary. His hand stopped at a stained glass window depicting the Last Supper. "I'm planning to be baptized."

Mary Beth was confused for a second. Sam was already baptized. Once as a young child and again for good measure during his freshman year at Sovereignty University, where they called it a "believer's baptism," designed to make sure you graduated with eternal salvation to go along with your diploma. Then Mary Beth realized what he was saying.

"Wait. You mean here?"

Sam's fair skin turned pink around his throat, as though being strangled by an invisible hand.

"Yeah," he said, meekly.

Mary Beth recoiled at the notion. Though a cynic who was probably more agnostic than anything, Mary Beth was culturally evangelical and considered Catholicism an archaic relic of the past. Plus, she knew a conversion could be a deal-breaker for Sam's current school.

"What's Sovereignty University going to think about you becoming Catholic?"

Sam took a step back and moved partially behind Sid. "Uh … I'm actually planning to …"

"Transfer," Sid said, finishing the sentence when Sam trailed off.

"What?" Mary Beth couldn't believe what she was hearing. She'd clearly been set up here and was feeling both blindsided and betrayed. Two emotions that instinctively made her dangerously angry.

"He's been accepted at Georgetown University," Sid said. "One of the best schools in the country. It's a great opportunity."

"Accepted?" In order to be accepted, you had to apply, which meant Sam had been conducting this escape plan in secret for quite some time.

"Why is this the first I'm hearing of this?"

She gave Guadalupe her "Et tu, Brute?" look. The old woman shook her head, held up her palms, and backed away.

Sid stepped forward. "Sam's way too smart to be wasting his time at some local little Bible college."

Now Mary Beth saw what was going on. This had been Sid's idea.

"Did you put him up to this?" she asked, feeling a rising fury in her chest.

"Mom, he just wants what's best for me," Sam said, trying to stick up for his granddad.

Mary Beth silenced Sam with her hand and said, "You know what, Sid? I think I will have that word in private now."

06

THANKS TO HIS FUND-RAISING prowess, Sid Cain had a key to a private church office where he and Mary Beth went for a quiet word. It was a dark room lined with shelves of dusty, leather-bound books. In the center was a round conference table and chairs where Mary Beth declined Sid's invitation to sit.

"Let's dispense with the bullshit," she said. "I know you've never liked me, Sid. And that's fine. Given who my parents were, I don't blame you."

"That's not true."

Sid tried to protest, but Mary Beth wasn't having it. "Save it," she said. "Bill told me all about it, okay? And like I said, I get it. But after Bill died, I could have made it so you never got to see Sam again. Instead I bent over backward to make sure you two have always been close. So for you to stab me in the back like this and convince Sam to transfer to some Catholic school more than two hundred miles away is really low."

"It's not *some* Catholic school. We're talking about

Georgetown University. It's a great opportunity. And, I absolutely do think he should take it. But this was all Sam's doing. Not mine."

"Riiiiiight," Mary Beth said. "I guess it was just divine inspiration."

"Maybe," Sid said, turning up his palms. "But I actually think that lawyer Sam's been working for after school may have had something to do with it."

That notion hit Mary Beth like a bucket of ice water. The lawyer Sid referred to was Patrick Connelly, the guy she'd dated before Bill and a teensy, tiny bit on the side while she and Bill were officially an item. It had been complicated. So complicated that when Mary Beth got pregnant during her senior year of high school she wasn't entirely sure which one was the father. Bill seemed like the odds on favorite and immediately proposed after hearing her "good news," so she convinced herself it was him and never said a word about there being any parental ambiguity. Patrick wasn't speaking to her at the time and was already away at Georgetown—a fact that, Mary Beth suddenly realized, made him an obvious culprit for engineering her son's planned defection. Patrick had returned to town during the Old Wengo Affair, during which Mary Beth confessed her long-suppressed belief that he, not Bill, was actually Sam's father. Patrick pledged to keep the secret but also cultivated ways to get to know Sam, who had recently been clerking for him part-time.

"Son of a bitch," Mary Beth said. Patrick must have been the one behind this. The reference to him, especially by Sid, had thrown Mary Beth. Although Bill had never suspected anything about Sam's parentage—thank God—Sid had often made little comments about how his grandson didn't favor his side of the family at all. Then he would lock eyes with Mary Beth the way she did with a suspect when trying to determine whether she was being lied to.

For the moment, Sid seemed relieved to have redirected her

ire. "What you said about me never liking you isn't true, either," he said. "Don't you ever quote me on this, but I believe you're the best sheriff this county's ever had."

Mary Beth gave him her don't-bullshit-me look.

"I'm serious. Sure, I had my doubts at first, given who your mother is. But you really proved yourself when you took over from Bill. And despite what the paper said, I knew for a fact you weren't dirty."

"Oh yeah? How do you know that?"

Sid looked around the empty room, like he was deciding whether or not to share a confidence.

"Okay," he said. "Don't get mad. It was a long time ago. But I tested you."

"You what?" Mary Beth had no idea what in the world he could be talking about.

Sid smiled, looking kind of proud of himself. "Back when you first came on as sheriff. You took down a big drug bust with Ben Goforth. An apartment on College Avenue, I think it was. Recovered a lot of money and drugs."

Mary Beth remembered it well. One of her first major scores. They'd recovered eighty grand and a brick of cocaine. She also remembered what Goforth had said to her. A little song and dance about temptation. Hinting at the dangers of underpaid, overworked cops coming across such big sums of money and product and how easy it would be to just report half of what they recovered and pocket the rest.

"It's not like the crooks can complain," he said. "And if they did, who'd believe them?"

Mary Beth was brand-new on the job at the time and completely inexperienced. She remembered how desperate she'd been to prove herself to the deputies she'd inherited—especially grizzled old veterans like Goforth. So he must have been extra surprised when she said, "Benny, it's a good thing I know you're just joking. 'Cause if I ever hear you say anything like that again, I'll not only fire you, I'll put your fat ass in jail."

Now she realized Sid had put Goforth up to it.

"That was you?" she asked.

Sid held up his hands. "Forgive me, Mary. But I just had to be sure. It was enough of a shock to find out my son was dating and then quickly engaged to Mountain Mamie's daughter. Then all of a sudden you were the damn sheriff. I just had to be sure you weren't working for your mama, you know? That the fox wasn't inside the henhouse, so to speak."

Mary Beth wanted to be mad, but she really couldn't blame Sid for thinking all that. She certainly would have if the situation had been reversed.

"So why are you trying to drive my son away from me now?" Mary Beth asked, turning back to the subject at hand.

"Don't you think it would be good for him to expand his horizons?"

"You never thought that about your son," Mary Beth countered. "You kept Bill in your shadow his whole life."

"Yeah, and looked what happened to him."

Mary Beth was taken aback.

"And I'm certainly not saying that was in any way your fault, of course, but—"

"But what?"

Sid looked embarrassed. "You know the old coal miner's myth," he said.

Mary Beth had no idea what he was talking about. "What myth?" she asked.

Before Sid could answer, there was a loud knock on the door, followed by Guadalupe's voice, sounding panicked. "Sheriff! Sheriff!" Mary Beth opened the door to the church conference room. There was Guadalupe, trying to catch her breath, chest heaving like she'd just dashed up a flight of stairs. The old woman took Mary Beth's hand. "Please. Come quick."

Guadalupe led Mary Beth toward the entrance of the church, where a crowd was gathered around Father Gonzalez, who looked like he'd been beaten all to hell. His black priestly uniform was ripped in several places, and he had a nasty gash on his right knee that was bleeding down his shin.

"What happened?" Mary Beth asked, just as Sid was catching up to them.

"He was attacked," Guadalupe said.

"Attacked? By whom?"

"The men. They—" Father Gonzalez had to pause to catch his breath. He was a fit-looking man in his thirties, but his chest was heaving and his whole body was trembling. Mary Beth recognized that he was in shock.

"I'm calling for an ambulance," she said. "We're going to need to get you checked out."

"No." Father Gonzalez sat upright.

"They killed him, sheriff."

"Who?"

"Brad Mayhew."

Mary Beth didn't know who that was, but many of those gathered gasped and recoiled with horror. Sid said, "He's one of our members. On the fund-raising committee."

It occurred to Mary Beth at that point that they might have an active-shooter situation.

"Maybe we should get Father Gonzalez somewhere more private to talk," Sid said.

Mary Beth already had her cell phone out and was calling Izzy. "No one's going anywhere until we know it's safe," she said to Sid. Then, as soon as Izzy answered, "Iz, we've got a situation at St. Michael's. Reported homicide. Not sure yet what we're dealing with, but I need as many cars as we can get here, quick."

Izzy didn't waste time asking questions. "On it."

Mary Beth hung up and turned to Sid, the retired former sheriff, whom she deputized with the responsibility of keeping everyone right where they were while she went and checked the sanctuary to make sure it was safe. She hiked up the leg of her slacks to access her ankle holster, where she kept a subcompact Beretta she called her hummingbird. Mary Beth unsheathed the tiny weapon and went into the sanctuary. After determining it was empty, Mary Beth returned to the front vestibule and ordered everyone to move inside the sanctuary so she could keep them contained while they cleared the rest of the building. By that time, sirens could already be heard in the distance. It was just a few more moments before Izzy arrived, along with deputies Skipwith, Stephenson, and Morgan. Mary Beth had them search the grounds while she went back to the sanctuary.

Some of the color had returned to Father Gonzalez's face by the time she arrived. Sid gave her a quick download on the information he'd been able to obtain during her absence. "This morning the father and Brad were out in the parking lot setting up traffic cones, like they do every Sunday, when a van pulled up and men with guns abducted them. They took their wallets and cell phones. Put bags over their heads. Duct-taped their hands, etc. Eventually, it sounds like they decided to let Father Gonzalez go."

At this point, the priest picked up the story. "Brad swore to them that I didn't know anything."

"Know what?" Mary Beth asked.

"I don't know," the priest said. "I have no idea what they were talking about. Although I know Brad has been very troubled lately—worried about something. He'd come to me a number of times over the last couple of weeks for spiritual counseling but was always vague. Unwilling to really unburden himself. I'd suggested that today after service he allow me to take his confession. And he had agreed but . . ."

"But somebody had other ideas," Mary Beth said.

"Yes, it would appear so," Father Gonzalez responded. "Anyway, after all of Brad's protesting on my behalf, some of the men expressed reservations about killing a priest unnecessarily. A phone call was placed, the situation was explained, and whoever they called must have told them to let me go. They cut my hands free just before they pushed me out of the van in a wooded area outside of town."

Sid was shaking his head in disbelief. "Oh, Father, I'm so sorry." He placed his hand on the priest's shoulder.

"Did you hear any names mentioned?" Mary Beth asked.

"Only Brad's. They all called him Mayhew."

"How about during the phone call?" Sid asked. "Did they identify themselves at all? A nickname maybe?"

Father Gonzalez shook his head. "No. The man who placed the call just said, 'Hey, it's me.' Something like that."

"What can you tell me about the van—its appearance?" Mary Beth asked.

"It was a white van. No windows on the side. Like a work van."

"Were there any decals or anything on it?"

"No. No, I don't think so. None that I noticed, anyway."

"Could you describe any of the men who grabbed you?"

Again Father Gonzalez shook his head. "They all wore dark clothes and masks."

Mary Beth reached up and scratched the top of her head, wishing she had her hat. She thought better with her hat on.

Father Gonzalez said, "But I did see the man who shot Brad."

Mary Beth and Sid both looked at each other, surprised. Earlier Father Gonzalez said he knew someone had killed Brad Mayhew, but since he'd described being released, Mary Beth assumed he'd been making an assumption about Mayhew's fate. Now he seemed to be saying something different.

"You're saying you actually saw someone shoot Brad Mayhew?"

Father Gonzalez made the points of the cross. "Yes," he said. "That is what I'm trying to tell you."

07

THE GRAND JURY LOOKED just as confused as Mary Beth had been when Father Gonzalez first told her he'd witnessed Brad Mayhew's murder. She tried to explain. "After Father Gonzalez was thrown out of the van, he was lost in the woods and wandered around for some time until he heard screams off in the distance. He followed the sound and eventually came to a ridge where he was able to see down into a clearing, and there was the white van and the men who abducted him, who had Brad Mayhew tied to a tree and were beating on him. Father Gonzalez said he saw another vehicle pull up. A white Mercedes SUV. And a bald-headed Caucasian man got out, approached Mayhew, and spoke for a few moments with the masked men, saying something Father Gonzalez couldn't make out. Then the man pulled a pistol from his waistband and shot Mayhew in the forehead."

Alexander Pomfried had moved uncomfortably close to the witness chair. Close enough that Mary Beth got a whiff of his musky cologne.

"What happened next?" he asked.

"Father Gonzalez ran," Mary Beth said. "He didn't know if he'd been seen or heard, or if they were chasing him, but he wasn't taking any chances. He ran until he eventually found his way back to the church."

Pomfried leaned in, getting even closer. "Was Father Gonzalez able to take you to the scene where he'd witnessed this torture and execution?"

Mary Beth was a little annoyed by the fact that Pomfried was asking questions he clearly knew the answers to. But she reminded herself that this was all for the jury's benefit. And although so much about the Velino case had subsequently become public knowledge, you never knew for certain what people did or didn't know.

"It took nearly all day to find it. Father Gonzalez wasn't able to take us right to the spot or anything. But we were eventually able to locate Brad Mayhew's body. Still tied to a tree."

"Can you describe his appearance?"

Mary Beth winced at the memory.

"Badly beaten," she said. "Fatal gunshot wound to the head. And there was a leather pouch that had been hung around his neck."

"Did you inspect this pouch?"

"Of course."

"Can you tell the jury what was inside?"

"Thirty silver dollars," Mary Beth said.

Pomfried pivoted around to face the jury. For some reason he really wanted to focus their attention on this detail.

"Thirty pieces of silver," he said. "What the good book tells us Judas Iscariot was paid for betraying Christ."

Ms. Nelson, in the front row of the jury box, covered her mouth.

Pomfried asked, "What, if any, significance did you draw from this discovery?"

Mary Beth shrugged. "I guess someone felt like they had

been betrayed by Brad Mayhew. And whoever that person was took themselves pretty seriously."

Mary Beth didn't want to say any more about how her view of that detail had changed in light of later discoveries.

Pomfried asked her to identify who all was present with her when they'd found the body. She listed the deputies she recalled being there, along with her and Father Gonzalez.

"There was someone else with you as well, wasn't there—a civilian you'd allowed to tag along?"

"Oh," Mary Beth said, realizing who Pomfried was talking about. "I wouldn't say he was a civilian. Sid Cain was the retired sheriff. At the time, I thought of him more as law enforcement *emeritus*. He was there when we first encountered Father Gonzalez and said he wanted to help, so—"

"So he rode along with you, Father Gonzalez, and Deputy Skipwith, is that correct?"

"Sounds right," Mary Beth said.

She failed to see what that had to do with the price of tea in China, but Pomfried was smiling like he'd just suckered her into a serious admission.

"And it was during this car ride, wasn't it, *Miss* Cain, that Sid Cain expressed his belief that you had killed before and would be willing to kill again?"

Mary Beth didn't know whether to laugh or scoff. Sid had never said any such thing to her. Not as far as she could recall. But the result of her surprise at the question was to her looking dumbfounded, mouth agape, which she realized too late might make her look guilty to the jury.

"We're waiting for an answer, Ms. Cain," Pomfried said.

Mary Beth regained her bearings. "My answer is: that's just about the dumbest thing I ever heard."

"Do you deny it?"

"Absolutely."

"I'm not asking about whether what was said is true. Just

whether it was said. Do you deny that Sid Cain leveled that accusation?"

Again Mary Beth hesitated too long before answering. The whole thing just seemed so out of left field to her. "Yes," she said, finally. "I deny that Sid ever said anything at all like that to me."

Pomfried smiled again, as though he'd just lured her further into his trap. "Tell me, Ms. Cain," he said, turning his back to her in order to face the jury. "Do you consider Deputy Skipwith to be an honest person?"

"Yes." That question seemed to come out of nowhere, too, but at least Mary Beth answered it without pausing. Skipwith was dumber than shit, but he was certainly honest.

"I thought so." Pomfried waddled his fat butt back toward counsel's table, where he had a television hooked up to a laptop, both of which were on a rolling cart. With some awkwardness, he rolled the cart out into the well of the courtroom and positioned it where both Mary Beth and the jury could see.

"This is a video of prior sworn testimony in this matter, given by Deputy Skipwith."

Pomfried pressed Play, and an image of Skipwith, the skinniest, youngest member of the force, popped up. He looked sheepish and pale, blinking incessantly and twisting his long, Ichabod Crane neck back and forth before speaking.

"It was all kind of weird," he said. "We'd been driving around a long time, and the sheriff started badgering Mr. Sid. I guess she thought he'd never really liked her much—you know, like back when she and Mr. Bill were married—and she wanted to know why. Then finally, Mr. Sid said he thought she'd killed people and might do it again."

Mary Beth did her best not to react, but she wanted to scream, *What the hell?*

In the video, an offscreen Pomfried could be heard asking Skipwith how Mary Beth responded to the accusation. To which he replied, "She kind of admitted to it."

Mary Beth's heart dropped, suddenly feeling like she'd been set up.

Pomfried stopped the playback, looking awfully satisfied with himself. "What do you have to say now, *Miss* Cain?"

Mary Beth was gobsmacked. Sid had never accused her of murder. And she certainly had never admitted to it. She was about to just give up and say she had no idea what to say—which wouldn't have sounded good—when she finally realized what had happened, and it struck her as so funny she actually laughed out loud.

"Something about homicide that you find amusing?" Pomfried asked.

Mary Beth laughed louder. She couldn't help it. The more the reality of what had occurred set in, the more it tickled her. She had to ask for a moment to compose herself.

Pomfried was put out by the fact she was enjoying this. "Whenever you're ready to explain," he said.

Mary Beth finally got her laughter under control. "I'm sorry. I just finally figured out what it was Skipwith was talking about. He just really misunderstood what he heard."

Pomfried hiked his pants indignantly. "Is that right? Maybe you'd care to elaborate."

"Sure." Mary Beth took another moment to make sure she wasn't about to launch into another laughing fit. "Right before we first discovered Father Gonzalez, Sid and I had been talking about my son, Sam, and the possibility of him transferring to another school, far from home. I was against it, and Sid was in favor of it. And I did tell Sid that I believed he had never really liked me. Going back to my marriage with Bill. He said that wasn't true and mentioned something about some old coal miner's myth that he didn't get a chance to explain because Father Gonzalez showed up at the church and we got interrupted. So later that day, after we'd been driving around for hours trying to figure out where exactly it was that Father Gonzalez had been when he witnessed Brad Mayhew's execution, I came back to the conversation and asked Sid to finish what he'd been saying."

"Which was?" Pomfried asked.

Mary Beth chuckled again at how badly Skipwith had garbled what was actually said, turning his testimony into a terrible game of judicial telephone.

"It's really kind of stupid," Mary Beth said. "Sid even admitted that it was. But apparently it's something the Scots-Irish people who settled this area brought with them—the idea that somehow redheaded women are bad luck."

Pomfried looked confused.

Mary Beth said, "Back in the day, women weren't allowed down at the coal mines. So the only time they ever showed their faces there was when their husbands had been killed in a cave-in. And in Ireland you've got a lot of redhaired women. So over time it just got to be that when the miners saw a redheaded lady, it meant someone had died."

Pomfried was flabbergasted. "But Deputy Skipwith said you admitted to—"

"Deputy Skipwith was busy watching the road, and only half listening. What happened was, Sid started talking about this old myth. And how he knew it was stupid. But there had been a lot of people around me who had died. My father, Bill, my brother. And Sid was saying that with how dangerous things had gotten around Jasper Creek lately, and with me going after Velino, he couldn't help but feel that Sam might be safer someplace else. I reluctantly had to agree that there was some truth to that."

Pomfried's mouth actually fell open. He started twice to try and speak, then decided to remain quiet and took his time returning the television cart to its prior position, acting like he hadn't just had his ass handed to him in front of the jury.

Mary Beth taunted the pudgy prosecutor. "I sure hope you've got something better than that, Pomfried. I'd hate to think you've wasted these poor people's time trumping up charges against me over this kind of ridiculousness."

Pomfried turned back to Mary Beth, looking so angry that it seemed like steam might come out his ears. "Oh, don't you worry, Sugar," he said. "We're just getting started."

08

AFTER RECOVERING Brad Mayhew's body, Mary Beth and Izzy had brought Father Gonzalez back to the station and sat down with him in an interview room. The priest was shivering, probably more from nerves than temperature, but Mary Beth placed her coat around his shoulders anyway, hoping it would comfort him.

"Here you go, Father," she said, still feeling odd referring to him in a paternal fashion, as the priest was about a decade younger than Mary Beth and had a youthful appearance, with a thin, hipsterish beard to go with his dark, wavy hair. Mary Beth patted him on the back. "Just sit here for a minute and relax," she told him. "Izzy and I will go and get you a cup of coffee."

The two officers stepped out into the hall to go over how they were going to handle this most important of interviews. When Father Gonzalez told them he'd seen a white Mercedes SUV pull up to the scene and a bald white man get out and perform the coup de grace on Brad Mayhew, Mary Beth just about shit her pants she was so excited. The man described had to be Leonard Velino. There was no doubt. The only question was whether

Father Gonzalez would be able to positively identify him in a way that would hold up in court.

While at the scene, the priest had been able to show Mary Beth and Izzy the basic area where he'd been situated when the shooting happened, on an elevated ridge approximately one hundred yards away from where Mayhew's body was found. Izzy had suggested they climb up there and take a few photos from what would have been Father Gonzalez's vantage point, for evidentiary purposes, but Mary Beth quickly nixed that idea, knowing it would just illustrate how great the distance was and thinking that the priest's testimony, minus the visuals, would play much better at trial.

"I know you're not going to want to hear this," Izzy said, "but now would be a great time to try and bring in the Feds. Give this to them and let them put together the big RICO case against Velino's operation."

Mary Beth was waiting for the punchline. When none came, she said, "You're joking right?"

"No. Velino's not some local shitkicker. Prosecuting someone like him is a big undertaking."

"And?"

Izzy gave her that worried-slash-disappointed, I-don't-know-why-I-even-try-because-you-never-listen-anyway look. He might have been under five feet tall, but he always had a way of gazing at Mary Beth that felt like he was looking down at her.

She bopped him on the shoulder. "Don't you see, Iz? That's the beauty of a murder charge. It's a purely state crime. As state as it gets. No way the Feds can come in and take it away from us, as long as we limit the prosecution to Mayhew."

She could tell Izzy had determined that arguing was pointless. "Well, we may be getting ahead of ourselves, anyway. Father Gonzalez has yet to officially identify Velino as the shooter. Guess we should go ahead and put together a six-pack." Izzy was referring to a standard method of police identification, where the witness was presented with photos of six different people and asked if one of them was the person they saw. This process was where cases were often won or lost, as defense attorneys typically attacked them on constitutional grounds and tried to get them thrown out for being unfairly suggestive. Thus, the gold standard was to videotape the procedure to show that nothing was done to coach the witness.

"Go ahead and put one together," Mary Beth said. "And make it good, Iz."

"Might be hard to find photos of five other guys who look like Velino."

"Throw in one of Uncle Fester if you have to," Mary Beth said with a smile.

"Yeah, maybe Voldemort, too."

"No," Mary Beth said. "Velino looks way too much like Voldemort. No way Father Gonzalez could ever tell them apart."

Izzy gave her a thumbs-up and went off to put the photo array together. Mary Beth decided Izzy should be the one to handle the identification so he could testify about it. Mary Beth had so often been accused of unconstitutionally sweating confessions out of suspects she might prove a liability to the prosecution if they had to rely upon her testimony over this key issue. But she could make sure Father Gonzalez would deliver.

As soon as Izzy was gone, she hit a button to turn off the camera mounted in the corner of the interrogation room and reentered. The priest looked up, noticing she wasn't carrying anything other than the file folder she had tucked under her arm.

"It will be just a minute on the coffee," Mary Beth said. She sat down and faced the priest in a manner that demonstrated the seriousness of what she was about to say.

"Father, I want you to know that I believe very strongly that you have been chosen by God to do something extremely important."

Father Gonzalez had been hunched over but sat up straight. "Oh, yes?"

"Yes," Mary Beth answered. "You see, our county has been in the midst of a crime wave led by a ruthless drug trafficker from Detroit named Leonard Velino. He's responsible for an untold number of deaths in this community, from overdoses to street-corner violence. And you have a chance to put an end to all of that if you are able to identify him as the man who killed Brad Mayhew."

Father Gonzalez exhaled, blowing out his cheeks. "I was some distance away. I'm not sure—"

Mary Beth held up a finger to silence him.

"Don't lose faith on me," she said. "Just take a look here."

Mary Beth opened up the folder she'd been carrying and pulled out several surveillance photos of Velino, including multiple ones of him getting out of or into his white Mercedes SUV.

"Now I can't tell you that this is the man you saw, Father. But what I can tell you is that this is Leonard Velino, who is a lifelong criminal, a mob-connected drug trafficker who's been accused of personally murdering numerous people. This is the face of evil incarnate, Father. And he just so happens to drive a white Mercedes SUV. Just like the one you saw."

"What could he have to do with Brad Mayhew?"

"I don't know the answer to that yet. But I intend to find out by the time we get to trial. All I need from you right now is for you to sear the image of this man's face into your brain."

"It could be him, certainly, but I'm not—"

"That's the vehicle you saw, right?" Mary Beth tapped hastily on the photo.

"It looks like it, yes."

"How many white Mercedes SUVs do you think there are in Jasper County?"

The priest shrugged.

"If there's two or three, I'd be surprised," Mary Beth said.

"This is a Ford or Chevy kind of community. And what are the odds of there being another white Mercedes SUV, driven by a pale-skinned, bald-headed murderer?"

Father Gonzalez nodded. He understood.

"No one is asking you to lie here Father. If there was any chance in the world that Velino wasn't our bad guy, I wouldn't be in here doing this. But there is no chance of that. It's one hundred percent. Now, some cowardly witnesses wouldn't want to get involved and might try to shuck the responsibility that God and circumstance had placed on them by saying they aren't sure who they saw. In which case, Lenny Velino would just go right on killing and wreaking havoc upon our community, pushing his junk on kids. But not someone like you, Father. A man who looks after his flock. That's why I believe—no, *believe* is not the right word. That is why I know God chose you to be the one to witness what happened. Do you understand what I'm saying, Father?"

The priest sat back in his chair. Mary Beth watched his chest rise and fall as he absorbed the full import of what she was asking of him. "I understand," he said.

"Good." Mary Beth stood and patted him on the shoulder. "You are a good man. And you are about to save a lot of lives." Mary Beth pointed to the door. "I'm going to go out, and in a few moments, I'll come back in with Deputy Baker, who is going to show you some photos. And this conversation that we just had needs to fall under your priestly code of confidentiality. It stays between you, me, and God, okay?"

The priest nodded.

Mary Beth clasped her hands in a praying gesture and bowed her head toward Father Gonzalez. Then she slipped out of the interview room, turned the camera back on, went to the break room to pour the priest a cup of black coffee, and was back just as Izzy was returning with a folder containing six photos of bald white men, one of which was their suspect.

"How's this?" he asked, showing the array to Mary Beth.

She studied them. The men ranged in age. Two were likely in their late twenties. Three others were middle aged, closer to Velino, who was fifty-four. None of the others were as menacing as Velino, but Mary Beth thought the images were close enough to pass constitutional muster.

"That will work," she said. "Now remember, when we get in there, we can't do anything to suggest anything to Father Gonzalez. No prompting. No coaching. And we need to tell him it's possible that this array doesn't contain a photo of our suspect."

"I know," Izzy said. "I just hope you're prepared to be disappointed. As far away as Gonzalez was from the murder, I'll be a little surprised if he's able to positively ID the shooter."

Mary Beth placed a hand on Izzy's shoulder and said, "Oh, ye of little faith."

They reentered the interview room. Mary Beth sat back and let Izzy take the lead. Before displaying the photos, he gave the witness a standard admonition. "Father, it's possible that none of these photos is the man you saw. It's also possible that none of these is a suspect. I don't want you to feel any pressure to try and please us one way or another. Just take a good look and tell us if you recognize anyone here as the shooter."

Izzy flipped open his manilla folder and slid it across the table. Inside were two rows of three photos each, all mugshots, with the name placards cropped out.

Father Gonzalez took his time looking at each one, then he raised his head and met Mary Beth's eyes for a moment.

Shit, she thought. Either the witness wasn't able to pick out Velino, despite her effort to burn his ugly-ass image into the priest's brain, or he'd lost his nerve, or—worse—he'd had an attack of conscience.

Mary Beth maintained a poker face, not wanting the camera to catch her doing anything to signal the witness.

After staring into her eyes for a cold few seconds, Father Gonzalez looked back down and pointed to the photo on the top right.

"That one."

Mary Beth breathed a sigh of relief. He'd fingered the right guy.

"How sure are you?" Izzy asked.

The priest looked back at Mary Beth as he answered. "One hundred percent."

Mary Beth felt every muscle in her body clench. She wanted to shout for joy or give someone a high five and maybe a good chest bump but knew that any such reaction could be used against the prosecution at trial. Instead she offered a muted thank you. She wanted to move quickly to end this interview, quit while they were way ahead, but Izzy wasn't ready to turn it loose.

"Do you know who this man is, Father?"

Mary Beth quickly answered the question for him. "His name is Leonard Velino. He's a suspected drug trafficker. *Prior to today*, had you ever heard that name?"

The question was carefully framed and elicited the desired response.

"No," Father Gonzalez said. "Prior to today, I had never heard of him."

Izzy gave Mary Beth a sideways glance to let her know he didn't approve of her interjection but moved on to what appeared to be his point, which, as usual, was one of caution. "He's a very dangerous person, Father. Someone who has reportedly harassed, intimidated, and possibly even killed witnesses."

The priest did a double take and stared at Mary Beth with a panicked expression, like he was silently asking her what in the hell she had gotten him into. Mary Beth did feel some compunction about the dangerous position Father Gonzalez would be in as the star witness against Velino, but she also knew it was necessary and that she would do everything in her power to protect him.

She pulled a metal chair out from the table, scraping it against the floor, and sat down opposite the priest. Mary Beth pointed a thumb back at her own chest and said, "I'm a very dangerous person, too, Father. And I pledge to you that I will protect you from this monster." She couldn't help thinking about Mr. Percy and how her failure to keep him safe would haunt her until her dying days.

"You will?" Father Gonzalez's nervousness was apparent but so was his bravery. Mary Beth knew she would give her life, if necessary, to protect him. And she wouldn't make the same mistakes again. She'd tried to keep Mr. Percy's identity a secret, referring to him only as a confidential informant in the warrant application. Someone who would have never needed to testify if she'd found Velino with the drugs she'd expected to be there. Anonymity wouldn't be an option with Father Gonzalez, however, as the only eyewitness to a murder. So Mary Beth would have to provide him with around-the-clock protection. It was something her department had never done before, but extreme times called for extreme measures.

Mary Beth put her hand to her heart and said, "With God as my witness, Father, I will keep you safe."

09

GETTING THE ARREST WARRANT for Leonard Velino was easy. The question was how to execute it. Mary Beth had a couple more shock-and-awe ideas, but Izzy cautioned, "Velino isn't the type to go quietly. And he's surrounded by armed murderers at all times."

So that got Mary Beth thinking. She snapped her fingers and said, "I know. Let's tell him I want to make a deal."

"What kind of deal?" Izzy asked.

"One that's bullshit. But everybody thinks I'm dirty, right? So let's use that. Get the word to him through some kind of back channel that I'd like to discuss an arrangement that will cut down on some of the ancillary crime and havoc he's been wreaking, and in exchange I'll ease up. The pressure we've been applying must be causing him headaches. He'd probably welcome a powwow right now. Might even be able to get him to come into the station."

"You'll never get him to come into the police station."

"Maybe not," Mary Beth said. "But wherever it is, we insist that everybody come unarmed, then we arrest him."

Izzy thought it over. "I like it. There's just one little problem."

"What's that?"

"We don't have any back channels to Velino. Who's going to handle the reach-out?"

Mary Beth frowned. "Yeah, that is kind of the bitch." She had an idea about that but didn't like it. Without any other plans springing to mind, however, she went ahead and said, "Suppose we could go to *the* bitch. See if she might be willing to help."

"In exchange for what?" Izzy asked. They both knew Mary Beth was referring to her mother, Mountain Mamie, who never did anything out of the goodness of her heart.

"Self-benefit," Mary Beth said. 'Velino's her competition, but her people operate in the same world. She has to have an emissary who can reach out to him, saying we want some kind of trilateral talks between Detroit, what's left of the McCray County Mafia, and me. We'll pitch it as a summit to broker a power-sharing arrangement. But the whole thing will be a ruse to get the drop on Velino and arrest him for murder."

Izzy reluctantly agreed with the plan and offered to go with Mary Beth to speak to her mother, but the sheriff declined—intent on doing the dirty work herself. So that evening, under cover of darkness, Mary Beth made the hour or so drive into Dulcimer, Kentucky, past trailer parks and enclaves of impoverished hovels, before arriving at her seventy-five-year-old mother's white palatial estate that would have fit right in on *MTV Cribs* with its Greek-inspired portico fronted by an ornate fountain in the center of a circular cobblestone driveway. From prior, unpleasant visits, Mary Beth knew the interior of the lavish home included a casino, bowling alley, a few random stripper poles, and a "hookah" room—which apparently had nothing to do with all of the prostitutes her mother employed. Out back was a lavish pool with an always-staffed swim-up bar and multiple Jacuzzis.

When Mary Beth got there, the security staff was busy

directing a long line of limousines and valeting various expensive sedans for what Mary Beth would soon discover was an "Eyes Wide Shut Party" where well-to-do guests came wearing party Venetian-style masks to hump their brains out with prostitutes and swingers, just like in what Mary Beth was pretty sure must be the only Stanley Kubrick film her mother had ever seen.

After flashing her badge a few times and explaining her relationship to the lady of the house, a security guard escorted Mary Beth to an upstairs study where Mamie was enjoying a cocktail with her latest boy toy, a twenty-something Tupac-lookalike wannabe rapper who went by the handle G Money.

"Geoffrey, dear," Mamie said, using G's full first name when she saw Mary Beth, "why don't you give my daughter and me a few moments alone to talk."

"Cool," he said and offered Mary Beth a fist bump on his way out. She declined.

That November, Mary Beth had endured the most awkward Thanksgiving dinner of her life, she and Sam at Mamie's long table. G Money had shown up late, looking all squinty eyed, and when he passed the mashed potatoes, Mary Beth caught a whiff of sweet-skunky weed that was strong enough to give her a contact buzz.

"You should be nice to Geoffrey," Mamie said to her daughter. "He just might end up being your stepdaddy one day."

"I wasn't nice to the last two or three. Why start now?"

Mamie sighed and fanned herself with a hand laden by three gaudy rings, each from a past husband. "Well, you're not wearing a mask, so I suppose you're not here for the festivities." The old woman had been born and raised on a coal pile in McCray County but loved Scarlett O'Hara and thus spoke with the embellished affect of a Southern belle—which never failed to grate on Mary Beth's nerves.

"Not hardly," Mary Beth said. "I was wondering what the local sheriff might think about your little orgy."

Mamie smiled. "I believe he's in a room down the hall, plowing that new Brazilian girl, if you'd care to ask him."

Mary Beth shook her head. Mamie said, "Why don't you just get on with it, dear? You only ever come to see me when you need something. What is it?"

"Leonard Velino," Mary Beth said.

Mamie smiled. "Ah, yes. I knew this day would come. You miss your dear old mama now, don't you?"

"I wouldn't go that far. I'm not welcoming you back. But I know some of your guys still have some remaining operations in old McCray and that Velino's been pounding the shit out of them. Seems like it would be in both our best interests if we could put him out of business."

Mamie's broad smile had diminished to a thin, tight line. She no doubt had been expecting more of a red-carpet invitation. "What did you have in mind?" she asked.

Mary Beth shared her idea about setting up a meeting as a pretext for safely arresting Velino on murder charges.

Mamie seemed uninterested. "Oh, I don't know."

"What's that mean?"

"We off the record?"

"Yeah, yeah. Say what you need to say," Mary Beth told her.

"Well, truth is, I'm mostly out of the drug business. At least in West Virginia. I get a little tribute here and there from the boys I set up, but it's more passive income for me at this point. I'm finding that the blackmail opportunities from these little parties are quite lucrative."

"But you still have the contacts. You could set the meeting, right?"

"I could. But what I'm telling you is there's not much in it for me. I get very little from the existing drug business in Old McCray. So arresting Velino does a lot for you and nothing for me. So why would—"

"Good God," Mary Beth said. "Fucking mother of the year."

"There's no need to be sarcastic, dear. I'm merely pointing out that your offer is not really an offer at all. Your negotiating skills are lacking. I thought I taught you better than that. You've got to dangle the carrot. For instance, if I were permitted to move back into my home, maybe boost my operation, then—"

"Not happening."

Mamie batted her eyes. "Then what do we have to discuss?"

Mary Beth knew this would be painful. Conversations with her mother always were.

"If there's nothing in it for me, then it sounds to me like you are not offering a deal. You are simply asking for a favor," Mamie said.

Before Mary Beth could interrupt, her mother continued, saying, "And since I have always supported my children, a favor is something I am happy to do."

Mary Beth held her breath, waiting for the other shoe to drop. Mamie held her gaze with the plastic smile of a beauty contestant.

"That's it?" Mary Beth asked.

"That's it. All you had to do was ask."

Mary Beth considered a few verbal jabs before deciding it was best to just take yes for an answer and said, "Thank you."

When she turned to leave, Mamie said, "Of course you'll owe me a favor in return at some point."

Mary Beth shook her head. She knew just how dangerous it could be to owe Mamie anything, especially a favor. Her better angels were telling her to walk away, but her blood lust for Velino was too strong to let that happen. "Yeah, okay," she mumbled.

"Good. Well, it's always a pleasure to see you, dear."

"Whatever."

Mary Beth tried again to leave when Mamie said, "Oh, there's just one more thing."

Mary Beth stopped. She knew this had been too easy.

"Your cousin, Tommy," Mamie said. "I believe there's still a warrant out for his arrest over that unfortunate little misunderstanding with your brother."

That unfortunate little misunderstanding was a near massacre. A confrontation between Sawyer's well-armed and completely unregulated militia versus a battalion of federal officers and troops ready for a siege. Mary Beth averted an all-out war by apprehending her brother, but after she secreted Sawyer out of harm's way through an old mining tunnel, she found her cousin Tommy and one of his buddies waiting for her on the other side. They rescued Sawyer and left Mary Beth handcuffed to a tree, where the Feds found her and charged her with aiding Sawyer's escape.

"You're damn right there's still a warrant out on Tommy," Mary Beth said.

Mamie gave Mary Beth her motherly look of disappointment. "Well, I think it's time to let bygones be bygones. All that mess is long over with. And Tommy's family. I'm sure he's tired of being on the lam and would love to come home."

Tommy was technically family, though distant. A second or third cousin, once or twice removed, Mary Beth was never really sure. Didn't matter. Mary Beth knew that the relevant connection was the fact that Tommy had been one of Mamie's chief lieutenants when she was running drugs in McCray.

"Does that count as your favor, if I make the warrant go away?"

Mamie waved off the question like she was swatting a fly. "Don't be ridiculous. That's not a favor, dear. That's just a little old accommodation. For a family member. I just think it would be nice is all."

"Suppose I say no, then."

Mamie grimaced. "Oh, I don't know. Without my help, your Mr. Velino's likely to get word you're looking for him and go to ground. Maybe head back to Detroit. You might never see him again."

That prospect sounded pleasant at first, but Mary Beth knew

that simply running Leonard Velino off wouldn't necessarily solve her problems. He could direct his drug operation from Detroit just as easily as he could from nearby. Plus, she wanted to collar the son of a bitch so badly the idea of letting slip away wasn't something she could abide.

"Fine," she said. "Tell Tommy he's in the clear."

"Excellent. Oh and—"

Mary Beth exited quickly after that and closed the door behind her before her mother could add anything else. She navigated through halls of debauchery, past people in tuxedos and evening gowns, and in various states of undress, some randomly fornicating right there out in the open. Once outside, she enjoyed a great breath of fresh air, then got in her car and drove quickly away.

It was a little after ten p.m. when she hit Jasper Creek and decided that there was one more unpleasant conversation she wanted to get out of the way that evening. So she hung a left on Mulberry down past the Go Mart and headed up past the Mountain View Country Club to an upscale neighborhood of custom homes called Boulder Ridge, where all the doctors and lawyers and big business owners lived. It always struck Mary Beth as funny, seeing those mansions way up there. In the coal town she'd grown up in, the rich people lived on what little bit of flat land there was, while the poor folks had the homes that clung to the sides of the mountains. But in Jasper things were often reversed, as the rich opted for isolated, elevated perches that allowed them to look down on everyone else.

Mary Beth parked down the street from a three-level Spanish-style home, a mixture of white stucco and red brick with terracotta roofing that passed for exotic in Jasper Creek. It wasn't nearly as big as her mother's home, but it was awfully big and ostentatious, in Mary Beth's opinion, with its three-car detached garage, connected to the main house by a walkway with brick arches.

Mary Beth followed that path and then banged hard on the dark wood double-front doors.

"Police. Open up."

Patrick Connelly answered, looking like he was ready for bed, dressed in navy-blue pajama pants and a white undershirt. He looked good, Mary Beth thought. But she always thought that, and it didn't matter. She wasn't there to pay him any compliments.

"Mary? What's—"

"We need to talk," she said, sternly.

Patrick looked worried. "Okay. Come in."

When he turned around, Mary Beth seized hold of his right arm, wrenched it behind his back, and drove him down to the ground, face first.

Before Patrick could ask what in the hell she was doing, Mary Beth had her knee in the center of his back and wrapped her arms around his throat like a boa constrictor and started to squeeze.

"Georgetown? Fucking Georgetown, Patrick!"

Georgetown University was Patrick's alma mater. The place he had left her for, and now her son Sam was about to as well. Mary Beth knew that despite Sam's stellar grades and test scores, you didn't get into a place like that without a great recommendation like the one she was certain he'd gotten from Patrick.

"It wasn't my idea," Patrick managed to say between gasps for air.

Mary Beth released her grip long enough to flip Patrick onto his back so she could stare into his eyes to see whether or not he was lying. She had him pinned down there when she asked, "Oh yeah, well, whose idea was it, then?"

"It was all Sam's, I swear. I don't want him to leave any more than you do. I was finally getting to know him."

Mary Beth saw truth in Patrick's eyes. Truth and fear. She had to admit that what he said made sense. Patrick had always hated

Jasper Creek, and West Virginia in general, but had moved back there in the hopes that he could be close to her and Sam, with the understanding that he would always keep secret the fact that he was Sam's biological father.

"Maybe it was," Mary Beth said. Sam had been clerking for Patrick, working part-time in his little law firm, and had been quite taken with the attorney. She could see Sam wanting to emulate this new role model by going to the same school.

"But you helped him get in," she said.

Patrick didn't deny it. "What was I supposed to do, say no when he asked me for a recommendation?"

Mary Beth paused to think about that, and Patrick took advantage of her hesitation. He flipped her on to her back, putting his full weight on top of her. Instinctively she thought about kneeing him in the groin but paused when he kissed her. She kissed him back at first, then pushed him away.

She sat up and crossed her arms. "You knew about this and didn't tell me," she said.

Patrick sat up next to her. "He asked me not to. Sam wanted to tell you himself."

It was another defensible response, but Mary Beth wasn't quite ready to stop being angry yet. She habitually viewed all things that displeased her as a betrayal and personal attack.

"You're going to pay for this, Connelly."

"Oh yeah?" Patrick gave her that cocky shit-eating grin of his that simultaneously infuriated and excited her. "Did you bring your handcuffs this time?"

Mary Beth held his gaze for a moment, debating how to respond. She got to her feet, and Patrick stood to face her. They were nose to nose when she said, "Don't I always?" and held up the silver metal restraints so Patrick could get a good look at them before she kissed him.

10

IT WAS A LITTLE AFTER MIDNIGHT when Mary Beth slipped out of bed and started looking around for her clothes. The first thing she found was a tiny pistol that she strapped to her ankle before putting on her underwear. Patrick was awake, watching her. Normally he would have enjoyed the sight, but his heart was heavy with the thought of her leaving.

"Why don't you just spend the night?" he asked as Mary Beth retrieved her bra from beneath the bedside table.

"Appearances," she said. "The sheriff sleeping with a criminal defense attorney? It doesn't look good."

"Is that all we're doing—sleeping together?"

"Here we go," she said. "Mr. Romantic. You're not going to propose again, are you?" Mary Beth turned a circle until she spotted her pants on the far side of the room.

"Maybe."

Mary Beth smiled at him. She hopped into her pants one leg at a time as she approached the bed and leaned down. Patrick thought she was going to kiss him, but she'd spotted her shirt draped above the headboard and retrieved it instead.

"You're sweet," she said. "But I already was married. I'm not putting Sam through that."

There it was. The ghost of Bill Cain. Mary Beth was always so determined to honor his highly romanticized memory. If only she knew what Patrik had learned at the end of the Maria Ruiz case, when he had been briefly appointed a special prosecutor to convict the hitman who killed Maria, a young girl who'd been missing for years before her body was discovered along with the remains of her unborn child.

When Mary Beth and her men went to arrest former deputy Randy Law, the man who allegedly hired the hitman. Patrick had a test run on the DNA of Maria's fetal remains against the control database of the county's law enforcement officers and personnel. Randy was the assumed father of Maria's baby, and since Randy killed himself before being apprehended, the case was considered closed by the time Patrick received the DNA results. He could still envision them in his mind.

PROBABILITY OF PATERNITY: 99.9998%
CHILD: Fetal Remains - Ruiz, Maria
FATHER: Cain, William

It appeared that Randy had been doing some of Bill's dirty work for him. Getting Raul to hide the fact that it was actually Bill Cain who'd impregnated Maria.

"I just think it would be nice is all," Patrick said as Mary Beth was buttoning her shirt.

"What's that?"

"If the three of us could have dinner together sometime. Go to a movie. Maybe a ballgame."

Mary Beth inspected her other pistol, a Glock .22, before reholstering it on her gun belt and securing the safety strap. "The three of who?" she asked.

"Who do you think? You, me, and Sam."

Mary Beth looked up. Now Patrick had her attention. "We had a deal," she said. "I agreed to let you come back here on the express condition that you'd never breathe a word to Sam."

That was true. Patrick had agreed never to let Sam in on their secret. That he, Patrick, was really Sam's biological father. But that didn't mean they couldn't have more of a relationship.

"I'm not going to tell him about that," Patrick said. "I'd just like to be able to tell him I'm your boyfriend."

Mary Beth laughed.

"What?"

"I don't know," Mary Beth said. "Boyfriend. It just sounds funny. Like we're sixteen again or something."

Patrick was hurt by her response. "Well, aren't I?" he asked.

Mary Beth bent down and kissed him. Patrick let her for a moment, then pulled back, realizing she was placating him. Shutting him up.

"Don't get so sensitive," she said.

"Well, am I or not?"

Mary Beth laughed. Patrick lay back on the bed and rolled the other way, facing the wall.

Mary Beth pushed him over enough to lie down behind him. "Yes, you are my boyfriend," she said. "If you pass me a note after gym class asking me if I want to go steady, I'll check the box for *Yes*, okay?"

"Yeah, sure. Whatever."

"Come on now, don't be like that."

"I said whatever. It's fine. Go on and go."

"Patrick." Mary Beth coaxed him to roll over and looked into his eyes. For a moment her shields were down, and she let him really see her. This was the Mary Beth that only Patrick knew. The vulnerable girl inside of all that armor.

"I just want to protect Sam," she said. "And I feel like I owe it to Bill. Truth is I was never a good wife to him. I didn't love him, and I think he knew it."

"Mary, if—"

She put her slender finger to his lips to silence him. "I wasn't a good wife to him because I loved you. And I think he knew that, too. Maybe a lot of people did. I just don't want Bill to be remembered like he was some cuckolded sap."

With that, she'd won Patrick over. As long as he knew that she loved him, had always loved him, just like he had always loved her, he could live with it being just their secret.

He kissed her and said, "I understand."

Mary Beth finished getting ready and let herself out, slinking back into the night. This had been their pattern for months: clandestine meetings and late-night rendezvouses.

Patrick did his best to get back to sleep but was troubled by the thought that protecting Mary Beth and Sam's memory of Bill Cain wasn't the only reason he'd decided to keep Bill's affair and murderous cover-up a secret. There was also a fear. A distinct feeling that if he were to pull on that Bill Cain thread any further, something much larger might unravel.

Bill had been killed in a drug bust. Randy Law, Bill's best friend and accomplice, had earned a reputation as a supercop when it came to drug busts, many of which had come at the expense of the McCray County Mafia. Patrick couldn't help but think how Bill's death sure did solve a lot of problems for Mamie. Next thing you knew, Mary Beth was sheriff, Randy Law was off the force, and instead of having her operation raided, Mamie was suddenly in a position to point law enforcement toward her competitors.

What if Mamie was the one who had Bill killed?

It boggled Patrick that Mary Beth had never put these pieces together, but then again she always did have a blind spot with the people she cared about.

Patrick was still thinking about all that the following morning when he arrived at the law office he'd purchased from Alexander Pomfried after the old barrister took the district attorney job.

The office had been converted from an old Victorian-style home located on the traffic circle around the Jasper County courthouse that sat in the center of town. Patrick parked in the tiny driveway next to the Subaru Outback his assistant drove. Sam wouldn't be in until later. The shopkeeper's bell on the front door rang as Patrick entered and waved hello to Dottie, the secretary he'd inherited from Pomfried. Patrick walked past her desk, through a narrow hallway. To the left was a dining room with a grand fireplace. The space had been turned into a conference room with a long table and chairs that didn't leave much room to maneuver around. Past that was the kitchen where Dottie had already brewed a pot of coffee.

Patrick poured himself a cup and shuddered to think of the conflagration that could occur if Mary Beth ever came to believe that Mamie was behind Bill's murder. If those two women were ever at open war with each other, it would be a battle that would make the Old Wengo Affair pale in comparison. And Patrick already wore the guilt over his role in causing that mess, like an albatross around his neck. He'd just wanted to help Mary Beth get out from under federal investigation by proposing a deal to wipe her slate clean in exchange for Sawyer's arrest.

That had been innocent enough, but when the lead prosecutor didn't go for it, Patrick decided he needed to make Sawyer a more valuable prize, so he gave Mamie some inside intel on a planned public works project in exchange for her manipulating Sawyer to up the ante with the Feds. Thankfully, Mary Beth had managed to subdue the situation before it got truly out of hand, but still, people had died, and Patrick knew their blood was at least partially on his hands. He wasn't about to risk anything like that again by sharing his suspicions about Bill and Mamie with Mary Beth.

Patrick took his cup of coffee back into his office, where a big, framed photo of Clarence Darrow at the Scopes Monkey Trial hung over his desk. Patrick had found the picture at a flea market in Galax, Virginia, and immediately felt drawn to it. Clarence Darrow, the hotshot Yankee attorney, unfazed by his hostile reception in Tennessee. Patrick could imagine what that must have felt like, as he was the forever outsider in Jasper Creek, the city slicker lawyer inside the rural lion's den.

Patrick sat down and started writing out his daily to-do list on a fresh legal pad, when Dottie appeared at the door, looking concerned.

"Mr. Connelly, there's some men here to see you."

Patrick wasn't expecting anyone, but he often got walk-in clients. That was the point of having an office next to the court-house. People got in trouble over there, and his was the first sign they would see on their way out, while in need of representation.

"They're in the conference room."

"Okay," Patrick said. "Is something wrong?"

"No. No," Dottie said. "They told me they wanted to consult with you about a criminal matter. Just gave me a bad feeling, is all. But I guess that goes with the territory."

Wasn't that the truth. Patrick still had not fully adjusted from his old life as a US attorney, litigating land-use cases on behalf of the government in high-rise office buildings and austere federal courthouses, far removed from the kind of daily grime he now encountered as a small-town jack-of-all-trades attorney who had to take whatever opportunities came his way. For the first time in his life, Patrick had overhead to worry about.

"Did they look like they have money?" Patrick asked, cutting to what necessity had dictated was the only relevant intake question.

"Yes," Dottie said, shaking her head. "They certainly do."

"Well, then, I'm happy to meet with them," Patrick said. "Please let them know I'll be right there."

Dottie left, and Patrick took a few more minutes to download his daily to-dos while he still had them in his mind. Then he pulled another fresh legal pad from a desk drawer that he secured inside a black padfolio that had a small stack of his business cards tucked in an inside pocket.

Patrick entered the conference room and found three men. Two were the size of NFL linemen and dressed like undertakers in black suits with black ties. Each was seated with both palms laid flat on the conference room table, staring at him blankly. Behind them was a slender, bald-headed man in navy slacks and pinstriped button-up shirt who had his back to Patrick. He'd been studying the fireplace when Patrick walked in but turned and offered his hand.

"Leonard Velino," he said in a raspy voice, as though he had a bad cold. "It's nice to meet you."

Patrick shook the man's hand. "Patrick Connelly. Please, have a seat."

They joined the man's two silent partners, who stayed motionless, like stone gargoyles, seated on opposite sides of Velino.

"What can I do for you?" Patrick asked.

Velino turned his head to the side, cracking his neck, and when his collar parted, Patrick noticed a sizable scar just below his Adam's apple.

"It's come to my attention that I'm going to be arrested."

"Oh." This was unusual. Clients usually sought Patrick out after they'd been arrested. Not before. "On what charge?" Patrick asked.

"Murder."

Patrick gulped.

"The murder of Brad Mayhew," Velino said. "But I am completely innocent."

Patrick felt his insides churn. He'd sat across the table from a fair number of criminals since going into private practice but none charged with anything nearly as serious as murder, nor were any of them as menacing as this potential client and his two bodyguards.

"How do you know you're going to be arrested?" Patrick asked.

Velino looked annoyed by the question. "That's not import-ant. What is important is that I have legal representation as soon as possible. I intend to fight these bogus charges." Velino snapped and pointed at Patrick. "That's where you come in."

At that point Patrick would normally be thinking about how big of a retainer to charge, but something inside told him to stay as far away from this guy as possible. He deflected.

"Where are you from, Mr. Velino? By your accent, I'm guess-ing that, like me, you aren't from around here."

"Detroit," Velino said.

Patrick was afraid of that. He'd heard scuttlebutt around the courthouse that all the recent drug activity and associated crime traced back to an outfit that had moved in out of Detroit. This wasn't some traffic ticket, or petty larceny, or simple drug possession. Patrick had a feeling this guy was a serious player, and that wasn't a league he was ready to get mixed up with.

"To be honest with you, Mr. Velino, I've never defended a murder case. I don't think I'm the best person to help you. Afraid I'm going to have to pass."

Patrick held his breath and did his best not to look away as he gazed into Velino's eyes. There was a sinister fire there. They were, Patrick thought, the eyes of a killer.

Velino remained quiet for a long moment, during which Patrick struggled to withstand his gaze. Then, just as Patrick was about to break and look away, Velino tapped the table and said, "Well, I appreciate your honesty, Mr. Connelly. And your time. My associates and I will just see ourselves out."

They all stood, and Patrick thanked Velino for understand-ing. He walked the men to the door of the conference room, where Velino stopped and said, "Oh, there's just one more thing. Jimmy."

One of enormous men flanking Velino punched Patrick in his stomach so hard it dropped the attorney to his knees. Patrick thought at first he was going to throw up, but before he could, the other bodyguard seized him by his hair and yanked his head back so he was staring up at Velino.

"You passing on my case wouldn't have anything to do with you balling the sheriff, would it?" Velino asked.

Patrick didn't have enough air in his lungs to ask how in the hell Velino knew about his relationship with Mary Beth. No one knew about that.

"Yeah, that's right," Velino said, reading Patrick's mind. "I know all about it. And that's why you're going to be the one to get her to back off."

Patrick knew there was no way he could do that. He'd be scared to ask Mary Beth to fix a speeding ticket, much less tank a murder investigation.

"I can't," he said.

Velino nodded to Jimmy, who kicked Patrick in the side so hard it lifted him off the floor. He rolled on his back, gasping for air.

Velino knelt over him. "Oh, you can," he said. "You're going to represent me like your life depends upon it. Like that bitch sheriff's life depends upon it. Like maybe even the life of her boy depends upon it. You know, the one who works for you? The one you treat like a son."

Patrick could tell by Velino's inflection that he somehow knew the truth about Sam. But that was impossible. Only he and Mary Beth knew that Patrick was Sam's father. There was no way that Velino, this stranger, could know. And yet somehow he did.

"Who are you?" Patrick asked.

Velino smiled a jagged, yellow-toothed smile. "I'm the fucking devil. And you," he said, poking Patrick hard in the chest, "are now the devil's advocate."

11

AT NOON, ALEXANDER POMFRIED called for a short, thirty-minute lunch break in Mary Beth's grand jury testimony. She couldn't believe that was enough time for the pudgy prosecutor to feed his face but of course kept her snide remark to herself. No need to add fat shaming to the parade of horribles being laid at her feet.

Everyone else made their way to an area restaurant, but Mary Beth knew there was no way she'd be able to eat. She stayed behind in the courtroom, looking around, reflecting. There were framed portraits of esteemed jurists hung around the room that dated back almost to the Civil War, when West Virginia first became a state. Mary Beth made note of the fact that two of them were Pomfried's ancestors. She also took note of the heavy metal door, the prisoner's hold, that looked like a bank vault, and feared that someday soon she might find herself on the wrong side of all that steel. Then she spent a few solemn moments studying the state seal on the wall, next to an engraving of Lady Justice, holding her scales and sword.

For so long she had felt like she was that lady—the actual

embodiment of the law. Mary Beth just couldn't believe it might soon all be over.

The break passed too quickly. The jurors were reassembled and seated quickly after lunch, and Pomfried wasted no time in resuming his examination.

"Ms. Cain, before the break, I believe you were telling us about your initial interviews with Father Gonzalez. Was he able to make a positive identification of the man he saw shoot and kill Brad Mayhew?"

"He was," Mary Beth said.

"Could you describe for the jurors the process of how he made that identification?"

This was yet another example of why any sane criminal defendant would assert their Fifth Amendment privilege and decline to testify before a grand jury. Mary Beth had used improper means to coach Father Gonzalez to be sure he could identify Leonard Velino, the man Mary Beth knew had to be the shooter. She didn't think there was any way Pomfried could know that but couldn't be one hundred percent sure. If it was going to come out anyway, it would be best for Mary Beth to volunteer the information to demonstrate her honesty. After all, the murder charge she was being targeted for was a whole hell of a lot more serious than influencing a witness, something Mary Beth was pretty sure happened in big-city investigations all the time. But if Pomfried didn't know about it and she volunteered the information, she'd be unnecessarily saddling herself with yet another infraction.

Faced with that crossroads, Mary Beth decided to remain coy. "Deputy Baker primarily handled that aspect," she said. "But basically, Father Gonzalez was shown an array of photos of different people—what we call a six-pack—and from that array, he identified Leonard Velino as the man he saw."

Pomfried stared at her to see if she wanted to add anything else to her answer. When she remained silent, he eventually asked, "How confident was Father Gonzalez in his identification?"

"Very," she said. "One hundred percent."

"Even from that distance? Wasn't Father Gonzalez over a hundred yards away?"

Shit. He knows something. Mary Beth thought again about confessing her little pre-interview session with Father Gonzalez, where she'd shown him multiple photos of Velino while explaining that he had to be the guy.

Ultimately, however, the smart-ass smirk on Pomfried's face compelled her to stick to her guns. "Lenny Velino was a very distinctive-looking man." she said. "He had the kind of face you never forget. And Father Gonzalez was a young guy with 20/20 vision."

Pomfried scratched at the sizable goiter of skin hanging beneath his chin.

Mary Beth held her breath as she stared back at him.

"Still," he said, "you would agree that Father Gonzalez's testimony was the sole piece of evidence that you had linking Leonard Velino to the Mayhew murder?"

"It was the key piece of evidence," Mary Beth said, instinctively not wanting to concede that there was nothing else tying Velino to the crime. How many other bald-headed, murderous drug lords could there be driving white Mercedes SUVs around their bucolic county?

"Did you have any other witnesses?"

"No."

"Did you have any confessions?"

"No."

"Ever find the murder weapon?"

"No."

"Did you have any physical evidence linking Mr. Velino to the scene?"

"We did find some tire tracks that we were able to match to Velino's vehicle."

"Michelin tires that also matched thousands of other vehicles, correct?"

Wow. Pomfried was really channeling his old criminal defense days. Instead of answering the question, Mary Beth said, "Mr. Pomfried, we had an eyewitness. An honest to God priest. Witnesses don't get any better than that, which I'm sure is why you, yourself, signed off on the prosecution."

Mary Beth thought she'd get him flustered there, but Pomfried didn't flinch. "Oh, it was a legitimate case to bring, certainly. Which is why Ms. Boggs in my office was assigned to it. My point was simply whether you would agree that the case hinged upon Father Gonzalez's testimony?"

Mary Beth really couldn't argue with that, as much as she'd like to.

"Yes, that's fair," she said.

"Thank you," Pomfried said, as though he'd been forced to pull teeth to establish the most obvious of facts. He took a minute reviewing some notes on a legal pad.

Mary Beth got the impression he was intentionally jumping around a bit to keep her off-balance and unable to predict the points he was trying to make.

"Can you describe Mr. Velino's arrest for us?"

Again, Mary Beth hesitated, making silent calculations about what Pomfried might already know and when and if she should proactively come clean over some of her questionable tactics. Using a ruse to arrest someone wasn't a problem, but Mary Beth's reach-out to her mother and planned cover story of brokering a deal with Velino would remind the jurors of all the corruption she'd so often been accused of. Mary Beth decided to omit all of that, especially since none of it ever came to fruition.

"Mr. Velino actually surprised us by surrendering before we could go and arrest him," she said.

"Indeed he did. Gave a pretty highly publicized press conference about it, too, didn't he?"

Mary Beth still smarted over the memory as she shook her head.

"You'll need to answer yes or no so the record is clear."

"Yes," Mary Beth said.

"I'd like to play a clip of it for the jury." Pomfried waddled back to his table, where he still had the rolling cart with a TV and laptop and repositioned it where both the jury and Mary Beth could see it. When he hit Play, Mary Beth saw Patrick Connelly standing before a bank of microphones next to Lenny Velino, backed by four men dressed in black suits with black ties, all wearing sunglasses, like they were the heist team from *Reservoir Dogs*.

Good afternoon. My name is Patrick Connelly. And it is my honor to represent Mr. Leonard Velino, who is standing here with me today. We have called this press conference because it has come to our attention that an arrest warrant has recently been issued, charging Mr. Velino with the murder of Brad Mayhew, a Jasper Creek citizen who was savagely and tragically killed several days ago. We are here today to state, unequivocally, that Mr. Velino is one hundred percent innocent of these charges. In fact, these men gathered here, who are members of his staff in the security company he operates, can all verify and will testify that Mr. Velino was nowhere near Jasper Creek at the time Brad Mayhew was killed. Furthermore, we will produce evidence that, for some time now, Mr. Velino has been the victim of a coordinated pressure campaign of harassment by the Jasper County Sheriff's Department, targeting him based upon some youthful indiscretions in his past, for which he long ago paid his debt to society, as well as what we believe is simple racism and stereotyping due to Mr. Velino's Italian American heritage.

In conclusion, we intend to fight these charges and can pledge to you that we fully expect Mr. Velino to be completely vindicated from any allegations of wrongdoing.

Patrick nodded to Velino, who started unbuttoning and removing his shirt, followed by his pants. Photographers snapped numerous photos, as Velino did a 360-degree turn, showing off his skeletal body and ghostly white skin.

In just a few moments, my client will voluntarily surrender. But before he does, we'd ask all of you press assembled here to take careful photos of the physical condition Mr. Velino is currently in, because we fear that law enforcement in this county is so prejudiced against him and has become so corrupt that they are likely to try and beat some type of false confession out of him.

Pomfried stopped the playback. "You can't have been very pleased by this little press conference," he said.

It had been one of the great shocks of Mary Beth's life to turn on the TV and see Patrick Connelly, the man she loved, standing there, metaphorically wrapping his arms around someone she considered to be the most despicable criminal she'd ever encountered. It took a great deal of effort to swallow all that emotion when answering Pomfried's question. "I took it as typical defense attorney nonsense," she said. "They all profess their innocence. It's just par for the course."

"It didn't get under your skin, being accused of racism and harassment, and him being so worried that you might try to beat a confession out of Velino that the man stripped down on live TV?"

The truth was it had pissed Mary Beth off royally. She had never beaten a confession out of anyone. She'd threatened it a few times but had never actually done it. Her strategic impulses were telling her to go ahead and admit that the press conference bothered her. The jury would know that it must have, and thus there'd be no reason to deny it. But Pomfried still had that smug look on his face, and Mary Beth couldn't help resisting the answer he was seeking.

"I really didn't give it too much thought," Mary Beth said.

"Really?" Pomfried looked at the jury in disbelief.

"Really," Mary Beth said. "I was more focused on building the case than anything in the media."

Pomfried turned back to her. "Let's talk some more about that case. Were you ever able to establish a motive?"

"Not definitively," Mary Beth said. "We know that Brad Mayhew had been very involved in the fund-raising and construction of St. Michael's new cathedral. And since construction is one of the classic vehicles for money laundering, and Mr. Mayhew had reportedly been troubled about something he was planning to confess to Father Gonzalez right before he was killed, we suspect that he may have been involved with cleaning some of Velino's drug money."

"You suspect," Pomfried said derisively. "Isn't that the kind of thing you'd normally want to nail down before bringing a murder case?"

"Your office brought the murder case," Mary Beth shot back.

Pomfried raised a hand of truce. "I'm not being critical, Ms. Cain. I just want the jury to understand the reality of the pressure you were under. So, please answer the question. Isn't establishing a strong theory as to motive, and gathering evidence supporting that theory, something you would normally want to nail down before bringing a murder case?"

"Yes, of course, but there wasn't time."

"Why not?" Pomfried asked.

Mary Beth turned up her palms. This part wasn't her fault. "Because they Blitzkrieged us," she said. "Normally, when you arrest someone on a charge like this, you've got a year or two to continue to investigate, gather evidence before trial. But Velino surrendered before we could even arrest him. Then he demanded a speedy trial. They put us to the test before we would normally have been ready to go."

Mary Beth had to admit it was a really good strategy. Unfortunately, Patrick had turned out to be a much better criminal lawyer than Mary Beth thought.

12

DESPITE THE FACT that Assistant District Attorney Jeannie Boggs had been successfully trying cases for twenty years, she still got nervous before every trial and convinced herself she was going to lose. Mary Beth had sat through enough of her pretrial brooding sessions that she didn't think much of it when Jeannie sat her and Izzy down in a small courthouse conference room and said, "We're in trouble."

Mary Beth had arrived a little late that morning and missed the preliminary motions but sat through jury selection. Once that was over, the judge called a break, and Jeannie insisted on having a private word.

"What's the problem?" Mary Beth asked.

"You missed the motions *in limine,*" she said, referring to the evidentiary hearing held at the outset of a trial. Jeannie slammed a written motion down on the table.

IN THE CIRCUIT COURT OF
JASPER COUNTY, WEST VIRGINIA

STATE OF

WEST VIRGINIA

    vs.   *case no. 25cr00526*

LEONARD VELINO

DEFENDANT'S
<u>Motion in Limine</u>

Now comes the Defendant, by and through undersigned counsel, and pursuant to Rules 404 and 609 and moves the court to prohibit the State from introducing evidence of any of Defendant's or Defendant's witnesses, alleged prior bad acts, including but not limited to, criminal charges that did not result in a conviction, or prior convictions that are more than ten years old.

Patrick Connelly
Patrick Connelly

Mary Beth didn't see what the big deal was. It was a pretty standard motion. The defense always tried to limit bad character evidence, using lawyerly words and phrases like *propensity* and *conformity therewith*. The basic rule, however, was simple. You couldn't bring up a bunch of stuff the defendant did in the past to argue that he was and is basically a shitbag and thus is probably guilty of the current charges. All rules had their exceptions, however, and judges would often let you bring up prior bad acts for another valid purpose, such as establishing motive. In this case, the plan had been to show that Velino was a lifelong criminal and drug trafficker who had been intimidating and silencing witnesses against him for decades, in order to suggest a motive for killing Brad Mayhew. The prosecution would argue that there was enough circumstantial evidence for the jury to conclude that Velino had been laundering drug money through the church construction project and killed Mayhew to prevent him from revealing that information.

"The judge screwed us," Jeannie said.

"What do you mean?" Mary Beth asked.

"I mean he kicked all of it. All of Velino's prior convictions, plus the numerous charges for witness tampering and your whole investigation of him since he's been in Jasper Creek."

Mary Beth suddenly understood Jeannie's concern and shared it. She knew the judge might keep out some of the really old convictions and charges that never resulted in convictions, because the witnesses disappeared. But she was certain that, at a minimum, she'd be able to detail her months-long investigation of Velino to establish that he was the kingpin behind all the recent drug activity in Jasper County.

"He can't do that," Mary Beth said.

"He's a circuit court judge. He can do whatever he wants," Jeannie replied. "He said that Mr. Velino is being charged with murder, not drug trafficking. And that unless we were ready to go ahead and charge Velino with the whole RICO conspiracy, then this trial would be limited to the facts strictly dealing with the Mayhew murder."

Mary Beth did her best to remain calm, but her emotions had been all over the place since Patrick dropped a megaton bomb on her by not only representing Velino but coming after her department with the same kind of aggressive nastiness that Pomfried used to employ. It had left her not only bewildered but heartbroken. Especially because things had been going so well with Patrick before that. She'd actually been considering bringing their relationship out into the open. But now Patrick wouldn't even talk to her. No explanation, no nothing. Just some bullshit text messages insisting that they keep their distance until the case was over.

Izzy pointed at the motion. "Connelly combined a 609 motion with his 404. What did the judge say about that?"

Mary Beth understood what Izzy was asking. The 404 motion had to do with whether the State could affirmatively introduce evidence of the Defendant's prior bad acts. Rule 609 applied to witnesses who testified and thus addressed whether such evidence, even though excluded under Rule 404, could be used in the event that Velino or any of his lying alibi witnesses chose to take the stand. Such a decision often opened the door to bring out things you otherwise couldn't.

"Connelly is smart," Jeannie said. "He argued both motions together to give the judge the perfect opportunity to split the baby. He granted the 404 motion but denied the 609. At least for now. Said he would have to wait and see how the testimony goes if the defense puts on any witnesses."

"So, that means all the other evidence could come in, right?" Izzy asked.

"Potentially," Jeannie said. "If Velino testifies, then I think the door is wide open. But I'd be shocked if Connelly puts him on the stand. It's less clear how far the judge would let us go if it's just the alibi witnesses who testify."

"But you'd be able to at least get some of the stuff in, wouldn't you?" Mary Beth asked.

"Yes. Should be able to."

The sheriff clapped her hands. "Then we're fine. Patrick already said on TV that they're going to testify. He has to put them on."

"He doesn't have to do anything," Jeannie said. "It's the state's burden of proof. Connelly doesn't have to put on any evidence at all. Much less be consistent with his statements to the media."

Mary Beth felt a smoldering sense of unspeakable betrayal flame up inside her. If Patrick got Velino off of these charges, she might literally kill him. She didn't mean that metaphorically, either. The rage she felt was so intense that it had her thinking about untraceable poisons she could put in Patrick's food. *If I were to rip his nuts off, I wonder if I could have them taxidermied and hung on my wall,* Mary Beth wondered.

"I think we just need to focus on the evidence we know we can present," Izzy said. "We've got an unimpeachable eyewitness with Father Gonzalez. And Connelly hasn't been able to produce anything to support Velino's supposed alibi. He says they were out of state at the time, but they haven't come forward with any receipts, credit card bills, security video, phone records, noninterested witnesses, or anything else that can verify it."

As was so often the case, Izzy's comments brought Mary Beth back from the ledge her emotions had taken her to. "That's right," she said. "Father Gonzalez should be enough. After he's done testifying, the jury will be convinced. And if Patrick puts any of those so-called alibi witnesses on the stand, you'll tear them apart, Jeannie."

The prosecutor seemed more beleaguered than bolstered by Mary Beth's confidence in her abilities. "I just wish I'd had more time to work with Father Gonzalez," she said.

Her lack of access to the state's key witness was Mary Beth's doing, as she'd kept the priest holed up at a secret location that only she and Izzy knew about. "We've had to take extreme precautions," Mary Beth said.

"I understand," Jeannie responded. "But I'm going to need to meet with him this evening to go over his testimony again. I need to make sure he's prepared for the merciless cross-examination he's likely to get from Connelly."

What Mary Beth was thinking but couldn't say was that part of the reason she'd limited the prosecutor's access to Father Gonzalez wasn't just for his safety, but also out of concern that if Jeannie probed too much, she might learn about the improper way Mary Beth had helped ensure he was able to ID Velino. At the time, Mary Beth believed Father Gonzalez would just be one piece in a much larger case they could continue building against Velino prior to trial. But now that Patrick had rushed them into court and cut off the evidence they could offer, she realized that the whole endeavor would come down to whether Father Gonzalez could withstand cross-examination. If Gonzalez broke or capitulated at all on how certain he was that Velino was the shooter, then the case was over. All Patrick would need was that one little break in the dam, and reasonable doubt would rush in like a deluge and swamp their case.

"I can have Father Gonzalez back here in a few hours," Mary Beth said. She stood to leave, calculating how long it would take her to get to the out-of-state hotel where she'd stashed the priest.

"Where are *you* going?" Jeannie asked.

"To get your witness."

"No you're not. The judge's ruling means we've got to really streamline our case, and you're my first witness. I'll need you to detail the Mayhew murder investigation and show off all the gruesome crime scene photos. I want to hit the jury with those right out of the gate so they'll be wanting somebody to pay for it."

"Right," Mary Beth said. "Izzy can go get Gonzalez, then."

Izzy started to stand until Jeannie raised her hands. "Izzy can't go, either. He's my second witness. I need him to reinforce the initial investigation to give me an excuse to show the victim photos to the jury again, then I need him to describe the process by which Velino was identified as the shooter."

Mary Beth started to say that she could handle the identification since she was present when it happened, but she realized, much to her chagrin, that Izzy was the better witness for that aspect since there were a lot fewer instances of past improprieties he could be cross-examined about.

"Could you change up the order of your witnesses?" she asked.

"No," Jeannie said, emphatically. "I'm already having to switch a lot of things up on the fly. I need to manage what's left of this case correctly. There's always peaks and valleys to a trial. I want to start out by having you describe the murder investigation. Show the jury the pictures. That will be a high point. Connelly might take a few digs at you after that on cross, but then we'll come back with Izzy to bolster what you've said, show the pictures again, and describe the identification process. By that time, the jury will already have heard multiple times what Father Gonzalez saw, so it will be imprinted in their minds. We get him up there in his priest collar, looking like the holy image of virtue, to place his hand on the Bible and bless all that you and Izzy have said, and we'll be riding high. After that will be his cross-exam, which is the real make-or-break part of the case. We survive that, and we end it on a high note by putting Mayhew's widow on the stand to evoke the jurors' sympathy. By that point, we should have them fully primed to convict."

Mary Beth saw the logic of what Jeannie had laid out and agreed it was a good case strategy in light of the judge's ruling. But it meant that someone other than her or Izzy would have to be told of Father Gonzalez's whereabouts.

"Okay, shit," she said. "Izzy, who do we have on right now who we could send to fetch the priest?"

Izzy thought about it for a moment. "Could send Goforth."

Mary Beth considered that. Ben Goforth was as reliable as any of her other guys, which wasn't necessarily saying much, but chauffeuring a witness to the courthouse should have been within his level of ability.

"Okay," Mary Beth said. "Tell Benny where he can find Gonzalez, and tell him I want him protected. The priest is to have a deputy by his side at all times until this trial is over."

"Got it," Izzy said.

While Izzy left to find Goforth, Mary Beth started worrying that maybe he'd been right all along and they should have reached out to the Feds months ago for help in building a more comprehensive RICO case against Velino. *Too late now*, she decided. *It is what it is.*

The gun was already loaded, aimed, and cocked. Time to shoot.

PATRICK CONNELLY FELT like he was in the center of a circular firing squad. Everywhere he turned were killers. His client. His client's henchmen. Even his sheriff girlfriend, who was certain to unleash a fury on him like he'd never seen, if, by some legal miracle, Velino beat the murder rap.

Patrick would lose Mary Beth for sure now. It had taken so long to regain her trust after the Old Wengo Affair, he didn't think there was any way he could ever do it again. Not after this.

With years of therapy under his belt, Patrick understood all too well about the mommy issues he harbored, having lost his mother to the depths of a mental illness that had her institutionalized for significant periods during his youth. He suspected that on some level, that was what attracted him so completely to Mary Beth. She had that same level of volatility and intense emotion as his mother, both positive and negative. To him, Mary Beth was like the sun, who could light up his world or burn him just as easily. Taking the Velino case was sure to invite a scorched-earth response. The thought of losing Mary Beth and, by extension, Sam triggered an instinctual sense of panic inside Patrick that was palpable. He felt like a little kid who'd wandered off and suddenly realized he was lost.

It was a feeling Patrick had been wrestling with all morning, made worse by how little sleep he'd had while preparing for trial. Getting ready to go in front of the jury was hard enough when the client wasn't a merciless psychopath who was constantly threatening to kill you. Patrick had been lucky to get a few hours' rest over the last several days.

Somehow he managed to make it through the preliminary motions and jury selection. But as soon as the judge called for a break, he raced to the bathroom to throw up. Fortunately, the courthouse bathroom was relatively clean, as he had to get down on both knees in his Brooks Brothers suit to let it fly. Patrick retched until the meager contents of his stomach had emptied. When he exited the stall. one of the male jurors was standing by the sink gawking.

"You okay, man?"

Patrick was forbidden to speak to the jurors. Not even so much as a hello was countenanced. So he just smiled, nodded, and navigated around the man to the sink. He was splashing water on his face when he felt a sickening grumble in his stomach and knew he was about to start evacuating from the other end. At least the juror had dried his hands and was on his way out by the time Patrick tore back into the stall. He barely got his pants off fast enough to avoid a truly embarrassing accident. He also hadn't taken the time to make sure there was actually some toilet paper inside the black plastic dispenser. Patrick held his breath as he reached up into the round contraption. He felt paper. Thank God. It was ridiculously thin paper, but it would do.

Patrick cleaned himself up, then spent several minutes at the sink vigorously scrubbing his hands while giving himself a silent pep talk. *You can do this. You have no choice. They'll kill Mary Beth and Sam if you don't.*

He repeated those lines like a mantra as he passed through the hall and into the courtroom where a guard let him into the holding cell. There, handcuffed to a metal bench, sat Velino. He'd been denied bail and was still a guest of the county, but the judge had allowed him to wear regular clothes throughout the trial, which in Velino's case was a blue, button-up Oxford and slate-gray slacks. He looked up at Patrick with his standard sinister sneer.

The guard closed the heavy door with a thud, leaving them alone. Patrick said, "We're in trouble. The judge screwed us."

Velino waved him off. "That can wait," he said. "Did you bring it?"

"Bring what?" Patrick asked.

"The phone, numbnuts."

"Oh, yeah." Patrick reluctantly opened his briefcase. He pulled out a prepaid mobile phone and handed it over.

Velino snatched it and started dialing. This had become their ritual. Before every meeting with Velino, his associate Jimmy, who had become Patrick's virtual shadow since taking the case, would give the lawyer a burner cell phone to smuggle inside. Unlike phone calls from the jail, attorney meetings couldn't be recorded and took place in private rooms where no cameras were allowed. Thus, Patrick was given a different phone moments before entering, so there was no way he could tip off police and allow them to set up a tap. Then, after using the phone to conduct some business, Velino would destroy the burner before giving the remains to Patrick to smuggle back out. That way no one could see who he called. Patrick was able to overhear what Velino said, but it was all in a vague, Mafia code. "You know the guy? The place? The thing?" It was all indecipherable to Patrick without the ability to hear the other side of the conversation.

This time Velino seemed to have a little more urgency than usual. "Where are we on the thing?" he said into the burner.

"No. No. That's not good enough … I don't care how. You need to find it … Ask our guy … Yeah, yeah. Okay. Clock's ticking, you know what I mean?" Then he paused, menacingly. "Oh, yeah, hang on—"

Velino covered the phone and looked at Patrick. "Is Opie coming to court today?"

"Who?"

"Opie. You know, the redheaded kid who works for you."

Patrick assumed he meant Sam.

"You know," Velino said with a sneer. "The one that looks like his mom and acts like you."

Yeah, that was Sam. Patrick had been rolling this mystery around in his head ever since first meeting Velino and still for the life of him couldn't imagine how the mobster could possibly know the truth about Sam's parentage.

"How do you—"

"Don't bother asking, 'cause I ain't answering, counselor. Just tell me, is he out there or not?"

"No," Patrick said. "When I took your case, I told him it was best if he stayed away until the trial was over."

Velino raised an eyebrow. He'd warned Patrick that if he did anything to tip Mary Beth or Sam off to the nature of his indentured servitude, there would be deadly serious consequences.

"I told him it was because his mom is so involved in this case," Patrick explained.

Velino nodded. He uncovered the phone and scooted closer to Patrick to make sure the attorney heard what was said.

"You still got a line on Junior? Good. Keep it. Anything goes sideways, you know what to do." Velino ended the call. He smashed the phone against the bench and tossed the remains back to Patrick to hide.

"Look," Patrick said. "Do what you want with me but—"

"You just win my case and you won't have to worry about it."

"That's the problem," Patrick said. "The judge's rulings this morning put us in a really bad spot."

Velino scoffed and made a masturbatory gesture with his uncuffed hand. "Whatever," he said. "We won that shit. He kept out all the stuff that bitch attorney wanted to say about me."

"Yeah," Patrick said. "But he left the door wide open if we put on any of our witnesses. My guess is the judge will let them backdoor a lot of that stuff in during the defense case."

Velino shrugged. "So don't put on a defense case."

Patrick had thought about that and ultimately dismissed it. "No defense case means no alibi. No alibi means this case comes down to a priest who will swear on the Bible he saw you shoot the victim."

Velino looked at Patrick like that was exclusively the attorney's problem. "Guess you'll just have to think of something else."

"What else is there?"

Velino shrugged. "That's your job."

Patrick hung his head. This whole situation was absolute torture.

"Hey," Velino said, sounding actually encouraging, almost kind. "Let me tell you something." Velino gestured for Patrick to come sit next to him.

"I'll stand."

"Sit down, jackass. I don't bite."

"No, really."

"Sit."

Patrick relented and did what he was told. The gangster put his free arm around him and spoke in an avuncular fashion.

"When I was coming up on the mean streets of Detroit, I used to get my ass beat almost every day. Skinny white kid. I was easy pickings. You know what I mean? Then one day I watched this other kid go down, and he was a good-sized kid, a lot bigger than me, but he was scared, see. He thought he was going to lose the fight, so after throwing a few blows he just kind of went into a defensive shell and waited for it to be over. And I remember really thinking about that. About how most people beat themselves. They give up because they think they're going to lose. Now, maybe this guy was going to lose anyway, but he could have inflicted a lot more pain if he kept swinging."

Patrick thought he knew what Velino was saying. There was a presidential campaign going on, and he'd thought something similar about how primary candidates kept dropping out just because some poll said they would lose.

"Anyway," Velino said, "the next time I got jumped, I vowed that I would never stop swinging. I would scratch, claw, bite—you name it. Be a Tasmanian devil from start to finish. I'd go home with the guy's balls in my back pocket if I had to. And once guys knew that, I didn't have to fight anymore because I got a reputation for being tough. For being willing to do things others wouldn't. And that's how I eventually got hooked up with a crew."

"So, you're saying … what, exactly?" Patrick asked.

"I'm saying, the way you win is you refuse to lose. Do the things the others aren't willing to. Cross those imaginary lines. Fear. Shame. Tradition. Whatever it is that keeps them boxed in. They're all worried about being decent. Fuck decent."

Patrick wasn't sure exactly what to make of that. It felt like he was receiving fatherly advice but from a member of the Manson family. Velino smiled and said, "'Cause if you don't win, you know what will happen."

14

A DOUBLE BANG on the heavy metal door meant the judge was ready for them to reenter and take their places before the jury was welcomed back to the courtroom. Velino stood, done with the conversation. The deputy came in, uncuffed Velino from the bench, and escorted him to the defense table. Velino's goon squad was seated behind him, in the first row. Patrick stood in the doorway of the prisoner's hold, watching Velino whisper something to Jimmy.

Mary Beth was seated behind the prosecutor. Patrick did his best not to make eye contact with her. He'd been warned repeatedly not to go to the cops. Velino's man Jimmy was watching him closely, and Patrick didn't want any sideways glance to be misinterpreted as some kind of signal. Early on during his forced representation of Velino, Patrick had thought of ways to get a message to Mary Beth to let her know what was going on, but Velino seemed to have a supernatural level of information and had convinced Patrick that any such efforts would be futile.

"Even if you told the sheriff and she rounded up all my guys,"

Velino had warned, "it wouldn't make a difference. We'd just send more. The only way you'll ever be safe is to win my case."

Patrick wanted to scream. To run. To hide in the bathroom puking and shitting some more. Anything other than being where he was. But he had no choice. If he didn't get Velino acquitted from what seemed like a slam-dunk murder beef, then he, Mary Beth, and Sam would all end up dead.

"Need you to step up, counselor."

"Huh?"

The courtroom bailiff was motioning for Patrick to move forward so he could close the door to the prisoner hold.

"Oh," Patrick said. "Yes. Sorry."

He paced stiff-legged to the defense table, feeling like a pirate walking the plank. When he sat down, Velino leaned over and whispered, "Jimmy would like to have a word with you after court. Make sure you're properly motivated."

Patrick swallowed hard, knowing what that meant. It would be the fourth beating he'd suffered since taking the case.

Then the bailiff called the courtroom back to order. "All rise."

Judge Parsons reentered, told them to be seated, and took his place behind the bench. He was the same judge Patrick had on the Raul Kowalski case. A man straight out of central casting. Judge Parsons was a tall white man in his sixties who had balded to the point he no longer bothered with a comb-over. He had a prominent nose where he perched a pair of half-moon reading glasses that he peered over as he asked whether the state was ready to proceed with opening statements.

"We are, your honor." Jeannie Boggs was standing, looking confident.

Shit, opening statements. Patrick was completely uncertain of how to proceed. He'd been hoping to tell the jury this was a simple case of mistaken identity and that multiple witnesses would establish that Leonard Velino couldn't be the shooter because he was in another state at the time, negotiating a contract for his security company. Add to that the complete lack of physical evidence tying Velino to the crime, other than a vehicle description and tire prints that could have belonged to virtually anyone, and the lack of any provable motive, and the state's case boiled down to pure supposition. Conjecture. Nothing remotely close to proof beyond a reasonable doubt. But with the judge's evidentiary rulings that morning, he could no longer do that. Sleep deprived and strung out from worry, Patrick was still scrambling to come up with a backup plan as the prosecutor addressed the jury.

Jeannie Boggs started out by telling the story of Father Gonzalez. His background. His good works. The pastoral counseling. The soup kitchens. The prison ministry. The meals he delivered weekly to the elderly and disabled. She had him ready for canonization before telling jurors of the horrors he'd faced on the day in question. With the skill of a thriller writer, Jeannie Boggs took the jury through every moment of his arduous ordeal. How he'd been kidnapped along with Brad Mayhew, a church member he'd been counseling. Jeannie described how Father Gonzalez witnessed Mayhew being tortured.

"That was when this man"—Jeannie fired a vicious point at the defendant—"Leonard Velino, pulled up in his very distinctive white Mercedes SUV. Got out. Walked up to his men." As Jeannie said this, she gestured to the menacing crew assembled behind Velino. Patrick should have objected, as there was no evidence to establish that those employees of Velino's security company had been the masked men responsible for Mayhew's kidnapping, but he didn't react quickly enough and was stunned by the ferocity with which Jeannie pointed a second time at Velino.

"Then the defendant—this man, right here, with his very distinctive appearance, a man Father Gonzalez will tell you he could see clear as day—this man pulled out a pistol and shot Brad Mayhew in the head, killing him."

A female juror in the front row shook her head with disgust. Patrick saw the man next to her cross his arms. After that, for the first of what would be multiple times throughout the trial, Jeannie showed the gruesome crime scene photos to the jury and forecasted the evidence they would hear about the investigation leading to Velino's arrest.

Despite all the judges' admonitions about how the attorneys' opening statements were not evidence and how jurors should not reach any conclusion until the end of the trial, Patrick could see in the jurors' eyes that by the time Jeannie retook her seat, they were ready to convict.

Patrick scribbled a note to Velino, telling him his guys needed to leave.

Velino shook his head no, then whispered. "They're here to make sure you do your job."

"They make you look like a gangster," Patrick whispered.

Velino sat back, thinking about that, then gestured with two fingers for Jimmy to lean over the railing. Velino whispered something to him, and he and the other guys quietly slipped out of the courtroom.

"Mr. Connelly, is the defense ready to proceed with its opening?" the judge asked.

What the defense was ready to do was shit its pants. But Patrick obviously couldn't say that, so he did his best to project an air of confidence as he stood and said, "Yes, your honor."

Patrick walked into the well of the courtroom and stood just a few feet from the jurors. He wanted to get close enough to make a connection but not so close as to make them uncomfortable. Then he began his opening the way he had practiced, without any idea of what he would do once he got to the part where he had planned to talk about Velino's alleged alibi.

"That was a compelling opening statement," Patrick said. He tipped an invisible cap to the prosecutor and said, "Ms. Boggs is a very good storyteller."

The jurors nodded in agreement.

Patrick looked down at the floor and bit his lip as though deep in thought. It was a rehearsed move but looked genuine. What he called his "look of sincere reflection." It was important, Patrick knew, that he become the avatar of the defense, so that it was him the jurors thought of, rather than the sinister-looking Velino, and thus, he needed to be viewed as completely earnest and trustworthy.

When Patrick looked back up at the jury, he said, "But you know, as Ms. Boggs was talking, I started thinking to myself that sometimes the most important parts of a story aren't the things you're told. It's the things the storyteller chooses to leave out."

The number four juror, who'd been shaking her head with contempt a moment ago, looked intrigued, like she was willing to hear Patrick out.

"For instance," he said, "I didn't hear Ms. Boggs say anything about a murder weapon. Maybe I missed it, but in a case that needs to be proved beyond a reasonable doubt, I thought we'd hear something about a gun being recovered that was linked through ballistics to the bullet that killed Brad Mayhew. I thought we'd hear how the state could also link that gun to the man they—" Patrick tried firing his own accusatory point at the prosecution's table, but when he did, he accidentally locked eyes with Mary Beth and saw nothing but pure fury, which caused him to lose his nerve. His point wilted into a half-hearted gesture as he mumbled the words "charged with the murder."

Patrick lost his train of thought. His mind went completely blank for a moment, causing him to panic and making it impossible to remember the next point he wanted to make. He feigned a coughing fit to give him an excuse to return to the defense table and side-eye his notes while taking a drink of water from the flimsy plastic cups the court provided.

He saw *CSI* scribbled there, and it came back to him. Patrick wanted to take advantage of the fact that many jurors were familiar with the *CSI* TV shows and had come to expect a more high-tech level of investigation than most police departments could realistically provide.

"Excuse me," he said, upon resuming his place in front of the jurors. "I started thinking about all the things we didn't hear during the state's opening and got kind of choked up." Patrick intended it to be funny, but no one laughed. He said, "I also didn't hear anything about crime labs or scientific analysis of evidence. Didn't hear one word about motive. Again, maybe I missed it, but in a case that is supposed to be proved beyond a reasonable doubt, I thought we'd hear something about why the defendant is believed to have done what the state is accusing him of. But I'm afraid you're not going to hear much about that at all during this trial. In fact, based upon the state's opening, I don't believe you are going to hear testimony to establish that Mr. Velino even knew the victim, much less that he had a reason to do him harm."

Patrick paused for another moment of insincere reflection.

Once he felt he'd held the pose long enough, he said, "As we go through this trial, I want you to listen to the testimony, of course, but I also ask that you pay attention to what you don't hear. And at the end of the case, you'll have to decide whether what has been presented is really proof beyond all reasonable doubt. Or if it's possible that their lone eyewitness—a man with no special training or powers of observation, a man who was probably in shock, a man who was positioned a considerable distance from the events he says he witnessed and separated by all kinds of trees and leaves, et cetera—*might*, just might, have gotten it wrong."

Patrick saw expressions of acknowledgment among several of the jurors. He'd made a good point. They looked like maybe they were willing to hold off closing the door on this case. Patrick had managed to open it a crack. He decided to try and nudge it just a little farther by saying, "That's all it takes in a criminal case, remember. If, at the end of this trial, you have any reasonable doubt. If you think it's possible that the state's witness was mistaken, then we'll ask you to follow the law and return a verdict of not guilty."

Patrick took a minute staring the jurors down after that. He went down the row, looking each one in the eyes, trying to solicit an unspoken agreement that they would indeed follow the law and flush the case if the state didn't meet its burden.

There was a whole other section to the opening Patrick had planned, but he decided it would be better to quit there than try to ad-lib a revision in light of the judge's evidentiary rulings. The result was probably the shortest opening statement he'd ever delivered, but he felt like he'd done well enough. Especially considering the pressure he was under.

When Patrick turned and looked back at his client, however, he could tell that Velino was dangerously unimpressed. Patrick walked reluctantly back to the defense table and sat down. Velino leaned over and whispered to him, "That's it?"

"What else is there?"

"Why didn't you call that priest a fucking liar?"

"Because he's a priest," Patrick whispered back. "The jury won't believe he's lying. But we may be able to convince them he's mistaken."

Their side conversation was interrupted when Jeannie Boggs stood and announced that Sheriff Mary Beth Cain would be her first witness. *Great*, Patrick thought, not relishing the idea of having to cross-examine her. Meanwhile, Velino wasn't done whispering his critique of Patrick's legal strategy. "That priest is lying," he said. "That bitch cop put him up to this. I know it. You need to go after her, hard."

Patrick nodded. Velino seized hold of his thigh, pressing his fingernails in close to Patrick's groin.

"I'm serious," Velino said. "I don't care if you are tapping that. You better rip that bitch a new one."

"Okay, okay." Patrick said it just to get Velino to back off, but as he settled in and did his best to focus on the testimony, he had to admit that his client might have been right, in terms of strategy. Patrick didn't think he could make the priest look like a bad guy, but he could definitely drag Mary Beth and her department through the mud. Continue along the same lines he had in his initial press conference, where he'd accused the sheriff's department of harassment. That might just be the only way to win the case and save Mary Beth's life.

But when Patrick looked up, he and the sheriff locked eyes again. This time, however, instead of a murderous stare, he saw that Mary Beth's eyes were welling with tears, full of hurt and betrayal. *Shit.* Now that they were face-to-face, Patrick knew he wouldn't be able to attack her in all the unfair ways that other defense attorneys had in the past. Even if it was the only way to save both their lives.

He would have to think of something else.

Fast.

15

BY THE TIME MARY BETH took the witness stand in the Velino trial, she was as anxious as a politician taking a polygraph. It wasn't the stress of testifying. She'd done that countless times. Prosecutors liked to put her on as their first witness in big cases because she'd typically been involved in all aspects of the investigation and could tell the whole story from start to finish. What was bothering Mary Beth this time, however, was the immense pressure she was feeling to convict someone as dangerous as Leonard Velino and the fact that the gangster had maintained a sinister grin throughout the morning's proceedings like he knew something Mary Beth didn't.

Combined with that unsettling feeling was the bewildering sense of betrayal Mary Beth had been wrestling with since Patrick took Velino's case and froze her out of his life. The whole thing blew her mind. All she'd gotten from Patrick were a few rigid text messages about them needing to keep their distance, to "build a Chinese wall between them," until the case was over. Not a word had been spoken between the two since. Patrick had even had his secretary tell Sam to stay away from the law office until after the trial.

Mary Beth had mostly been fuming mad over the low-down backstabbing, but as she reflected on it while raising her right hand and swearing to "tell the truth, the whole truth, and nothing but the truth," she damn near started to cry. The sheriff looked over at Patrick, expecting to see that cocky smirk, but the coward looked down and away as soon as she made eye contact.

"Sheriff Cain," Jeannie Boggs said, "I'd like to start with when you first learned that Brad Mayhew had been killed. Can you tell us about that?"

"Of course." Mary Beth launched into the tale of what had happened at St. Michael's that morning. It was not where she and Jeannie had planned to start. The hope was to kick the story off much sooner with the months-long investigation into Velino's suspected drug operations and the numerous other dead bodies encountered along the way. But the judge had put the kibosh on that, limiting their presentation to the facts strictly related to Mayhew.

It didn't take long before Jeannie had Mary Beth discussing the crime scene and pulled out the blown-up photos of Mayhew's corpse. She placed them on multiple easels arranged in front of the jurors. The judge allowed Mary Beth to get down from the stand so that she could indicate to the enlarged photos while answering Jeannie's questions about the crime scene and condition of the body.

By the time Mary Beth retook her seat, she'd taken the jury right up to the part of the investigation where Father Gonzalez came in for an identification.

"No further questions at this time," Jeannie said. The prosecutor would pick up the story with Izzy as her next witness. First, however, Patrick Connelly got to cross-examine.

Jeannie Boggs sat down, leaving the macabre crime scene photos in place. A more seasoned defense attorney would have immediately asked that they be taken down, so the jury didn't continue to stare at them during cross, but Patrick kept quiet, head down, scribbling notes on his legal pad.

"Your witness, Mr. Connelly," the judge said.

Mary Beth bristled. She didn't like being called Patrick's anything. Not anymore. Not ever again.

She was ready to do battle, but Patrick surprised her with how he kicked off his examination. "Sheriff Cain, you've told the jury about the day Brad Mayhew's body was discovered. I'd like to go back in time a bit, because you'd actually been trying to build a case against Mr. Velino for quite a while, correct?"

Mary Beth had to suppress a laugh. Unless she was wildly mistaken, Patrick had just kicked the door wide open for her to discuss all of Velino's suspected crimes that the judge had kept out. She looked to Jeannie Boggs, whose wide smile told Mary Beth to cream the son of a bitch.

"Well, actually—"

That was as far as Mary Beth got before the judge silenced her. "Counsel, approach the bench."

The attorneys stepped forward. As Patrick passed by the witness stand, Mary Beth noticed just how peaked his complexion had become. He didn't look well. She wondered if he was sick.

The judge had a tiny noise-canceling fan next to a stack of statute books that he switched on so the jury couldn't overhear their conference, but Mary Beth was close enough to make out most of what was said.

"Mr. Connelly," the judge began, sternly, "you spent the morning trying to exclude evidence of the larger investigation into Mr. Velino, and now you are soliciting testimony about that very subject? Care to explain yourself?"

Patrick wiped a sheen of sweat from his forehead, even though it was a little chilly inside the heavily air-conditioned courtroom. "We've had a change in strategy, your honor."

Patrick tried to leave it at that, but the judge wouldn't let him. "You'll need to say more if you want to get this evidence in."

The defense attorney looked back at his client, then dabbed at his brow with the back of his jacket sleeve as he turned back to the judge. For the first time, Mary Beth got the feeling that Patrick wasn't ill. He was nervous. Nervous like she'd never seen him.

"Judge … uh, we want to put on our alibi witnesses. And we know that if we do, this evidence is likely to come in anyway. So, better the jury hears it from us first."

The judge wagged a finger. "But that is the problem, Mr. Connelly. My ruling this morning, based upon *your* motion *in limine*, prevented the prosecution from admitting this evidence. The jury didn't get to hear it from them. Now you bring it out on cross, and it makes it look like the state was hiding something when they weren't. Is it your intention to argue that the state had tunnel vision in targeting Mr. Velino for this crime because of their investigation into other matters?"

Patrick raised an eyebrow like that was not what he'd been thinking at all but was a good idea. *What is he thinking?* Mary Beth couldn't figure out his strategy.

While Patrick struggled to answer the question, the judge said, "I'll not allow you to sandbag the state in this fashion, Mr. Connelly. No more than I would allow them to do it to you. I—"

"We don't object," Jeannie Boggs interrupted. "We want the evidence in, too, judge. I would have preferred to do it during my direct examination, but if it comes out on cross, that's better than not having it at all."

The judge grimaced. He didn't like lawyers doing end-runs around his rulings. But since both attorneys were in agreement, he ultimately was as well. "If you are sure, Ms. Boggs."

Jeannie was chomping at the bit. "Absolutely, judge."

"Very well, then. Let's proceed."

Patrick glanced briefly at Mary Beth before turning from the bench. He had the most tortured expression, which really left her feeling confused.

What in the world are you up to, Patrick Connelly?

The judge instructed Patrick to repeat his prior question.

"Sheriff Cain, isn't it true that you had already been investigating Mr. Velino for some time prior to Brad Mayhew's murder?"

"Yes," Mary Beth said. "We had been investigating him for nearly a year prior."

Patrick slid his chair a little farther away from his client. "Investigating him for what?" he asked.

Mary Beth looked at Velino, who was glaring at Patrick as though he might lunge at him at any second. She thought about holding back with her answer but ultimately couldn't do it. "You name it," she said. "Drug trafficking, murder, extortion, conspiracy, bribery, corruption. We believe Mr. Velino is essentially the criminal mastermind behind the massive influx in drugs and violence this county has seen recently." Mary Beth paused, expecting there to be some objection or direction to stop, but none came, so she kept going. "Our information is that Mr. Velino is a gangster connected with organized crime out of Detroit. The number of crimes he's been suspected of are almost too many to list."

"Let's focus on murders, then," Patrick said. "How many people do you suspect Mr. Velino of having killed?"

Again, Mary Beth instinctually felt like someone would stop her from answering. The question seemed like such a gift to the prosecution. No longer was she confined to what she could prove but was being asked to lay out all that she simply suspected.

"The number of murders Mr. Velino is believed to have personally committed is at least twenty. It goes all the way back to when he was a teenager and first started working as a hitman for the mob. Then, of course, there are the ones we think he ordered to be carried out by others."

Has this been Patrick's plan all along? Mary Beth wondered. *Is he throwing the Velino case on purpose to assure I'll get my conviction?* It certainly seemed that way. But then Patrick veered back toward the tunnel vision argument the judge referenced during their bench conference.

"Would it be fair to say that building a case against Mr. Velino has been your top priority in recent months?"

"It was certainly one of our top priorities."

"And are there other law enforcement agencies, in Michigan and other states, for instance, who have been attempting to build cases against Mr. Velino over the years?"

"There are."

"Has Mr. Velino ever been convicted of killing anyone?"

"No, just robbery, assault, drug possession, and possession with intent to distribute." Mary Beth ticked the convictions off quickly. She knew she was pushing her luck by mentioning them, but Patrick didn't seem to mind.

"Those are all lesser crimes than murder and carry smaller penalties, correct?"

"That's correct."

"Convicting Mr. Velino in this murder case would be a much bigger deal, right?"

"Murder is a more serious charge, sure."

"I imagine that you and all the other agencies who have investigated Mr. Velino over the last thirty years would love to have convicted him of those murders you described, right?"

"Objection!"

Jeannie Boggs was on her feet. "Your honor, she can't answer how other law enforcement agencies felt."

Judge Parsons sustained.

Patrick moved on, asking, "Sheriff Cain, can you explain how it is that all these various agencies have been investigating Mr. Velino for all of these killings without ever securing a conviction?"

Jeannie stood like she was about to object but seemed to change her mind at the last minute and sat back down.

Mary Beth said, "Mainly because the witnesses against Mr. Velino always turn up dead."

"Do you suspect Mr. Velino of intimidating and killing witnesses?"

"Yes."

"He's also been suspected of juror intimidation, hasn't he?"

Before Mary Beth could answer, Velino leapt across the defense table and seized his attorney by the throat.

"You fucked me!" Velino yelled as the two men crashed to the floor. Jurors and onlookers screamed. Mary Beth shot up out of the witness chair and dashed toward them to try and intercede. Izzy and the courtroom bailiff beat her there. By the time she arrived to help, Izzy had Velino in a choke hold while the bailiff was doing his best to pry loose the mobster's grip around Patrick's throat.

With Mary Beth's help, they eventually got Velino's hands cuffed behind his back.

Patrick was gasping for air. He eventually got to his feet and leaned against counsel's table. After several moments, it looked like order was about to be restored when Velino lunged at his lawyer again, headbutting Patrick this time and then biting at him like a piranha. Velino went for Patrick's ear, but Mary Beth and the bailiff pulled him back, which resulted in the gangster catching Patrick down around his jawline, sinking his incisors in deep enough to draw blood before he was again subdued.

"Order! Order in the court!" Judge Parsons yelled. He sent the jurors back to the assembly room and told the bailiff to lock Velino in the prisoner hold.

A clerk had a first aid kit and was tending to Patrick's bloody jawline, while the judge asked the attorneys how they wanted to proceed in light of the defendant's outburst.

Mary Beth wasn't sure at first what the judge was asking,

but Jeannie Boggs got it. She was the first to speak. "The state strongly opposes a mistrial, judge. The defendant shouldn't be able to benefit from any prejudice that he himself caused."

"I tend to agree," Judge Parsons said, "but I'd like to hear from Mr. Connelly on the subject."

Mary Beth started to curse Patrick under her breath, thinking that maybe all of his self-defeating questions were designed to intentionally provoke Velino's outburst as an excuse for a mistrial. But Patrick quickly eschewed that notion. With a white square of gauze now taped to his jaw, Patrick stood and said he did not want a mistrial, either.

"In fact, judge," he said, "I don't even want a continuance. If it pleases the court, I'd like to get the jury back in here as soon as possible and proceed."

Mary Beth, who was often wrong but almost never in doubt, had to admit she was mystified as to Patrick's strategy. *Maybe he's losing it*, she thought.

The judge deferred to Patrick's desire to proceed. After a brief recess, the jury was brought back in with futile instructions to disregard the outburst they'd witnessed. The judge also allowed Velino to reenter but insisted he be restrained by handcuffs and a bite collar to prevent any more attacks.

When the questioning resumed, Patrick picked up right where he'd left off, asking the sheriff to describe the multiple witnesses against Velino who had turned up tortured and murdered—much like Brad Mayhew. Mary Beth started going through that parade of horribles. By the time she got to describing the most recent instance, her old friend Mr. Percy, whose eyeball had been delivered to her home, Mary Beth figured the state was assured the biggest slam dunk conviction in the history of jurisprudence.

Jeannie Boggs certainly looked confident. She declined to redirect after the cross was over and winked at Mary Beth as she exited the stand.

But as the sheriff passed by the jury, she saw something that shook her. Twelve expressions of abject horror. Not disgust or disdain over what they had heard, but fear. Palpable fear. The people in that box, the everyday citizens of Jasper County, were scared to death as Velino glared at them, looking like Hannibal Lecter, in his restraints and bite mask, sitting next to an attorney who had blood-soaked gauze stuck to his face.

It was only then that Mary Beth finally understood what Patrick had been up to this whole time. Though she could barely believe he would do something so unconscionably unethical. The point of Patrick's cross-exam had been to threaten the jury. He was intimidating them right there in open court, under the judge's nose, with the enthusiastic encouragement of the prosecution, by detailing the extreme and violent lengths Lenny Velino would go to in order to escape justice. Patrick wanted the jury to know what they were up against. He wanted them to recognize what Mary Beth had been unwilling to—that Leonard Velino was a kind of evil that the law wasn't equipped to handle. Many agencies had tried and failed. Norms and rules and basic decorum couldn't protect witnesses from a man like him. They couldn't protect a church elder like Brad Mayhew. They couldn't even protect Velino's own attorney.

If those twelve people were to have the audacity to find Velino guilty, God only knew what might happen to them.

16

NOW IN FRONT of the grand jury, Mary Beth was seated in the same witness chair she'd been in the day Velino attacked Patrick in open court. She'd just finished describing that event when Pomfried asked, "Is it your belief that Mr. Connelly was seeking a jury nullification?"

"I'm not sure I know what you mean," Mary Beth said.

"A jury nullification. Meaning, Connelly was basically asking the jurors to violate their oaths. To find Velino not guilty despite overwhelming evidence of guilt, because they were afraid of him."

Again Mary Beth weighed just how forthright she should be. Ultimately she decided to shoot straight. "I thought he wanted to scare them. Then when Father Gonzalez testified, I assumed he would go hard against the identification and see if he could back the priest off of how certain he had been that Velino was the man he saw. If that didn't work, he'd put his bogus alibi witnesses on. Either way he'd have some plausible argument for reasonable doubt and hope the jurors were so afraid of Velino that they'd latch onto it like a life raft and return a verdict of not guilty."

"Thank you," Pomfried said. "For the record, I think that's what he was doing, too. I believe he was telling those jurors that the system was not equipped to handle a man like Leonard Velino. Would you agree with that?"

Mary Beth had thought almost those exact words but didn't want to admit it. "I don't know."

"Sure you do, *Miss* Cain. He was telling the jury that the law has restrictions, limitations, restraints. And a man as shameless and ruthless as Leonard Velino can blow right through those gaps and do harm to witnesses, jurors, prison guards, lawyers, even police officers or their families. Isn't that right?"

Again Mary Beth had a hard time arguing the point but hesitated to concede it. "Well, witnesses, at least."

"Ah yes. Let's talk about witnesses, *Miss* Cain. Tell the jury what happened after your testimony concluded."

Mary Beth decided to stay within the confines of the question and not skip ahead. "Chief Deputy Baker was called to the stand. He described putting together the six-pack photo array from which Father Gonzalez identified Leonard Velino as the man who killed Brad Mayhew."

That had been a real nerve-racking part of the trial. Mary Beth had to pray that what she'd done to coach the identification wouldn't get exposed.

"Was there any cross-examination of Deputy Baker?"

"Some," Mary Beth said, "but it didn't really lead anywhere."

"And what occurred after Chief Deputy Baker finished testifying?"

"The plan was to call Father Gonzalez next."

"That may have been the plan, but please tell the jury what happened."

Mary Beth paused. She had to fight back a crushing sense of guilt. "Well," she said, "we ran into a problem."

"That's one way to put it. Please explain."

Mary Beth took a deep breath. It was a hard subject for her to discuss, wrapped as it was within such deep feelings of remorse, regret, and seething anger. To keep those emotions under control, Mary Beth spoke in a cold, detached manner. "Deputy Goforth had been sent to an undisclosed location where Father Gonzalez was being held, to bring him back just in time for his testimony, and ..."

"And? Go on, please."

"And he never made it back."

Again, Mary Beth had to pause to collect herself. She'd taken such care with Father Gonzalez, stashing him in fleabag motels in Virginia, Kentucky, and North Carolina, moving him every couple of weeks. Only she and Izzy had known his whereabouts. The poor priest had been completely cut off from his church community, not even given a chance to say goodbye before he was whisked away into protective custody.

The last time Mary Beth saw Gonzalez was just days before the trial began, and he didn't look well. The priest's beard was overgrown, his hair unkempt, his complexion sallow, and he'd gained weight from lack of exercise and a diet consisting mostly of fast food. "It feels like purgatory," Father Gonzalez had told her.

"It will all be over soon," she had assured him.

Even then it broke Mary Beth's heart that she'd put Father Gonzalez in such a tough position. But they'd gone too far to turn back. And convicting Velino was too important. If she could have changed places with the priest, she would have. She knew she would. But that wasn't possible. All she could do was promise to keep him safe.

Pomfried asked Mary Beth again what happened to Father Gonzalez. She managed to respond, describing it as best she could, limiting herself to the facts she knew, though it was the ones she could only imagine that haunted her most deeply.

Father Gonzalez had shaved that morning. They knew this because they later found evidence of it in the bathroom sink, and Mary Beth had suggested he do so in order to look more presentable to the jury. Most likely he had also spent some time reading the Bible, because the hotel copy was found on his unmade bed, open to a page in Psalms that included the passage Mary Beth guessed he might have been focused on, twenty-three, verse four:

Even though I walk through the valley of the
shadow of death,
I fear no evil;
For thou art with me;
Your rod and your staff, they comfort me

The words sent shivers down Mary Beth's spine. How often had she imagined herself as the shepherd of her county, protecting her flock. And hadn't she promised Father Gonzalez that she would be the one to personally escort him that day? That she would see him through his hour of darkness?

The priest must have been surprised when Deputy Goforth, a man he had never seen before, was the one to knock on his door that morning. Mary Beth knew this because during the time she'd been testifying and had her phone switched off, she had missed calls from the burner phone they'd purchased for Father Gonzalez and instructed him to use only to contact Mary Beth or Izzy. When he'd been unable to reach the sheriff, Father Gonzalez had called Izzy, who assured him it was safe to go with the deputy.

When Mary Beth got to the point of describing to the jury what happened after Father Gonzalez got into Goforth's cruiser, Pomfried stopped her.

"At this point, I think it might be most helpful to play for the jury the dashcam video."

With the grace of a warthog on roller skates, Alexander Pomfried repositioned his cart with the TV display, pushing it in front of the jury, and cued up the video. The camera was mounted in the center of the dash, angled slightly toward the driver's side, showing more or less the view that Goforth would have had as he drove. There was a time stamp in the top-right corner, indicating it was shortly before 1:00 p.m. when the cruiser exited off of I-77, past the rest area designed to evoke the region's mountains. Goforth could be overheard prattling on about the Mountaineers basketball team, how the university had done the coach wrong, when there was a loud metallic crash and the image spun to the left so violently that the picture dropped out for a moment. By the time it flashed back on, the horn was blaring as Goforth's unconscious body slumped against the steering wheel. His right hand, with the Jasper High class ring, was visible in the dashcam frame. Off to the right was a white, windowless van. Its front end was smashed from where it had collided with the rear passenger side of the cruiser.

Father Gonzalez's voice could be heard. "Oh, God. Oh, God. No. No. No. Get away!" There were sounds of struggle. Goforth's hand slid out of view, and the horn stopped. "Get away! Get away!" More commotion, then three gunshots that were later determined to have come from Goforth's gun, fired through the roof of the cruiser. Presumably Father Gonzalez had retrieved the unconscious deputy's pistol in a vain attempt to defend himself. More struggling sounds were followed by a blood-curdling squeal like a lamb about to be slaughtered as Gonzalez was pulled from the vehicle. The video ended with a fleeting image of masked men in dark suits wrestling the priest into the back of the van, before it pulled away out of sight.

"Those were most likely Velino's men we just saw there, abducting Father Gonzalez," Pomfried said. "Wouldn't you agree?"

"Nothing was able to be definitively established from the

video," Mary Beth said. "We sent it to the FBI for assistance, but even after a detailed analysis, they weren't able to firmly identify the vehicle or any of the assailants."

"But certainly you believe it was Velino's men who grabbed the priest to keep him from testifying in the Mayhew murder trial?"

"Yes," Mary Beth said. There was no point in denying it. She knew it, just as everyone in that jury box did.

"Velino kidnapped your witness?"

"Yes, I believe he did."

"He kidnapped a man you put in harm's way. A man you swore to protect, correct?"

"Yes," Mary Beth said, as tears welled up in her eyes.

"What happened to Father Gonzalez, *Miss* Cain?"

Mary Beth struggled to make the words come out. "He wasn't found for some time," she whispered.

"Come again?" Pomfried held his hand to his ear.

Mary Beth repeated herself, speaking more loudly the second time.

"But when he was found?"

Mary Beth shook her head. The memory was too painful.

Pomfried thundered away at her. "You have to answer the question, *Miss* Cain. What happened to Father Gonzalez?"

"He was dead."

"Not just dead, though, right, *Miss* Cain?"

Mary Beth didn't respond.

"He'd been tortured, hadn't he?"

Again Mary Beth couldn't bring herself to answer.

Pomfried charged aggressively toward her. "And not just tortured. He was crucified, wasn't he?"

Mary Beth felt tears of devastation and rage—white-hot rage—pouring freely down her cheeks.

Pomfried slammed a photo down in front of her. "Look at

him," he commanded. "This is what they did to Father Gonzalez, isn't it?"

Mary Beth couldn't bear to look at the photo. She'd seen enough dead bodies that she'd lost count, but none had ever shook her like the corpse of Father Gonzalez; the sheer brutality was unspeakable.

"I'd like to take a break," Mary Beth said.

"In a moment," Pomfried barked back at her.

Mary Beth was upset. And when she got upset, she got angry. And when she got angry, she lost control. And that was right where Pomfried wanted her.

"Knowing that Leonard Velino was responsible for this," he said, pointing down at the photo, "you wanted him dead, didn't you, *Miss* Cain?"

Mary Beth shook her head. She wanted to deny it but couldn't say the words.

"DIDN'T YOU?" Pomfried shouted, getting right up in her face.

"YES!" Mary Beth shouted back. She had leaned forward into her answer, curling her top lip, baring her teeth like fangs, as though she might bite Pomfried's head off if he didn't back the F up.

Yet the prosecutor moved in even closer, to the point they were almost kissing. "You wanted him dead, and you didn't care how it happened. If the law couldn't handle him, you were willing to take matters into your own hands, weren't you?"

Mary Beth knew she was making a mistake by saying any more, but she was too worked up to keep quiet. She'd already crossed an emotional barrier she couldn't retreat from. It just felt too righteous, too cathartic to admit the truth that everyone had to already know. "Yes, goddammit. I wanted Velino dead. And I was willing to kill the motherfucker with my own bare hands if I could get a hold of him."

Pomfried's eyes went big. He backpedaled a step, almost

tripping. He took a moment to let the sheriff's incriminating answer resonate throughout the courtroom.

Mary Beth's chest was heaving. Hot tears poured down her cheeks, eventually counterbalanced by a cold sweat that formed at the base of her neck as she realized what she'd just said. The sheriff regained enough poise to make an effort at damage control.

"I would have killed him, Mr. Pomfried. But I didn't."

The prosecutor seemed unbothered by this addendum to her prior answer.

He returned to counsel's table and took his time going through his notes. "Tell me something," he said, finally. "Did you ever suspect that Deputy Goforth was complicit in allowing Velino's men to abduct Father Gonzalez?"

"No," Mary Beth answered quickly.

That was a lie but a strategic one. Mary Beth had regained enough composure to avoid the truth on this subject. She had suspected Goforth. And it had taken extraordinary measures for her to satisfy herself that he was not in league with Velino.

Extraordinary measures.

All she could do at that point in her grand jury testimony was to pray that Pomfried didn't know about that, too.

17

MARY BETH KNEW Father Gonzalez was kidnapped to keep him from testifying, and the easiest way to make sure he stayed quiet forever was to kill him. The one thing that gave her hope was that the cruiser cam showed Gonzalez being taken alive and stuffed into the kidnappers' van. If they'd wanted him executed as soon as possible, they could have shot him right there inside Goforth's squad car. But they didn't. That meant there was a chance. Though with every hour, every minute, every second that passed, the odds of ever recovering Father Gonzalez alive dropped precipitously. Thus pride was no longer a sin Mary Beth could afford. She called the FBI for assistance.

By that afternoon, federal agents were already on the case, working with her deputies to go over any additional surveillance footage that could be recovered from neighboring businesses. Others went to round up Velino's known associates to try and sweat them for information. Once all of that was in motion, and there was nothing else Mary Beth could do, she and Izzy met with Jeannie Boggs in a small conference area next to the courtroom to find out what would happen with the trial in light of the Gonzalez abduction.

"There's really nothing we can do," Jeannie said. "Without the priest, there's no case. When we reconvene in the morning, the defense will make a motion to dismiss, and the judge will have to grant it."

"So … what?" Mary Beth said, unable to control her volume. "Velino just goes free?"

Jeannie held up her hands. "Yeah."

"Not happening," Mary Beth said. "Everyone knows he's behind this. The judge included."

"I agree," Jeannie said. "Everyone knows it. But we can't prove it. Velino was in handcuffs in the middle of the judge's courtroom when Father Gonzalez was abducted. He obviously didn't do it himself. So unless you've got a witness who can tie him into a conspiracy, then Velino is going to walk."

Jeannie had a plastic cup of water in front of her that Mary Beth slapped off the table, sending it splashing against the wall. Izzy put a hand on the sheriff's shoulder to keep her calm.

"We know it's not your fault, Jeannie," he said.

Mary Beth was too angry to acknowledge that obvious fact. The miscarriage of justice was too overwhelming.

Jeannie stood to leave. "I'm sorry, sheriff. I really am. But you'll get him on something else. I'm sure you will. It's just a matter of time."

Mary Beth didn't respond. She stayed quiet as Jeannie exited the conference room. Izzy walked around the circular table to where Jeannie had been just a moment earlier. He sat down facing Mary Beth.

"Don't you dare say it, Izzy. I swear to God."

"Look at me," Izzy said.

Mary Beth shook her head. The tentacles of guilt over Father Gonzalez were already wrapping around her, ready to pull her down into the abyss.

Izzy gently tried to lift her chin, forcing her to meet his eyes. She slapped his hand away. "Stop," she said.

"MB, it's time to ask for help. The Velino situation is too big for us to handle on our own. The FBI is already here working the Gonzalez kidnapping. It's time to turn the whole thing over to the folks who have the resources to deal with this kind of thing."

"Bullshit. It's not about resources, Izzy. We bring in the feds or some other jurisdiction, and it's just more people Velino can pay off or intimidate. This is about will. Who has the will to see it through."

"And that's you."

"You're goddamn right it is."

Izzy was clearly frustrated. "Look, you saw how scared shitless those jurors were in there, after Connelly told them about all the things Velino has done. Even if you bust Velino again, you think there's a local jury that will have the guts to convict?"

"I can keep the jurors safe," Mary Beth said.

"During the trial, maybe. But are you going to follow them around for the rest of their lives?"

"We can keep their identities a secret."

"Bullshit," Izzy said. "This is a small community. There are no secrets here."

Mary Beth pounded the table with her fist. "So what would you have me do? Just give up?"

"Asking for help isn't giving up, goddammit. This is the lie you always tell yourself. It's not all on you."

Mary Beth dropped her head and rubbed her temples. If it had been Patrick on the other side of the table who'd just gotten the upper hand on her in an argument, she would have acted desperate or sad, or cried if necessary, to regain the advantage, but that didn't work with Izzy. So instead she changed the subject.

"How's Goforth?"

"He's got a concussion," Izzy said. "Some bruises. I'm sure he'll be awfully sore tomorrow, but he's going to be all right."

Mary Beth made eye contact with Izzy again. "Do you think—"

"No."

"How can you be so sure?"

"He was driving the car that got taken down like a Scud missile."

Mary Beth had already considered that and found that detail inconclusive. "Yeah, but like you said, he's just a little banged up. How else could Velino's guys have known where they could find Father Gonzalez? We've kept him safe all this time, when just you and I knew his location. And within hours of us letting Goforth in on that secret, they were able to snatch our witness."

Izzy had obviously been thinking this through and had a response ready. "They knew we'd have to bring Gonzalez to court. They've probably been following all of us the last few days. Somebody must have tailed Goforth there, and when they saw him fetch Father Gonzalez, they launched a plan to nab him."

Izzy's explanation was plausible, but Mary Beth wasn't convinced. "I want to see Benny," she said. She needed to look Goforth in the eyes. She needed to be sure.

By the time Mary Beth made it to the hospital, Goforth was just about to be discharged. He'd already changed out of his hospital gown into the civilian clothes his wife had brought and was sitting with his missus as the nurse went over medication instructions and things to look out for.

Goforth stood when Mary Beth entered the room. "Sheriff, you didn't have to come."

Mary Beth was wondering whether she should have. Seeing Goforth's wife kind of knocked her off her stride and made her feel bad about coming there to interrogate him.

"I didn't mean to interrupt."

The nurse waved off the concern. "We were just finishing. You have any problems, Mr. Goforth, you give us a call. Otherwise you are good to go."

The Goforths thanked the nurse, who smiled at Mary Beth on her way out.

"It was nice of you to come out, sheriff," Mrs. Goforth said.

"Yeah, well, I just wanted to check in. How you doing, Benny?"

Ben Goforth tapped a fist against his forehead. "Just fine, sheriff. I used to play linebacker for Jasper High back when they taught us to tackle headfirst. This is nothing."

"Good," Mary Beth said. She thought about leaving it at that and looking for a polite way to exit, but her need to know whether Goforth was dirty was too great.

"Something wrong, sheriff?" the deputy asked.

Mary Beth took off her floppy-brimmed Stetson and held it in front of her like a shield.

"Actually, Benny, I was wondering if we could have a private word. I'd like to talk to you about what happened today. If you're up to it, that is."

Ben Goforth patted his wife on the knee. "Babe, why don't you go bring the car around, and I'll meet you out front in just a few."

Mrs. Goforth was country polite. She looked like a sweet little mamaw at first blush, in her light-pink pedal pushers and baggy white blouse. But she'd been a cop's wife for thirty years and gave Mary Beth the impression she could be plenty tough when she needed to be.

"He needs to take it easy," she said to Mary Beth, as she stood to leave.

"Understood," Mary Beth said.

Mrs. Goforth looked back at her husband. "Don't be long."

Goforth assured her he wouldn't and walked his wife out. He closed the door of the cramped little hospital room behind her and turned to face Mary Beth.

"I can't tell you how sorry I am about what happened today,

sheriff. I should have kept a better lookout. I just … I didn't see them coming."

Mary Beth didn't respond. She maintained radar lock on Goforth's eyes.

He squirmed under the silence.

"It's all kind of a blur, really. I don't even remember getting hit. There was just like a flash. Next thing I knew, I was in the back of an ambulance with a medic shining a light in my eyes."

Again, Mary Beth stayed mum.

"I asked about Father Gonzalez, but the EMTs, they wouldn't tell me anything. It wasn't until I got here and talked to Izzy that I really knew what had happened."

Mary Beth gave Goforth a few more beats of the silent treatment before saying, "Do you have any idea how they found you?"

"Who?"

Mary Beth didn't like that answer. "Who do you think?"

"Oh, yeah," Goforth said, embarrassed. "I mean no. No, I have no idea. I didn't say a word to nobody, sheriff. I swear."

Mary Beth watched him a little longer. Goforth was clearly uncomfortable with this conversation. The sheriff held his gaze in her tractor-beam stare.

"I'm putting you on administrative leave," she said.

"For how long?"

"Thirty days," she said. "To start."

Goforth scratched at the top of his potbelly stomach. "Come on, sheriff. I'm telling you I'm fine. Maybe a day or two to clear out the cobwebs might be a good idea, but I don't need no thirty days."

"It's not for you," Mary Beth said. "It's to give me time to make sure you aren't dirty."

"Dirty?" Goforth seemed appropriately appalled by the notion.

"Yeah," Mary Beth said. "I need to make sure you didn't sell out my witness."

"Sheriff, please, listen—"

Mary Beth held up a hand. "You might want to consult a lawyer before you say anything else, Benny."

She started to leave, but Goforth kept after her.

"No, sheriff. You've got it all wrong."

"I hope so," she said. "I really do. And if I'm wrong, I'm sorry. But if I'm right …" Mary Beth paused to put her hat back on. "If I find out you gave up Father Gonzalez, then Benny, any violence that man suffers as a result, you're gonna pay for it."

She turned the knob to leave, but Goforth put his thick, wide hand in the middle of the door.

"Wait."

"I don't have time to wait," Mary Beth said. "I've only got till morning to figure out to keep a cold-blooded murderer from going free. Now move aside."

Goforth didn't budge. The deputy was an out-of-shape, white-haired man who was close to retirement, but he had a couple of inches and at least fifty pounds on her all the same. He could give Mary Beth some serious problems if he'd wanted to. Especially in such tight confines, where the benefit of her greater speed and dexterity would be diminished.

Mary Beth was prepared to grab him by his privates if he tried something, but the only aggression Goforth showed was in the profuseness of his pleading.

"Please, sheriff. Please. I can't sit at home with you and everybody thinking I had something to do with this. It'll tear me up. Please just let me do something to prove it to you."

Mary Beth nodded to his hand, which was holding the door closed.

"Oh," Goforth said, embarrassed. He backed up physically but kept after her verbally. "Really, sheriff. I'll do anything. Anything you ask."

Mary Beth intended to leave him there, groveling, when an idea struck her.

"Anything, huh?"

"Yes, you name it."

Mary Beth rolled a notion around her noggin for a few more seconds, more focused on the logistics of what she was plotting than whether or not it was a good idea. The latter type of consideration was Izzy's department. And her personal Jiminy Cricket wasn't there at the moment, which was good, Mary Beth decided, because what she was thinking was something Izzy shouldn't know anything about.

"Okay," she said, putting a hand on Goforth's shoulder. "I've got an idea. You help me with it, and I'll know for sure that you're on the level."

18

AT 2:00 A.M. there was only a skeleton crew working the regional jail. It was well after lights out, and all the little shithead criminals were tucked snugly in their beds, locked into cells with visions of felonies dancing in their heads.

Like Santa Claus sneaking down the chimney, Mary Beth wanted to deliver a special present to Mr. Velino without being seen, so she made sure all the relevant cameras were switched off before making her way down through South Block, navigating a corridor of beige brick walls lined with metal cell doors painted battleship gray. When she got to cell 121, she undid the latch for a narrow rectangular metal window cover, opened it, and peered in through thick glass. Velino was asleep with his back to her, facing the wall. She rattled her handcuffs against the door loud enough to rouse him.

Velino rolled over and stared at her bleary-eyed. When she saw recognition in his expression, she held her middle finger up to the glass and said, "Wake up, dickhead. We need to talk."

Mary Beth undid another latch on the door, this one covering a horizontal, mail-slot-sized opening for passing things to prisoners. The sheriff flipped her handcuffs through it like a Frisbee. They fell at Velino's feet, where he was now seated on his bed.

"Put those on," Mary Beth said.

Velino picked up the handcuffs. Without argument he shackled himself to a steel bar in the back of the six-by-eight concrete room and tugged at the cuffs to show they were secure.

Mary Beth switched on her walkie and said, "Open 121." Two seconds later there was a loud metal click. Mary Beth opened the door, stepped inside, and closed it behind her.

"You know you're not supposed to talk to me without my lawyer present?" Velino said.

Mary Beth smiled at him. "That's your whole thing, isn't it, Lenny?"

"What's that?"

"That's your advantage. You're always going up against a system that has to play by rules, when you don't have any."

Velino didn't respond.

Mary Beth said, "Losing at trial? You'll just kidnap the state's chief witness."

"I've got the right to remain silent," Velino said.

"You've got the right to eat shit," Mary Beth said. "Fuck your rights. Look around you, Lenny." Mary Beth gestured to the hard, austere surroundings. "You're inside my world. This is the dictatorship of Sheriff Cain-istan. And I don't give a rat's ass about the rules, either. What do you think is about to happen here, Lenny?"

Velino smiled a wicked smile. He arched his back and slid his free hand toward his crotch. "Maybe you were wanting a little conjugal visit?"

Mary Beth wasn't amused.

"You're about to get Jeffrey Epsteined up in this bitch, unless you tell me where Father Gonzalez is."

If Velino was scared, he was doing a good job of hiding it. "Talk to my lawyer," he said.

"I wouldn't piss on your lawyer if he was on fire."

That elicited a chuckle from Velino. "Yeah, you two don't like to do much talking. Just a little—" Velino made a short punching motion with his free hand.

Mary Beth felt sickened by the notion that Patrick had shared the nature of their relationship with this scumbag. It seemed impossible to her that he would violate her trust that way. The only thing she could figure was that Patrick must have determined their romantic connection was a potential conflict he had to disclose. He had such a tortured sense of ethics. Trying to follow its labyrinthine path of logic was like watching a Rube Goldberg machine determine the difference between right and wrong. How else could Patrick have justified representing someone like Lenny Velino?

Well, not Mary Beth. Her moral reasoning was a straight, goddamn line, going from wherever she was to wherever she needed to get. And right now that was to Father Gonzalez. Velino would either lead her there, or he would regret it.

Mary Beth switched her walkie back on and said, "Bring them in." She opened the cell door and looked down the hall where little gears were grinding as the metal door at the end of the cell block slid open. On the other side was Deputy Goforth, toting a shotgun, marching four inmates dressed in orange jumpsuits who were chained together and shuffling like penguins. Each one was covered with jailhouse tats and swarthy-looking, who-gives-a-fuck beards that spread like crabgrass on their face and necks.

The sheriff stepped farther into the room, almost within Velino's reach, so the men could assemble in the doorway where Velino would see them.

"Where's Father Gonzalez?" she demanded.

Velino didn't answer, but she could see his pulse hammering away on the side of his neck. She had his attention.

"Maybe you didn't know it," Mary Beth said, "but Father Gonzalez was pretty involved in prison ministry. He personally baptized each one of these men. So what's about to happen, Lenny, is I'm gonna give you one last chance, and one chance only, to tell me where Father Gonzalez is. And if you don't, then these guys are going to tear you apart like a pack of wild dogs."

"You're bluffing," Velino said.

"No," Mary Beth said. "I don't bluff, and I'm out of patience. Uncuff them."

Goforth handed her the shotgun. Mary Beth stepped past them out into the hall and lowered the rifle, ready to shoot if anybody got out of line. She knew it would be a lot safer to have a few other guards helping her with this, but there was obviously no established protocol for what she was doing, and there were only so many people you could bring into such an operation. Even the guard in the control room had just been told to take a break and didn't know what was going down. No one else did. Just Mary Beth and Ben Goforth and four very willing prisoners who all loved and admired Father Gonzalez.

"You boys fuck him up good now," Mary Beth said.

Goforth was unshackling the wrists of the prisoner closest to him when Velino said, "I don't know where Father Gonzalez is. I truly don't."

"That's the wrong answer, Lenny."

Mary Beth nodded for Goforth to continue. Each of the prisoners was cuffed to a belly chain that ran down to ankle shackles. Goforth finished unlocking the first man's wrists, then his ankles. Once free, the man moved to the far side of the cell. He stretched his neck and cracked his tattooed knuckles, while he waited for the others to join him.

Velino started squirming like his underwear was full of fire ants. "Wait," he said. "I don't know where Gonzalez is, but I might be able to find out."

The freed prisoner punched Velino with enough force that it would have flung the slender gangster off his bed, but his shackled wrist kept him from falling all the way to the floor.

"Stop." Mary Beth raised the shotgun. The prisoner backed away. Velino spit a glob of blood onto the floor. He sat up. Using his free hand, Velino reached into his mouth and wriggled a tooth free and tossed it on the floor.

"Is there someone you can call?" Mary Beth asked. "Tell them to let Gonzalez go?"

Velino looked at her a moment, then at the four men who were just itching to beat him to death. He used the back of his hand to wipe the blood at the corner of his mouth. "Give me a phone," he said. "And keep those motherfuckers away from me."

"Back up," Goforth ordered. The prisoner who'd struck Velino looked disappointed but complied. He offered Goforth his wrists and allowed himself to be reshackled.

Meanwhile, Mary Beth pulled out her cell phone and tossed it to Velino.

He caught it with one hand and laid it on the bed so he could dial, then picked it back up and held it to his ear.

Mary Beth couldn't hear the voice on the other end but someone must have answered. Velino said, "You still got him. Good."

Mary Beth felt her heart leap. Gonzalez was still alive. This crazy gambit might actually work.

"Things have gone sideways," Velino said. "Yeah. That's right. Tomorrow. Oh … not a burner." He ended the call and dropped the phone back on the bed.

"What the fuck was that?" Mary Beth asked.

Velino held up a finger like he needed a minute before answering.

"Who was that?' Mary Beth demanded again.

Velino pointed at her and then rubbed his head. Like maybe he was making a reference to the red hair.

At least I've got some, Mary Beth thought.

"You remember the first time we met?" Velino asked. "You told me about that old sheriff, Sid Hatfield, who took up for the miners. Went after the guys the mine owners hired to roust them?"

Mary Beth was not interested in reminiscing. "Where is Father Gonzalez? And who were you just talking to?"

Velino kept going, regardless. "I told you I knew about old Sid. And how he got shot and killed right on the courthouse steps, remember?"

"I'm losing patience, Lenny."

"Turns out there's another part to that story I just learned about. The dead sheriff's wife. You know this part?"

Mary Beth did not.

"It's very interesting. The wife had previously been married to the mayor, who was killed in the Battle of Matewan. After he died, she marries the sheriff, who gets killed not long after. I hear that, and I'm thinking this lady is some kind of bad luck. Everybody around her keeps getting killed."

He's stalling. Mary Beth was about to sic the prisoners on him again when Velino said something that stopped her.

"I hear the coal miners have a superstition about that. About redheaded women. You ever heard it?"

Mary Beth didn't respond. Velino said. "It's got to make you wonder. Your dad gets shot, your husband gets shot, your brother gets shot. Sure would be a shame to add your son to that list."

Mary Beth's blood ran cold. "My son?"

Velino gave her a blood-soaked smile. "That was my insurance agent I was just talking to. Took out a little policy to protect from accidents. You know, like if I were to slip and break my neck in the shower, or hang myself in my cell."

Mary Beth and Goforth looked at each other, neither quite understanding. The sheriff stepped closer and pointed the shotgun at Velino's chest. "What the fuck are you talking about?"

Velino smiled wider. "That was my man sitting outside your son's apartment."

Mary Beth nearly dropped the shotgun.

"That's right," Velino said, delighting in her reaction. "While you've got me at your mercy in here, my man out there is grabbing your little bitch-ass boy. And unless I walk out of here tomorrow a free man, after the judge dismisses my case, then you've seen that kid for the last time."

Mary Beth snatched her phone off of Velino's bed. She pulled up the call history to see the number he'd dialed.

"It's a burner," Velino said. "And I told him I wasn't calling from a burner so he knew to destroy his phone the second we hung up. Maybe you can trace it, maybe you can't, but it doesn't matter. 'Cause I'll tell you where he's at: 112 Waverly Street, apartment B."

Mary Beth was gripped by panic. That was Sam's address. She handed the shotgun back to Goforth and pushed past him, trying to speed-dial Sam as she hurried down the hall.

Come on, Sammy Pick up.

Mary Beth dashed down the southern corridor, through the open door down the hallway that connected with the jail's center hub. The call went to voicemail.

"Shit."

She got on her walkie and sent out the SOS. She prayed that one of her deputies working the night shift was close enough that they could get to Sam in time.

SAM HAD FALLEN ASLEEP on the couch that evening, while watching a documentary about Bob Lazar, the man who claimed to have reverse-engineered alien spacecraft at Area 51. Sam was dreaming about being on a similar team of scientists called in to investigate a recovered saucer with dead aliens inside. But as they were going through the ship, they were surprised to find some things written in English. Then, in a *Planet of the Apes*–type twist, they found a US flag hung up on the hull, with the year 3046 engraved, and determined that what we'd long assumed to be extraterrestrials, with their big head and eyes and their tiny gray bodies, were actually humans time traveling back from the future. The grays were what people evolved into after generations of staring at screens all day, living in mostly virtual realities, never going outside due to climate change and extreme weather and technology-fueled apathy, resulting in enormous brains and withered little physiques. Over time, humans had also become relatively genderless and mostly sterile, which was why alien abductions so often involved sexual violations. The people of the future were traveling to the past and conducting experiments in hopes of repopulating the species.

In the midst of this discovery, there was a loud banging sound. At first it was inside Sam's dream, something slamming against the metal exterior of the crashed saucer. But then, as Sam was startled awake, he realized the noise was someone rapping aggressively at his front door.

"Police," a man's voice shouted. "Open up."

At about the same time, Sam's phone went off, playing the Darth Vader theme—a ringtone that only played when his mother called. Before Sam could answer it, the door was kicked in by a big man in a Jasper County deputy uniform.

Sam jumped. "Jesus."

The deputy was pointing a flashlight and a gun at him, holding them together as one.

"Sam Cain?"

He didn't recognize the deputy's voice. But he didn't know all of them and didn't know any of his mother's coworkers well, other than Izzy.

"Yes," he answered.

"We've got to get you out of here. There's men coming to grab you."

"What? What men?"

The man holstered his weapon and moved into the room holding out his hand. "There's no time to explain. Come on, son," he said. "Hurry."

Sam hesitated. His phone stopped ringing.

"That was my mom. Let me just call her back and see what's going on."

"We don't have time, Sam. We've got to hurry. You can call her on the way."

The man's accent sounded strange. Something inside Sam told him not to trust him. He picked up his phone, determined to call his mom anyway.

"Just a second," he said. "Let me get my shoes on." While making a show of looking around for his shoes, Sam unlocked his phone and was about to speed-dial his mom when the Darth Vader march started up again. She was already calling him back.

"Let me just get this." He answered the call. "Mom?"

"Sam? Oh, thank God. Listen—"

Before his mother could finish her sentence, the man hit Sam in the ribs with a Taser. It was a jolt like nothing Sam had ever felt. He dropped the phone and collapsed onto the couch.

He could hear his mother shouting, "Sam! Get out of there!"

But Sam could barely move. The next thing he knew, the man was over top of him. He hit him with another Taser blast just below his collarbone. Sam had no ability to resist as the man zip-tied his hands behind his back, then pulled out a roll of duct tape and wrapped it twice around Sam's head, covering his mouth. Next a black bag came down over Sam's head.

All the while, Mary Beth was shouting, "Sam!"

Strong hands grasped Sam's shoulders and yanked him up. He could barely stand, so the man half carried, half shoved Sam across the living room and out of the apartment into the cool night air. The sound of his mother's shouting—"Sam! Sam! Sam!"—got progressively quieter, then faded out all together as Sam was scooped up like a baby and stuffed inside what he quickly surmised was the trunk of a car.

• • •

Sitting on the witness stand, in front of the grand jury, Mary Beth allowed herself a moment to imagine her son's abduction. It was the second time Sam had become a target, a victim, because of her. The first was when he was taken hostage by her brother, Sawyer, something that would never have happened if Mary Beth had simply turned the Moonshine Messiah over to the feds instead of trying to take him in herself. She should have learned her lesson after that. But Mary Beth was nothing if not stubborn. Her attempts to take the law into her own hands with Velino had made Sam a hostage once more.

Fortunately, his bondage was short-lived. The day after Sam was abducted, Velino's case was dismissed. An hour later, he was processed out. Goforth personally escorted Velino beyond the walls of the county jail in what became a prisoner swap. Mary Beth waited alone at a designated location. Where Sam was simultaneously dropped off by masked men in a stolen van.

Her boy was free. Physically. But Mary Beth knew Sam would never be the same. He already carried so many emotional scars from what had happened with Sawyer, and this event seemed to rip them all back open again. Fresh and raw. Sam was edgier after that but also quieter. More inside himself. And it seemed to Mary Beth as though some of the light in his eyes went out. Gone was that sparkle when he got especially jazzed about an idea. It had been replaced with an aloof kind of gaze that broke Mary Beth's heart.

Goddammit, why couldn't she have just left well enough alone? Or better yet, why didn't she just encourage Sam to go away to school like he'd always wanted to? Far away from her and whatever mischief she managed to cause.

"You still with us, *Miss* Cain?" Pomfried asked, trying to regain her attention.

"Oh, I'm sorry," Mary Beth said. "Could you repeat the question?"

"I was saying that it must have been hard for you to just let Leonard Velino go?"

You have no idea, Mary Beth thought. One of the most insufferable parts of Sam's abduction was that Mary Beth couldn't bust anybody for it without putting herself at risk. How could she explain the circumstances without revealing the vigilante torture she'd nearly carried out in Velino's cell?

That notion had her squirming in her seat, thinking about how to answer Pomfried's question.

The only way he could know is if Goforth told him. Mary Beth knew Pomfried had hauled Goforth and most of her subordinates before the grand jury before getting to her. What she didn't know was what they'd told him.

"Well, Ms. Cain. Was it hard for you to just let Leonard Velino go?"

The way he asked, it felt like Pomfried was trying to bait her. Maybe he knew how she'd nearly let four prisoners beat Velino and wanted to see if she'd come clean or dig her hole of lies even deeper.

Avoiding a murder charge was Mary Beth's main reason for testifying, and convincing the grand jury not to indict would require a high level of candor. But admitting to what she and Goforth had done—or nearly done—to Velino would be more than sufficient to get her fired and the county sued, and it would probably be the basis for an additional set of charges.

Mary Beth decided to play dumb and hope Goforth hadn't ratted her out.

"Releasing Mr. Velino was what the law required, Mr. Pomfried," she said.

"Yeah, but it must have been a bitter pill to swallow?"

"The judge dismissed the case," Mary Beth said. "I had no choice but to let Mr. Velino go."

"Really? That's all you have to say about the subject?"

Shit. Mary Beth hesitated, fearing Pomfried had the goods on her. *Goforth, you rat motherfucker.* She thought again about coming clean but was too far in to back down.

"I don't know what else there is to say," she responded.

Pomfried looked at the jury, indignantly.

"It didn't burn your britches? Stoke that famous Mary Beth Cain temper, just a little?"

Mary Beth did her best to keep her cool. "I wasn't happy

about it, certainly," she said. "But like I said, I had no choice in the matter." That much was true. "Besides, I figured it was just a matter of time before Velino committed some other crime that we'd be able to charge him for."

Pomfried turned back and stared at her. He remained silent, which was a rarity for the old gasbag.

Mary Beth knew what he was doing. It was a technique she often used herself in interrogations. Just keep quiet. Most witnesses can't stand the silence and will often fill it with the most incriminating things. But Mary Beth was no ordinary witness. She just sat and stared, content to remain that way for the rest of the day if Pomfried wanted to.

Finally Pomfried broke. "Okay," he said, clapping his hands. "I guess it's time to move onto the main event, then."

Mary Beth breathed a quiet sigh of relief. Pomfried moving on meant Goforth hadn't ratted her out after all.

Way to stay strong, Benny. Never doubted you for a second.

Meanwhile, Pomfried waddled in his seersucker suit back to the defense table, preparing for what promised to be the climactic clash in the day's testimony. The prosecutor took several moments sorting through documents, putting them back into folders, and squeezing them into his carrying case, which looked like a gray plastic milk carton on wheels with an extendable handle, like a rollaboard suitcase. He pulled a thick Redweld folder out of that case and dropped it onto the prosecution table with a thud.

Mary Beth had no idea what was coming. She feared that Pomfried had something good.

Within the Redweld folder were multiple smaller manila folders that Pomfried arranged on the table in front of him. He flipped one of them open, and Mary Beth could just make out enough to tell that it contained photos.

Pomfried cleared his throat and smiled at her.

"Ms. Cain, I think it's time for you to tell everyone what happened after Mr. Velino was released."

HONESTLY, NOTHING MUCH HAPPENED after Velino was released. Not at first. The drugs were still omnipresent in their community. Overdoses kept happening every day. And the street violence was constant. All the while, Velino continued to stay one step ahead of Mary Beth, no matter what she tried.

One day, while she was in the middle of yelling at a few of her deputies for their lack of success, she got a visit from the unlikeliest of visitors.

"There's a guy out here, says he's your cousin," Deputy Skipwith said from the doorway of Mary Beth's office. Izzy, Goforth, and Morgan were seated on the opposite side of her desk, and each seemed relieved for a pause in the ass-chewing they'd been receiving.

"Cousin?"

"That's what he said."

Mary Beth got up and walked past Skipwith into the hall, where a half wall separated the offices from the waiting room. Her visitor was seated out there, facing the opposite direction, so that all she could make out was the back of his bald white head. Her first thought was that Velino was playing a joke. There to taunt her.

"Son of a bitch," she mumbled, dropping her hand to her pistol, before realizing that even Skipwith would have recognized Velino. Mary Beth walked around the half wall, putting the pieces together in her head about the same time her eyes registered the fact that it was her *distant* cousin Tommy.

"Oh. You," she said.

The tachometer on Mary Beth's fury meter dropped, but only a few notches. Tommy wasn't a welcome sight, either. "You gotta lot of balls showing your face here," she said.

The last time the sheriff had seen Tommy, he was handcuffing her to a tree and aiding Sawyer's escape, leaving Mary Beth in a whole mess of trouble.

"I heard I was in the clear," Tommy said.

Mary Beth had almost forgotten about telling her mother that she'd rip up the outstanding arrest warrant they had on Tommy. She'd actually forgotten to do it but made a mental note to take care of that as soon as he left.

"I said you could come back home. That doesn't mean I wanted to see your ugly mug."

Tommy smiled. From the front, he didn't look anything like Velino at all. His fleshy head was a lot pinker and freckled, and Tommy actually had kind eyes.

"I came to deliver a message," he said. "From your mama." Tommy was wearing a denim shirt that was the same shade as his faded jeans, making him look like one long pair of Levi's.

"Great," Mary Beth said. "More good news."

"Is there somewhere private we could talk?"

Mary Beth nodded toward her office, knowing that whatever this conversation was, it probably wasn't something she'd want broadcast.

"Come on."

Izzy and Deputies Goforth and Morgan were still lingering

around Mary Beth's desk, waiting like abused puppies to see if she had more yelling to do.

"Is Velino in here?" she asked.

The deputies all looked at each other, confused.

"No!" Mary Beth shouted. "He's not. So get out there and start looking for him."

Goforth and Morgan scrambled quickly away. Izzy took his time exiting, giving Tommy a hard stare and Mary Beth a disapproving look on his way out.

Mary Beth shut the door behind him and told Tommy to take a seat. She walked around in front of him, leaned back against her desk, and said, "Okay, what's the message from Mommy Dearest?"

"Your Uncle Jimmy is dead."

Mary Beth didn't know Jimmy had still been alive. Last she'd seen him, he was in a sniper's nest outside Sawyer's militia compound that got taken out by a drone strike. Most assumed the old Vietnam War vet had perished. Though there'd been rumors he was still out there somewhere in the surrounding forest, living off his bushcraft.

"I thought he already was dead," Mary Beth said.

"No," Tommy told her "He was crazier than shit, no longer taking his meds, out in the wild living like Rambo. But he would still come around the old family homestead occasionally. Your mom told the guys to leave food out for him, like he was a feral cat or something. Anyway, a few weeks ago he stopped coming around, and when Mamie heard that, she sent some of her guys to look for him. Apparently, the animals had already gotten to him a little bit by the time they found him."

Mary Beth closed her eyes and observed a little moment of silence. Uncle Jimmy was a handful, but she'd always liked him. He was a real colorful character in her youth. Always called her Strawberry Shortcake, on account of her reddish hair. And he had been a true blue American hero at one point, coming back from the war with a chest full of medals. Jimmy didn't deserve to die all alone like that.

She walked around behind her desk and sat in her chair.

"I'm sorry to hear that."

"Yeah, we all are," Tommy said. "Anyway, the family's wanting to have a little memorial service up at the old homestead, and your mom would obviously like to attend. So she sent me here to see if she can get a special Sheriff Cain visa to cross the state line without you giving her any trouble."

There it was. Mamie would take any opportunity, even her big brother's death, to weasel her way back into West Virginia.

The sheriff gave Tommy her I'm-not-stupid look.

"It's just for the funeral, I swear."

Maybe Mary Beth should have resisted, but after months of dealing with Velino, her mother no longer seemed so bad. If Mary Beth was honest, she was actually a little nostalgic for Mamie's less violent machinations.

"When's this supposed to happen?" she asked.

"Saturday. Four o'clock. The plan is for a brief service and then a meal afterward. It will be small. Your mom didn't want to do anything that might draw attention. Jimmy's was a big name at one point, and she figured the last thing you'd want is another round of newspaper stories reminding people about the Old Wengo mess."

"Huh? That actually sounds kind of thoughtful. You sure it was Mamie who said that?"

Tommy chuckled and crossed his leg. "Daughters are always tough on their mothers."

"Daughters of sociopaths, especially."

Tommy laughed. He uncrossed his legs and leaned forward. "Between you and me, Mary, there's something different about Mamie since I got back. She's … I don't know … softer."

"Soft as a porcupine."

"I'm serious," Tommy said. "She's getting old, Mary. Her

memory used to be like a steel trap. But now you'll tell her something, and ten minutes later you've got to go over the whole thing again, like you never talked."

"Hmm." Mary Beth hadn't been around Mamie enough to notice any of that for herself. Her mom was getting up there in years, but Mary Beth always figured she was too damn mean to decline the way most folks did. Mountain Mamie had always been such a force of nature—the plague or tornado kind—that Mary Beth had a hard time imagining her as anything less than fierce.

"So how about it?" Tommy asked. "Will you give Mamie the green light?"

Mary Beth sighed. "I guess," she said. "But just the funeral. She can stick around for the dinner after, but no dessert. I want her wrinkly ass back across the state line by nightfall."

"You're too kind," Tommy said.

"I can change my answer to no if you like."

"No, no," Tommy said, raising his hands in surrender. "But your mom was hoping you and Sam would be there as well."

"Oh." That surprised Mary Beth. Her law enforcement status had long made her a pariah among most of her kin. And she'd largely kept Sam away from them, to the point that he'd be hard-pressed to name the majority of people who would likely be in attendance. The last family gathering was Sawyer's funeral, which Mary Beth and Sam had not been invited to for obvious reasons.

"Well?" Tommy asked. "What do you say?"

Reflexively, Mary Beth nearly declined, but something stopped her. A teensy little longing for what it was once like to belong to her own clan. They might have been criminals, but there was a time they'd made her feel protected—at least for a while.

"Come on. It'd be nice to have you," Tommy said.

Mary Beth wasn't sure he meant that or that any of the

others would share that sentiment, but she would like to pay her respects to Uncle Jimmy.

"I'll talk to Sam," she said. Since the abduction, her son had been mostly avoiding her calls. He was frustrated that she couldn't give him any straight answers about what had led to his kidnapping and intuited that his mother's cowboy ways were responsible for once again putting him in harm's way. The last time they spoke, he told her he was planning to leave Jasper Creek for good, and for the first time in Sam's life, his mother didn't argue with him.

"You do that," Tommy said. "Last time I saw Sam, he was about this big." Tommy held his hand at the level of Mary Beth's desk. "I remember he was reading some big thick book that was way too advanced for a kid his age. *War and Peace* or something."

"*Crime and Punishment*," Mary Beth said. "His dad was a cop. I think he picked it just based on the title."

"Yeah, I guess it would have been."

"Now he's saying wants to be a criminal defense lawyer."

Tommy laughed. "Sounds like you're not the only one who likes to stick it to your mama."

Mary Beth had never made that connection before, but Tommy had a point.

Her cousin gave her a one-finger salute as he stood. "Well, you know where we'll be," he said. "I hope you can make it."

"We'll see," Mary Beth said.

Tommy gave her a goodbye wave and said, "It was good to see you, Mary."

Funny thing was, he actually looked like he meant it.

AFTER THE VELINO CASE ENDED, Patrick Connelly remembered how a phone functioned and kept trying to call Mary Beth. But she refused to answer and eventually blocked his number altogether. The way she figured it, Patrick had refused to talk to her while the Velino case was pending, so the least she could do was return the favor by giving him the silent treatment until the day they put her in the ground.

Knowing that stubbornness was a dominant family trait, Mary Beth feared that Sam had the same kind of avoidance in mind for her, when her calls to her son about Uncle Jimmy's funeral went unanswered. Mary Beth decided to pay him a visit. Her first few knocks on Sam's apartment door went unanswered. Mary Beth started fishing around her purse for her key. Some might say she should respect her adult son's privacy, but Mary Beth paid the damn rent and saw no reason she shouldn't let herself in.

The door opened onto a kind of bachelor pad funk of unwashed gym clothes covered up by some-type of aggressively pheromone-laden cologne. Mary Beth quickly got enough of a look around to ascertain that Sam hadn't been there in a few days. The milk and several food items in the fridge were expired—though that was nothing unusual for her absent-minded son. But the fact that Sam's PS5 and VR headset were missing, as was his suitcase, was a dead giveaway that he had been crashing somewhere else since his abduction.

Mary Beth knew that hadn't been at her house. Sam had declined her multiple entreaties for him to move back home for a while. Sam was a bit of a loner, with no close friends she knew of and God knew the bookish, awkward kid didn't have the game to shack up with a girl, so that left one likely suspect: Guadalupe. Whenever Sam was feeling *a wittle homesick*, he sometimes preferred the company of his childhood nanny to his own mother, despite the fact that Mary Beth had carried and birthed and nursed and provided for the ingrate.

Mary Beth had entered the apartment still feeling pretty guilty about Sam's abduction, knowing it was her fault, but by the time she left, she had a pretty good case of the red ass going, and, per usual, the anger was starting to mask the guilty feelings quite nicely. This time when Mary Beth got back in her Camaro she flipped on the party lights and left sirens blaring, speeding all the way to the trailer park where Guadalupe lived. The park was on the outskirts of town and was officially called The Oaks but was more often referred to as the Barrio, since it was mostly populated by members of Jasper County's growing Latino community. Guadalupe had a nice double-wide near the back, under the canopy of a weeping willow tree. The old lady's Monte Carlo was parked out front, but there was no sign of Sam's car, as Mary Beth spun to a stop in the soft grass.

She switched off her lights and siren, and went and knocked on the door. Guadalupe had obviously been to the beauty parlor recently. When she answered the door Mary Beth caught a whiff of burnt-smelling hair from too much time under the heat lamp. Guadalupe was still stylish for an eighty-year-old, keeping her hair in a kind of pixie cut that had been freshly dyed magenta. As soon as she saw Mary Beth, Guadalupe started to cry and pulled the sheriff into a hug.

"What they did to our Sam was so awful," Guadalupe said.

Mary Beth wasn't in a mood to be sentimental, or share *her* Sam with anyone. But she was glad that at least Guadalupe apparently did not blame Mary Beth for the ordeal.

"Have you seen him?" Mary Beth asked while trying to free herself from the hug. "I went by Sam's apartment, and it looked like he hadn't been there in a while."

Guadalupe looked aghast. "How could he sleep there after what happened?"

Mary Beth agreed. Once someone snatches you out of your apartment in the middle of the night and stuffs you in the trunk of a car, it'ss hard to imagine that place ever quite feeling like home again. Mary Beth just wished Sam would turn to her in such situations.

"Has he been here?" she asked.

"No," Guadalupe said. "I told him he could stay, of course, but he said the only place he felt safe was at his grandfather's."

That made sense. As much as it hurt Mary Beth that Sam had not chosen her home as his safe haven, she had to acknowledge the logic of staying with Sid Cain. The retired sheriff not only had law enforcement training but an extensive arsenal, having collected more guns than a doomsday prepper. No doubt Sid could protect Sam just as well as she could. And, unlike Mary Beth, Sid wasn't a target for the Detroit thugs.

"Oh, okay," Mary Beth said. She was still feeling hurt but the tightness in her shoulders and clinch in her jaw loosened a bit, realizing that at least Sam was safe.

"Why don;t you come in?" Guadalupe said. "Let me fix you something to eat."

Mary Beth was feeling too emotional at the moment to enjoy any of Guadalupe's always excellent cooking. "That's very nice of you. But I really need to talk with Sam right now. I hope you understand. Another time."

"Yes, yes, of course," Guadalupe said. "Go. Go find your boy."

Sam was back to being Mary Beth's boy. That notion buoyed her soul as the sheriff hugged Guadalupe once more, initiating the embrace herself that time. After that she climbed back in her car and headed toward Sid's place, leaving the lights and sirens off.

Despite his economically modest career in law enforcement, Sid had married into some coal money inherited by his now deceased wife, and lived in an affluent neighborhood in South Jasper, in a historic two-story Tudor with a three-car garage. The home was on Brookside Drive, a quiet street that overlooked the Jasper Elks Lodge, where Mary Beth was forced to go politicking during election season. She parked along the street, taking note of the two vehicles in the driveway. One was Sam's little silver Honda Civic. The other was a truly sickening sight. A black BMW. Patrick Connelly's black BMW.

"Motherfucker." *What is the hell is he doing here?*

Mary Beth had been struggling mightily with guilt over not only Sam's, but Father Gonzalez's abductions–to people she'd put in harm's way–and it was fueling an intense and growing hatred for Patrick Connelly, telling herself that if he had never represented Velino, then maybe none of this shit would have ever happened. The sheriff flipped her lights and siren on full blare as an expression of her rage then marched angrily up to the front porch with half a mind to kick the damn door down. But it opened before she got there.

Patrick came out with his hands up. "Don't shoot."

Mary Beth hadn't thought of that just yet, but it might not be a bad idea, depending upon the answers she got to her questions.

"What in the hell is going on?" she demanded. "What are you doing here?"

"I just came to drop off some of Sam's things he left at the office?"

"Why? Did you fire him?"

"No, of course not," Patrick said. "But he's obviously not coming back now. He told me what happened."

Mary Beth didn't like the fact that Sam had confided in Patrick. It reminded her of when her son was little and would lobby Bill to intervene when he found Mary Beth unfair.

"Get out of my way," Mary Beth said. "I want to see my son."

She tried to push Patrick, but he held out an arm to stop her.

"He really doesn't want to see you right now, Mary."

"*Ex-cuse* me?"

"Sam's very upset."

The audacity. How could Patrick dare be the one to tell her that?

"And somehow you're the good guy in all of this?" she said. "You are the one who represented that fucking monster."

"Sam understands the difference between the criminal and the criminal defense attorney. He knows I'd never want this to happen."

"I don't know how you can sleep at night."

Mary Beth was so angry and hurt and frustrated, she honestly felt like she could strike Patrick in that moment or maybe spit in his face.

Patrick glanced back at the door like he didn't want anyone to overhear. "I need to tell you something."

"I don't want to talk to you."

Mary Beth tried again to push past him, but Patrick seized her by the shoulder and yanked her back forcing her to look at him.

"Well, I'm going tot talk to you. And you are going to listen, goddammit."

Mary Beth was taken aback by his sudden aggressiveness.

Patrick closed the front door. "Why do you think I took Velino's case?".

Mary Beth didn't like his tone, and couldn't figure out why in the hell he seemed frustrated with her. She was the one with a right to be pissed.

"I'm guessing a whorish love of money," she said.

"Think again," Patrick said. "I didn't get paid a dime."

"Then you're a stupid whore."

Patrick made a grunting sound, as though there was a wild animal inside him, desperate to get out. "I did it because he threatened to kill Sam if I didn't. And you. And me. Velino said he'd kill all of us if I didn't find a way to set him free."

Mary Beth was stopped in her emotional tracks by that. She backpedaled even more as Patrick started to explain. "Velino said that if I even told you about it, they would do it. And that there was nothing you could do to stop them anyway because even if you arrested all his guys, Detroit would just send more."

Mary Beth was reeling, trying to process this revelation.

Patrick read her stunned expression as incredulity. "You don't believe me? Look." He lifted his shirt, revealing a torso covered with purple and yellow bruises in various stages of healing. "They beat the shit out of me but never left a mark anywhere you might see in court."

"My God," Mary Beth said, feeling actual sympathy by that point, which was a pretty quick recalibration for her. Once she had a good mad going, changing course was like trying to turn a cruise ship. It normally took some time, but the sight of Patrick's battered body had accomplished the internal 180.

"Have you told Sam?" she asked.

"No," Patrick said. "I didn't know how to explain why he and you were both so important to me without revealing our secret." Patrick made a sound of exasperation. "But Velino sure as hell knew. He kept saying things like how Sam looked like you but acted like me."

That was an accurate description. Sam had his mom's fair complexion and strawberry-blond hair, but his build and book-ishness and mild-mannered personality were all Patrick.

"How could he possibly know about that?" she asked.

Patrick shrugged. "I guess he's got my house and phones bugged. Maybe he heard us talking about it. I don;t know. All I do know is that he had me followed the whole time I was work-ing for him. That's why I was too afraid to try and get a message to you to let you know what was going on."

A new sense of crushing guilty enveloped Mary Beth as she though back to how haggard Patrick had looked throughout the trial and all the smoldering looks and vengeful energy she'd pointed his way, not knowing that all the while he was going through hell to try and protect her and Sam.

"My God," she said, covering her mouth. "I'm so sorry. I had no idea."

Tears welled up in her eyes. Patrick pulled her to him and wrapped his arms around her. "Of course, you didn't. There's no way you could have known. It's not your fault"

He held her for a quiet moment in what felt like a healing embrace until Patrick said, "I just can't figure out why they would kidnap Sam like they did."

And just like that the guilt and defensiveness was back. Mary Beth pulled away.

Patrick mistook her withdraw as confusion and tried to explain. "I mean, it doesn't make any sense. Once Father Gonzalez disappeared, Velino's case was going to be dismissed. He was going to get released anyway. Why go after, Sam?"

Mary Beth wasn't ready to tell Patrick or anyone else the truth about that so she deflected by turning the tables. "Did you know they were going to grab Father Gonzalez?" she snapped.

Patrick looked appalled by the implication. "No. Of course not," she said.

"You're sure?" Mary Beth asked. "Don't hold back on me. If

there's anything you can tell me that could help locate the priest, I need to know."

Patrick took hold of her hand and held it gently. "There's nothing," he said. "Velino would have me smuggle burner phones into the jail, and I'd occasionally catch part of his conversations, but it was always in code. I had no idea what they were talking about."

"Dammit."

"Do you have any leads on Father Gonzalez?" Patrick asked.

The sheriff threw up her hands. "I don't know. The FBI is handling it now. We're just the local goobers who have screwed everything up. I should have just listened to Izzy and asked for their help from the beginning." Mary Beth rubbed her temples. "Everything is so messed up."

Patrick squeezed her shoulder. "It will be okay," he said. "The main thing is that Sam is safe."

Yeah, no thanks to me, Mary Beth thought. The rare moment of self-flagellation had her eyes welling up with tears again. Patrick moved in to hug her once more. She let him. Despite all the abuse he'd taken for her and Sam and all the additional abuse she was ready to heap on top of it, here he was comforting her. That was the thing about Patrick that amazed her most. He had a ton of obvious good qualities: handsome, intelligent, kind. But the thing that made Patrick truly stand out was his ability to take her shit without running away. It didn't take one of the shrinks Izzy was always pushing on her to diagnose the fact that Mary Beth had some obvious abandonment issues, having lost both her father and her husband. But some of the worst abandonments of Mary Beth's life were the everyday ones, when most people—her son included—just shied away due to her abrasive personality. She was simply too much for most people. Always had been. But she couldn't help it any more than a yappy dog could keep from barking. And Patrick, for some bizarre reason, managed to love her anyway.

Mary Beth laid her head against his chest for a moment. "I really want to see Sam," she said.

"Of course. Just let me go talk to him first."

Mary Beth thought about giving him a sarcastic thank you, but the truth was, if she wanted to patch things up with Sam, she really could use Patrick's help.

22

SAM WASN'T VERY TALKATIVE during the drive to Uncle Jimmy's funeral. They had taken Sam's car because Mary Beth's low-riding Camaro wouldn't do well on the gravel road leading up to the old homestead. But Sam had insisted that Mary Beth drive. She knew her way around and how to handle all the winding country roads. Plus, Sam said he didn't want her criticizing his driving.

It was after they'd crisscrossed the switchbacks down the Old River Mountain and the road started to level out through Honeysuckle Pass that Mary Beth realized Sam had earbuds in.

"Take that shit out of your ears."

She reached for Sam, who shirked his mom but pulled the tiny earbuds out.

"Fine. I can't get a signal out here anyway."

"That is so rude, Samuel. I've just been sitting here talking to my damn self for the last half hour."

"Sorry," Sam said.

"I can't believe you."

"I said I was sorry."

After a minute of silence, Sam took a weak stab at conversation. "Where are we, anyway?"

"Don't worry about it," Mary Beth said. "You just stay in your own little world. I'll take care of everything. Like always."

"Whatever, Mom."

They drove in silence for about fifteen minutes after that, Sam staring out his window to avoid eye contact. The kid had spent so much of his life with tunnel vision, laser-focused on a screen, Mary Beth couldn't imagine what Sam must have thought of the sights through downtown Mapleton, all the empty storefronts, the old-timey soda shop, and an abandoned theater with a formerly grand marquis. They did half a loop around the traffic circle at the center of town where a park and fountain had been erected in place of where the old federal courthouse stood for nearly a hundred years before Mary Beth's dumb-ass brother, Sawyer, had his followers blow it up.

That was when Sam finally broke the silence. "Are you sure this is going to be okay?"

"Is what going to be okay?"

"Me being around your family."

"They're your family, too," Mary Beth reminded him.

"Yeah, but you know what I mean. About Uncle Sawyer."

Mary Beth kept her eyes on the road. "If they're mad at anyone about that, it's me. Not you," she said.

Sam answered her in a whispery voice. "But I'm the one that shot him."

"Not how I remember it," Mary Beth said.

"Come on, Mom," Sam's voice was trembling. There were actually some real emotions behind that digital firewall inside the kid's brain. As crazy as it was, Mary Beth realized they had never spoken about it since it happened. And she thought maybe they should keep it that way.

"It's just the two of us," Sam said. "We both know the truth." Mary Beth recalled how, after escaping her custody, Sawyer had later broken into her home and taken both her and Sam hostage. A struggle ensued in which Sam used Mary Beth's gun to shoot and kill his uncle. Mary Beth controlled the aftermath, arranging the scene to make it look like she was the one who shot Sawyer in self-defense. She wanted to protect her son from any repercussions. Though she'd successfully protected him from any legal scrutiny or community stigma, she now realized she couldn't spare him the consequences inside his own mind.

"The *truth*," she said, "is Sawyer got what he had coming to him. That's all there is to it."

Sam nodded.

Mary Beth took a left off of Highway 52 onto Rural Route 19, which snaked back up the mountainside.

"I think about it all the time," Sam said. "Sometimes it's like it's all I can think about."

Mary Beth didn't know what to say to that.

"When that man came and grabbed me, I was so scared. I didn't know what in the world was going on. But after a while, just sitting there in the dark, not knowing what they were going to do, I started thinking that maybe I deserved it."

Mary Beth slammed on the brakes, sliding to a stop on the shoulder of the mountain road, sending a cascade of gravel down the hillside.

Sam flinched, like he was afraid Mary Beth might take a swat at him.

"Look at me, Samuel."

Sam faced his mother with tears welling in his eyes.

"You saved my life. Do you understand, me? Sawyer was going to kill me if you hadn't stopped him. I'm only here because of you."

Sam nodded timidly.

"And what I said wasn't right. That wasn't all there was to it. The full truth is that I was reckless. I thought I knew better than everybody else and tried to take the law into my own hands by sneaking Sawyer out of that compound, and that's how he was able to escape. I'm at least partly to blame for you being in that situation. Just like—"

Mary Beth stopped suddenly, not sure she wanted to finish her sentence. But Sam's sweet eyes prodded her along.

"Just like I'm partly responsible for what happened to you the other night."

She responded to Sam's quizzical expression without forcing him to ask the question they both already knew the answer to.

"I stepped outside the lines, and that's why Velino sent his men after you. If I'd just done my job the way I was supposed to, it never would have happened. I'm sorry, Sam. I'll never be able to tell you how sorry I am." Mary Beth's voice cracked a little, but she'd managed to say the words without bursting into tears.

Sam looked at her not with the disgust or reflexive anger Mary Beth was expecting but with something more like pity. It was the way Patrick sometimes looked at her, she realized. Like he knew she just couldn't help it.

"I'm sure you were doing what you thought was right," Sam said.

That did it. If Mary Beth's emotional homeostasis had been a balloon, Sam's statement was like a pinprick that left it in shreds. The tears came on quick and heavy. Next thing Mary Beth knew, her son was the one comforting her. Hugging her like he had when he was a toddler and his mama was his whole world.

"It's okay, Mom," he kept saying. "I'm okay."

And at the end of the day, that's all Mary Beth had ever really wanted. Where else did her unquenchable need to right the world's wrongs come from if not her innate desire to keep her boy safe? To keep him safe the way she had tried and failed to do for her baby brother Sawyer.

When Mary Beth composed herself, she said something to her son she had often felt but rarely expressed. They weren't the kind of words that were spoken in the world she grew up in.

"I'm very proud of you, Sam. You are brave and you're decent." Mary Beth snorted and wiped a remaining tear from her eye. "It's one of the reasons I've mostly kept you away from my family, because I didn't want them to try and take that from you. And believe me, they would try. They did it to me."

Sam hugged her one more time. When they were finished, she said, "You know, you are a lot stronger than I give you credit for. Stronger than me, maybe. I used to tell myself I was keeping you here to protect you. But the truth is, I was probably doing it more to protect me. If changing schools in the fall is really what you want to do—"

"You mean it? You're okay with me transferring?"

Mary Beth felt a little like she was giving a doctor permission to carve out a couple of her organs, but she did her best not to show it. "Of course," she said.

Sam hugged her for a third time, which probably exceeded their total number of embraces over the prior decade. Then Mary Beth said, "Let's just get through this funeral together, okay?"

"Okay, mom," Sam said smiling. "Let's go."

23

MARY BETH WAITED for a tractor-trailer to pass, giving it time to ease through the curve before she pulled back onto the road. Ten minutes later they were rumbling up the gravel driveway to the old Logan homestead, which was a three-story cabin Mary Beth's grandfather had built. It sat in a clearing on a thirty-degree angle against the wooded mountainside. On the lower end of the home was a second-story porch that had begun to sag. Mary Beth parked there next to a number of vehicles she didn't recognize other than the Ford F-150 truck she knew belonged to her cousin Raelynn because of its bumper stickers, *REDNECK PRINCESS* and *WARNING: MY BOOBS ARE BIGGER THAN MY BRAINS.*

Raelynn was Mary Beth's age, Uncle Jimmy's youngest child, and was the first to greet them when they went inside. True to her truck's advertising, she was sporting an ample amount of cleavage, dressed in a mourning outfit that consisted of a black, low-cut halter top and jeans.

"Look at this strapping young man," she said, fawning over Sam.

"How you doing, Rae?" Mary Beth asked.

"Okay, Mae B. How you?"

"Ah, you know. Still kicking."

"Well, that's something, ain't it?"

"Yeah, I guess so," Mary Beth said. "Hey, I'm real sorry about your loss, Rae."

"Thanks."

Raelynn smiled at her, and Mary Beth actually felt a moment of genuine warmth. Time was funny like that. When she and Raelynn were young, they'd been in more hair-pulling tussles than she could count—not to mention all of Mary Beth's ex-boyfriends Rae had bedded out of spite—but none of that seemed to matter at the moment. Raelynn just felt like an old familiar face. They had shared history, and at that stage of Mary Beth's life, that meant something.

"Well, come on," Rae said. "Everybody's out back. They're about to get started. Little Benji's doing the service."

Little Benji, who was six two, was one of Jimmy's grandson's. His daughter Janet's boy who, Mary Beth learned, had become a pastor and had his own church set up where the Sears used to be in a rundown shopping mall in Tazewell, Virginia. Apparently, Mamie had staked him, which meant she was probably laundering money through the operation, but at least they were saving some souls in the process.

There were about thirty people in attendance. First and second cousins Mary Beth hadn't seen in forever and a lot of their grown kids, whom she'd only seen as babies or never even met. The only notable absence was Tommy, who reportedly had come down with something.

Benji did a nice job with the service, keeping it light on the religion, given the unredeemable nature of his audience, and toward the end Mamie spoke, telling stories about what Jimmy was like as a boy. On days when it would snow, she said, they were too poor to afford boots, and Jimmy would give her a piggyback ride on the walk to school so she could keep her feet dry. And of course, everyone talked about how proud they were of Jimmy's exploits in Vietnam, becoming one of the most prolific snipers in US history.

When it was over they all sang some of the songs Jimmy had loved, "Amazing Grace," "Power in the Blood," and "The West Virginia Hills," finishing it up with his favorite, "Country Roads."

Mary Beth had never been much for nostalgia, but there was a moment when all their voices were blending together that reminded her of a time before she became aware of all the lines that would come to divide them. She almost felt like she belonged.

After the singing was over, some of the younger folks in attendance had a headstand competition in Uncle Jimmy's honor, since he'd been known for getting drunk and performing that feat at family reunions. Sam actually turned out to be pretty good at it. The normally antisocial kid seemed to enjoy getting to know some of his cousins.

There was a potluck meal afterward, and while everyone was inside eating, Mary Beth escaped the smell of baked beans to head out back and stroll through the family cemetery where Jimmy had recently been laid to rest. Her father was buried out there, too, and there was one other grave Mary Beth had never had the chance to visit before.

SAWYER BLAKE THOMPSON
"THE MOONSHINE MESSIAH"

Mary Beth stood there for a while looking at it, wondering if she'd have anything to say. No words ever came. Not from her. But a voice behind her said, "It wasn't your fault."

The sheriff turned to find her mother, Mamie, walking toward her, using a fingernail between her teeth to clear some silk left from the corn on the cob Janet brought.

"I know that," Mary Beth said, sounding more defensive than she intended. Her gut told her Mamie was going to contrive some kind of kumbaya moment to try and get on her good side. She figured that was at least part of the motivation for extending the invitation to Mary Beth and Sam in the first place.

"I'm not talking about that one," Mamie said, pointing at Sawyer's tombstone. "You obviously had no choice in shooting your brother. We all know that."

Mary Beth was a little surprised to hear her mother admit it.

"I meant that one," Mamie said, pointing to the tombstone for Mary Beth's father.

OLIVER WARD THOMPSON

"Dad?"

Mamie walked between the two headstones and said, "They're connected, don't you think? What happened to your father and how Sawyer turned out?"

Mary Beth thought Mamie bore a good share of the blame for Sawyer's upbringing, but she agreed that their father's death was the pivotal event when her once-sweet little brother became more or less a psychopath.

"I know you always felt responsible," Mamie said.

Mary Beth was fifteen at the time. Sawyer was eleven. As had so often been the case, she'd been put in charge of watching her brother and was supposed to keep him under control while the DEA surrounded their home. But when Oliver Thompson went to surrender, Sawyer broke free of Mary Beth's grip and charged after their father. It was what prompted a fidgety G-man to pull the trigger, killing Oliver right in front of his son.

"It wasn't fair of us," Mamie said. "We always made you watch your brother. God knows he was a handful. We just had so much going on in those days. Pressure coming from every direction. We honestly couldn't handle him, and we put too much of it on you."

Mary Beth felt a chill, hearing her mother acknowledge something she had always felt but never fully looked at before. It reminded her of the conversation she kept having with Izzy–why she always felt like it was all up to her. In a lot of ways, it always had been.

Mamie stepped a little closer. "I know you think we're about as different as oil and water," she said. "But I had to grow up too fast, too. My mother died when I was nine years old. They had me in the kitchen, playing lady of the house, cooking for my dad and brother before I was even in the fifth grade. When there was something to cook, that is. We were dirt poor in those days."

Mary Beth watched her mother suspiciously as Mamie slowly put her arm around her daughter. "Then I lost my husband, just like you lost yours," she said.

This wasn't the first time Mamie had tried to point out the parallels between their lives. It had Mary Beth fighting against herself. On the one hand, she was a little touched by what her mother had said about Sawyer and was just generally emotional and yearning to experience some actual connection. But she also knew from experience that when it came to her mother, it was best to keep her guard up.

Mary Beth timidly put her left arm behind Mamie's back. The two women looked quietly down upon the gravestones of their loved ones. Their men.

Then Mary Beth said, "Mom?"

"Yes, dear?"

"Do you want to cut the shit and just tell me what it is you're angling for?"

Mamie recoiled, holding a hand to her heart as though it might break from the offense.

"Mary Elizabeth, I am appalled. That you would think for one second that I—"

"Shove it up your ass, Mom. You've been buttering me up ever since I kicked you out of West Virginia. I know you want back in the game. And you know I need help. This whole Velino thing is more than I can handle. There, I said it. So let's quit beating around the bush."

It felt good to get it out. Mary Beth made a megaphone with her hands and yelled down the mountainside. "Do you hear me, Izzy? I. Need. Help. My name is Sheriff Mary Beth Cain, and I need somebody else's help."

"Sweetheart, you are losing it."

"Good. Great. I've lost it. I don't care. I quit. I give up. I must have, if I'm actually asking for your help. So …" Mary Beth gestured for her mother to speak.

"Dear, I don't—"

"You were about to do your whole speech about how we're so much alike, and how you've always just done what you had to, to support your children—"

"I have always supported my children," Mamie said, indignantly.

"Right. After making that pitch, you were going to suggest a way you might be able to help with my little Velino problem and put yourself right back running the McCray County Mafia's drug operation, right?"

Mamie raised her other hand, placing a double grip on her heart, while batting her eyes. She held that pose for about fifteen seconds before giving up the pretense. "Well," she said, "now that you mention it."

24

AFTER HIS CONVERSATION with Mary Beth, Patrick Connelly asked Izzy to sweep his home and office for bugs. The diminutive deputy discovered a figurative infestation. Covert listening devices in Patrick's living room, kitchen, and bedroom, and three more at his law office. The whole process took a couple of hours, so it was a little after lunchtime when Izzy finished his technological extermination and declared, in a voice mimicking the medium from *Poltergeist*, "This house is clear."

Patrick thanked him and tried to pay him for his time but Izzy wouldn't accept it. He had just been gone for a few minutes when Dottie, Patrick's assistant, knocked on the office door and said "there's a sheriff's deputy here to see you."

"Izzy must have forgot something," Patrick declared.

"No it's not Deputy Baker," Dottie said.

"No?"

"No, it's one of the other deputies."

Patrick was still thinking it had something to do with the sweep for listening devices. Maybe Izzy had asked one of his co-workers to meet him there and he was showing up late after the job was finished. But Dottie squelched that notion. "The gentleman said he needs to consult with you about a legal matter."

"Hmm." Patrick couldn't imagine what that might be about. Only one way to learn. "Please show him to the conference room," he said. "I'll be there in just a moment."

Patrick stalled for a few minutes after Dottie left. He liked to make prospective clients wait a little before meeting with them, to make it seem like he was busy and important.

When Patrick eventually entered the conference room, the deputy had his back to him, looking at the grand fireplace, holding the iron poker. It gave Patrick a flash of PTSD, reminding him of Velino.

Once the man turned to face him, however, Patrick recognized him as one of Mary Beth's older deputies. A man Patrick had seen before but whose name he didn't know until he got close enough to read it off the plate above his badge.

"Deputy … Goforth?"

"Yes, sir. Ben Goforth."

The men shook hands across the long conference room table wedged into what had once been a dining room in the historic downtown home, turned office.

"Patrick Connelly."

"Oh, believe me, I know. After the Velino case, everybody knows."

Patrick wasn't sure that was a good thing.

"Have a seat," Patrick said.

The deputy and attorney each took chairs facing each other. "What can I do for you?"

Goforth sighed. "I need to know where I stand on some things."

Patrick was expecting him to say more. When he didn't, Patrick asked, "What kind of things?"

"Things that have been bothering me."

"Can you be more specific?"

Goforth shifted in his seat. "Let me ask you, hypothetically, if someone were to tell you about something they'd done, something they shouldn't have done, you can't tell anybody, right?"

"It's something that has already happened? In the past?"

"Yeah."

"Then, yes. You are here consulting with me in my role as an attorney. So anything you tell me about a past crime is privileged."

Goforth winced. "Is it okay with you if we don't use that word?"

"What word? Crime?"

"Yeah, that one."

Patrick shrugged. "Sure. Let's just call it prior conduct, okay? Anything you tell me about prior conduct is privileged."

Goforth smiled. "Great. I like that a lot better. Conduct." Goforth said it with a sense of pride, like he'd just learned a new word.

"So what is the conduct you'd like to discuss?"

Goforth opened his mouth like he was about to tell his story, then ran into another thought he had to circumvent first.

"Let's say this *conduct* had something to do with someone you represented. Would that change whether or not you had to keep it a secret?"

Patrick took a guess. "Are we talking about Leonard Velino?"

"Hypothetically?"

"Yeah, sure. Hypothetically."

"Then, yeah. Let's say that *hypothetically* this—what was your word again?"

"Conduct?"

"Right, *conduct*. Let's say it has something to do with ... that guy whose name you just said." Goforth was pointing at Patrick like, *you said it, not me.*

Patrick paused a moment to consider the potential for conflicts in light of this new information. He no longer represented

Velino and, God willing, never would again. So there was no concurrent conflict. As far as the prior representation was concerned, jeopardy had already attached by the time the case against Velino was dismissed, so he could never be tried again for the Mayhew murder. Therefore, nothing Goforth told him should trigger an obligation to tell Velino if it became relevant to that case. Patrick figured he was ethically in the clear to listen to whatever Goforth had to tell him.

"Not a problem," he said. "You can tell me anything you want. My lips are sealed."

"Okay, great." Goforth's shoulders relaxed. "I don't know if you know this or not, but I was the one transporting Father Gonzalez to court in the Velino case when …" Goforth trailed off.

"I'm very familiar with what happened," Patrick said. "Are you about to tell me you know how Velino, or whoever it was, was able to intercept Father Gonzalez?"

If the answer was yes, it wouldn't be an ethical quandary in terms of his prior representation, necessarily, but as Patrick thought about it some more, he realized he'd be super motivated to turn that info over to Mary Beth to try and get back on her good side. Plus, if Goforth was the mole in her department, and Mary Beth found out Patrick represented him, she might view that as negatively as him representing Velino. He might have a conflict after all, for personal reasons.

Fortunately, Goforth pushed back from the table, raising his hands in surrender, and said, "It wasn't me. I swear." He paused, reflecting for a moment, then sheepishly added, "I just think maybe I know who it could have been."

"Okay," Patrick said. "Go on."

Goforth leaned forward and whispered, "I was supposed to have lunch with him that day, you see. Only then the sheriff needed me to go fetch her witness. So I called and told the man I'd have to take a raincheck. And he kept kind of pushing, you know? Asking questions. Saying couldn't we just meet up later, and I maybe let it slip that Sheriff Cain had me going all the way to Virginia, and it couldn't wait. Had to happen that morning."

"And this was on the day the trial was supposed to start?"

"Yeah."

"So you think this person put it together that the urgent errand you were running was to go get Father Gonzalez?"

Goforth tapped twice on the table. "That's what I'm thinking," he said.

Patrick was relieved. "Well, it sounds to me like you didn't do anything wrong. Not really. I think you need to tell Sheriff Cain what happened as soon as possible. This could be important to the investigation."

Patrick knew Mary Beth might be super pissed at Goforth, but she'd know he'd just been stupid, not corrupt. And not telling her would only make things worse if she found out later.

The deputy seemed like he had additional concerns, though. "Thing is," he said, "this wasn't the first time this person's been kind of nosy, you know, about what all is going on down at the station."

"What do you mean?"

"Like back when the Randy Law stuff all went down. And maybe a little before that, too. You know, we'd just be shooting the shit, trading war stories, mostly. But looking back on it, some of the stuff in the stories the paper ran about the sheriff could have ..." Goforth trailed off again, but the implications were obvious. He was realizing he may have been a useful idiot, unwittingly passing intel to someone who'd been working to undermine Sheriff Cain all along.

"Who are we talking about?" Patrick asked.

Goforth scrunched his nose as he answered. "The sheriff."

Patrick was confused.

"Not the current sheriff," Goforth explained. "The old one. Mr. Sid."

"Sid Cain?"

"Yeah. Sid and I are old buds. We've always kept in touch."

Patrick was initially dubious. He was no huge fan of Sid Cain, since he was the father of Patrick's romantic rival, but he appreciated the way Sid looked out for Sam. Sid had also supported Sam's desire to transfer to a better school and had gone to bat for him with Mary Beth, which was no small feat.

"What makes you think Sid would have passed that info on to Velino?" Patrick asked.

Goforth made a sour face as he said, "That's where you get into some more of that *conduct* we were talking about."

25

AFTER TWO YEARS OF LIVING on the lam, Tommy Wiggins was ready to make some real money upon his return, only to find out that the McCray County Mafia's drug business had gone to shit in his absence. The queenpin, Mountain Mamie, had been run out of the state and was now living it up in her mansion over in Dulcimer, Kentucky, hosting lavish parties, while the guys who'd built her fortune were barely scraping by back in old McCray. Times were changing, and not for the better. The good ol' boys were being pushed out of the drug industry just like they'd been cut out of the coal industry by big carpetbagger companies from up north with all their advanced machinery and technology.

Tommy could see it as clear as the mountains.

So while Mamie was busy burying her brother, he was having a sit-down with the competition at the Applebee's in Jasper Creek. The restaurant was an outparcel at a strip mall off Highway 460 that got a good bit of business with a Walmart Supercenter as its anchor store. Lots of people around, which was good, because these guys made Tommy nervous.

They took a corner booth in the back. Velino sat on one side of the table while Tommy was opposite him, squished between two of Velino's bodyguards, who likely weighed three hundred pounds apiece. Tommy could smell their sweat, dressed identically in thick black wool suits with black ties. Each wore sunglasses despite being inside.

Neither said a word when the waitress took their order. Velino told her his friends were on a diet and didn't talk much. Then the gangster requested a Bourbon Street steak for himself, extra rare, with a tall draft beer. Tommy was too anxious to eat, so he just ordered a rum and Coke. Then he started explaining why he'd asked to meet them, giving them a lot more detail than was probably necessary.

Right before the waitress brought Velino's food, Tommy was saying, "Retiring is fine for Mamie. She's made her fortune, and I don't blame her for wanting out. But I'm forty-seven. I need another thirty years of income, you know what I mean, Mr. Velino?"

Tommy paused while the waitress placed a sizzling skillet in front of Velino. She asked if they needed anything else. Tommy and Velino had barely touched their drinks, and both said they were good. Velino's silent partners stayed mum. So she left them alone after that.

Velino started sawing a bloody hunk of steak. "Go on."

Tommy shifted in his seat to try and get a little breathing room between the two men flanking him. Neither budged. "Anyway, like I was saying. I used to be a high-level guy. But the best Mamie's been able to offer me since I got back is a little mule money. A couple of times a week I pick up some weed, occasionally some pills, or meth from this crazy-ass wildcat who cooks it in a tin-can trailer out near Cottonmouth Ridge, and then I take the shit to a stash house Mamie's got set up near Crawdad Holler."

Velino laughed. "These fucking names you people come up with."

"Yeah, I know," Tommy said. "We're very creative. So anyway, that's all I've been doing since I got back. I drop off the stuff. And it sits there until a long-distance courier comes to take it away. You've pretty much muscled Mamie out of local distribution, so she's having to ship it out and gets a much smaller cut than she used to back when she basically controlled the whole distribution chain."

"Sounds like you've got a pretty easy job to me," Velino said.

"It is, but the money's shit. I used to practically run Mamie's whole operation. Had a real sweet deal, working out of this strip club she used to have called Mountain Flowers. But now I'm reduced to an errand boy."

Velino worked at severing another bite of steak. "Let's get to the part where this benefits me," he said.

Tommy leaned in. "Mamie's about to have a liquidation sale. She's fixing for one last major score before she rides off into the sunset. So, there will be a short window of time, about two weeks from now, where she'll have a few million dollars' worth of product in that stash house by the time I make my final drop. And I'm thinking—"

"I know what you're thinking," Velino said. "I knew that before we sat down. You're thinking about biting the hand that's fed you all these years."

Tommy squirmed under the weight of Velino's description.

"So tell me, Mr. Hillbilly Man, if I was to make a deal with you to go hit this stash house and cut you in on the proceeds, how do I know you're not going to double-cross me, just like you're proposing to double-cross Mamie?"

Tommy swallowed hard. That was a tough question to answer. "Because," he said, "Mamie's hand isn't going to feed me anymore after this. I need a future, Mr. Velino. I'm not just looking for a score. I'm looking for a career. I need to hitch my wagon to somebody who's not going anywhere anytime soon. An operation that's not just going to disappear when one person decides to hang it up."

Velino held Tommy's eyes as he took a drink of his beer.

"You could use somebody like me, Mr. Velino. I know this area. Know these people."

Velino had a hold of the oversize steak knife they'd given him and was turning it from side to side, watching how it reflected the light. "Tell me more about this stash house," he said. "What kind of security?"

"Just two guys. Nothing heavy. It's in a nice, quiet little suburban neighborhood, so as not to draw attention."

"How's it work with the drops?"

"The guys there know my ride. I back in the driveway and honk twice. They see who it is and open the garage door. I back into the garage, and they close it once I'm inside. We unload, and then I leave."

"The guys are in the garage when you back in?"

"Yeah."

"Both of them?"

"For me, yeah," Tommy said. "One guy is supposed to stay inside behind a locked steel door, while the other guy unloads. But like I said, these guys know me. They know I've got a bad back, and we keep the stuff loaded in heavy crates full of shit in case I were to get stopped. So when I make my drops, both guys always come out in the garage to help unload."

"That's convenient."

"Right," Tommy said.

"So how do you know there's not more guys inside?"

"Because I know." Tommy could felt himself relax a little. The crushing tension in the back of his neck eased up as he felt like he was finally developing a little bit of rapport with the Detroit mobster. "These guys used to work for me, Mr. Velino. We talk shop while I'm there. They look at me as speaking for Mamie and do what I tell them. So what I'm thinking is, when I make this last drop, you and your friends here come with me. A couple of you hide out in the back. I got a Jeep Cherokee, and if I lay the back seat down, there will be plenty of room. As soon as I'm in the garage, the guys always lean their rifles against the wall and are ready to unload by the time I hit the button to lift the back gate. You can easily get the drop on them before they have any idea what's going on."

"Tap. Tap," Velino said, firing a little finger gun in Tommy's direction.

"You won't even have to," Tommy said. "When that gate rises and they see these guys"—Tommy pointed his thumbs in opposite directions to indicate the beefy gentlemen pressed up against him—"pointing guns in their faces, they aren't going to fight you. Mamie doesn't pay these guys enough to go up against guys like you. Plus you'll have me. You could crouch down in the passenger seat, then we'll get out and I'll have my hands up and say you guys jacked me. I'm telling you, Mr. Velino, these tweakers Mamie has guarding this place won't be any trouble at all. They'll help us load the shit. Then you guys tie us up and leave. I'll tell Mamie you took me hostage and I didn't have a choice."

Velino moved some potatoes around the plate, soaking up some of the pooled blood.

"Okay," he said. "Let's take a ride and check it out. See if it looks good."

Tommy took a big gulp of his drink, slugging down a little liquid courage before saying, "I'm sorry, Mr. Velino, we can't do that."

The men on either side of Tommy squeezed in closer, pressing him down into his seat.

"What was that?" Velino said. "I'm not sure I heard you."

Tommy cleared his throat. "If I were to show you where the

stash house is, then what's to keep you from robbing it on your own and cutting me out?"

Velino stared at Tommy for a long, hard minute, waiting for him to capitulate. Somehow Tommy managed not to. Finally, Velino smiled, showing his sharp yellow teeth. "That's the problem with our business, isn't it, Tommy? We're all fucking thieves."

Velino and his henchmen all laughed, ominously.

Tommy said, "With all due respect, Mr. Velino, I don't think of myself as a thief. I'm just a guy trying to make a living."

Velino said, "Okay, working man. Tell you what. Let's go take a walk. There's something I want to show you." The gangster and his guards stood in unison. Velino pulled a wad of cash out of his pocket and peeled off a couple of twenties that he dropped on the table.

"Where are we going?" Tommy asked.

"Just outside," Velino said. "Won't take but a minute."

Tommy reluctantly followed Velino and his guys around to the back of the restaurant where they had a dark-blue windowless van parked near the garbage dumpsters. Velino led them around the van so they were between it and the brick corral that housed the dumpsters, shielding them from the view.

"Did you hear about that trial I had recently?" Velino asked.

"Yeah," Tommy said. "I heard about it."

"You heard they had some priest who was supposed to testify against me?"

Tommy nodded. He'd heard that, too.

Velino slid open the van's side door.

What Tommy saw inside hit him like a bat to the stomach. There was a priest, beaten all to hell and strapped to a thick wooden board, lying flat on his back, blindfolded, with a ball gag in his mouth. The poor man's arms and legs were splayed out like a cross, held in place by multiple industrial-length bolts that had been drilled through his appendages into the thick board. It was a gruesome crucifixion, one that could keep the suffering man alive for days, maybe weeks, before it would finally be over.

Tommy had never been so sickened and frightened in his entire life. After decades of working for Mamie, he had seen some shit, but never anything so savage. A cold ripped through him that froze his insides.

Velino nodded to one of his men, who hopped inside the van and put on a pair of work gloves before wielding a yellow DeWalt Power drill and retrieving an eight-inch deck screw.

"Oh, Jesus. God, no," Tommy said.

"Shut the fuck up, unless you want to join him," Velino said.

The presence of the big man inside the van stirred the priest out of his daze. He made muffled squealing sounds and squirmed like an earthworm on a hotplate but couldn't go anywhere. There was no way for him to escape what was coming.

Tommy tried to turn away, but Velino's other man grabbed the back of his head with one hand and turned his eyes to the van, forcing Tommy to watch as the screw was driven mercilessly through flesh and sinew and into the bone.

It was all Tommy could do not to throw up. When it was over, Velino slammed the van door closed. He turned to face Tommy, getting so close Tommy could smell the bloody steak he'd just eaten.

"Just so you understand," Velino told him. "If somebody crosses me, I don't forgive. And I sure as hell don't ever forget."

TOMMY THREW UP TWICE behind the dumpsters after Velino left. He thought there might be a third upchuck but was able to get himself together. Then he went back inside the Applebee's and did two shots of tequila at the bar to try and calm his nerves. After that he left and drove around for a long time, wondering what in the hell he had gotten himself into. Tommy did all the tricks. Changing speeds. Driving too slow on the highway and too fast on the neighborhood streets. Waiting at intersections with horns honking behind him until the light turned red, then gunning it. Pulling off into a cul-de-sac and parking for a while.

Only after he was absolutely sure he wasn't being followed did he head up to the overlook on Canebrake Mountain. It was a long, curvy drive. A favorite spot for high school parties on the weekends because you could see the cops coming long before they were able to wind their way to the top. And with a pair of high-powered binoculars, you could observe the stash house Tommy had told Velino about.

Tommy parked by the water tower and got out. Mary Beth and Mamie were already there, waiting for him.

"Well," Mary Beth said, "did he go for it?"

"You've got no idea what you're dealing with," Tommy said. "These guys are crazy."

"There's a lot of crazy going around these days," Mary Beth said.

Tommy thought about telling her about the priest but knew she'd go wild if he did. She'd try to save the poor bastard, bust Velino for taking and torturing him, and force Tommy to testify. There was no way he would do that. The scheme Mamie had sucked him into was dangerous enough.

"Did he take the bait, or not?" Mamie asked.

"Yeah," Tommy said.

"Excellent." Mamie turned to her daughter. "See, I told you."

When Mamie looked back at Tommy, she commented on his sour face. "What's the matter?"

"I'm just thinking about how I'm supposed to pull this off without getting killed," Tommy said.

Mamie looked disappointed that he doubted her. "You told them to hide in the back of your Jeep, right?" she asked.

"Yeah."

"Then they'll be looking behind them as you reverse into the garage. They'll be all juiced up. Adrenaline flowing. Ready to charge out the back. When you hit the button to raise the gate, and they hear that beep, and the latch comes undone, they'll be ready to go. You'll be in the front seat. So, just shoot them in the back."

Mamie said it with a soft, sweet voice, like she was reading a child a bedtime story.

"It will be at least three people. Maybe four," Tommy said. "That's a lot of people to shoot before getting shot myself."

"You'll have the element of surprise," Mamie assured him. "Just start by shooting whoever's closest. The ones farthest away will try to jump out the back. And if they make it out, I'll have a whole hell of a lot more than just two boys waiting on them."

Tommy sighed. The situation had him reflecting on when he ran Mountain Flowers and would tell the dancers how they could make extra cash working the trailers out back. "It's no big deal," he would say. "At the end of the day, we're all whores for somebody." The statement had never felt truer to him than in that moment. *The things we do for money.*

"And if I do this," he said, "you promise you'll set me up?"

"That's right," Mamie said. "Sawyer's gone, after all, and my wayward daughter here certainly has no interest in the family business. So after this, you'll be the heir apparent. I just want to make enough money out of this move that I can enjoy my golden years. But I'll immediately start transitioning everything over to you."

"And the sheriff is on board?" Tommy asked.

Mary Beth was wearing a black dress, having just come from the funeral. Her expression was one of mourning, but Tommy didn't think it had anything to do with burying her Uncle Jimmy.

"If this goes off the way Mamie has planned, then everything will go back to the way it used to be," Mary Beth said. "You keep your business within the confines of what used to be McCray County, and we should get along just fine."

Tommy kicked at a rock, taking his time like he was making a decision, but it was already made. He'd been working for Mountain Mamie since he was a teenager and had always done what she told him. No reason to stop now.

"Okay," he said. "Guess we have a deal."

"Just so you know," Mary Beth interjected, "I asked Mamie if there was somebody else she could get to do this, but she said Velino wouldn't buy it otherwise."

"That's right," Mamie said. "You can't sacrifice a pawn to take the king. If it was some low-level boy who came to him with this offer, Velino would smell a trap. But Tommy's my number-one guy. Someone dear to me. Not a person he would suspect me of putting in harm's way. Plus, given the circumstances, Tommy's got believable motivation. It's always someone in his position, a higher-up, who makes a move like this. In Velino's world, capos conspire against bosses all the time." Mamie rubbed her hands together, delighted by her scheme. "I think it's just perfect."

"And you're confident that once Velino's gone, Detroit won't just send someone to replace him?" Mary Beth asked.

"They might try," Mamie said. "But it won't be anyone as formidable. Nothing we can't handle. Besides, I told you, my information is Velino is a black sheep among his own people. They sent him down here mostly to get him out of the way. I don't think you'll have any Motor City mobsters shedding any tears over his passing."

Mary Beth didn't look convinced but didn't argue the point. Instead she said, "I still can't believe you sent Tommy to meet with Velino before we talked. What if I didn't agree?"

Mamie chuckled. "Please, dear. I know what you're gonna do before you do. It's a gift."

"Whatever," Mary Beth said. "Just make sure that when Tommy does this *final run* you've got him loaded up with drugs. Velino will inspect those crates to make sure it's not bullshit. It's got to look like Tommy's really contributing to a big score."

"Yes, yes," Mamie said, waving away the comment.

"I'm serious, Mom. I know how cheap you are. Don't send him out there with nothing but a fucking dime bag stowed in the back. He needs to be hauling some serious prison-time level of drugs for this to work."

Mamie looked disappointed by her daughter's concern. "Sweetheart," she said, "have I ever let you down?"

Mary Beth didn't dignify that with a response. Tommy could tell she didn't like any of this but was on board regardless. Getting rid of the Detroit outfit was too important. In everybody's interest. But Tommy wasn't entirely sure what was scarier, Velino or the thought of Mamie and Mary Beth working together.

• • •

Patrick Connelly had two problems. One ethical and one logistical. On the ethics front, he'd learned information from Deputy Goforth he was desperate to share with Mary Beth but was prohibited by attorney-client privilege. He had come up with a plan to navigate that little quagmire but was still running into the logistical problem that Mary Beth wouldn't answer his calls. So he decided to drive to the sheriff's house and force her to talk to him.

Mary Beth still lived in the same split-level house she and Bill had bought back in their twenties. It was the last one in a row of similar homes that sat on a quiet street, at the top of a hill where the road dead-ended into some wooded trails favored by four-wheeler enthusiasts. Mary Beth wasn't home when he got there, so Patrick waited for what turned out to be a couple of hours before the sheriff finally showed. She was driving her Camaro and rolling in hot, going much faster than necessary, and completely ignoring the sign that said *SLOW CHILDREN AT PLAY*. Patrick knew the sign meant to slow down because kids played near the street, but being the arrogant Yankee that he was, he thought about making a joke that all the neighborhood kids must be a little slow in the head.

As soon as Mary Beth got out of her car, however, he could tell she was in no mood for humor.

"What in the hell are you doing here?" she demanded. Throughout their trysts, they'd always met at his place because Mary Beth didn't want her neighbors to know she was hooking up, and she didn't look very happy to find him there now, even though hooking up was something that seemed unlikely to ever happen again.

Patrick paused before responding. It took him a minute to

soak her in. Gone was the typical cop uniform, replaced by a slinky but classy black dress. She looked good.

"You won't answer your phone," Patrick said, finally, bringing his eyes back up off her figure. "I really need to talk to you."

"I was at a funeral." Mary Beth walked past him in the driveway on her way to the front porch. "And I blocked your number," she explained.

"Why?"

"Because I'm still pissed at you."

Mary Beth unlocked and opened the front door. Patrick followed her inside.

"I explained all of this to you," he said. "I had no choice in representing Velino."

Mary Beth didn't slow her march through the foyer, passing a honeypot filled with dried cattails. "I know, but I'm still pissed."

Patrick followed her back to the kitchen, where Mary Beth poured herself a glass of water from the fridge.

"That doesn't make any sense," Patrick said.

"It doesn't have to." Mary Beth took a gulp of water and wiped her mouth with the back of her hand. "Listen, Connelly. If you betray me in a dream, you better wake up and apologize."

Patrick could see she was in no mood to be reasoned with. He might as well just get to the important part.

"I have something important to tell you."

Mary Beth was in the middle of another sip of water and motioned for him to go ahead and say it.

"Only, I can't tell you."

Patrick thought she would be intrigued, but she looked annoyed, rolling her eyes. "Great. Good talk. Thanks for stopping by." Mary Beth sat her water glass down on a round wooden kitchen table where she sat, kicked off her shoes, and started rubbing her feet.

This was not at all how Patrick imagined this conversation would go. "It involves a client," he said. "I need to run this info through Jeannie Boggs first and try to work out an immunity deal before I can share it with you. Can you convince Jeannie to grant me a Queen for a Day interview?"

Patrick was asking for a proffer session, where Goforth could tell the prosecutor everything he knew about prior crimes within the sheriff's department, during the Sid Cain era, where none of it could be used against the deputy. If the prosecutor thought it was valuable enough—and Patrick knew she would—then they could enter into an agreement whereby Goforth would receive immunity and retire with full pension benefits in exchange for his cooperation in future prosecutions. Patrick specifically asked for Jeannie because he knew from the Ruiz case that Pomfried had previously consulted with Randy Law about such matters and would have a conflict.

"What's this all about?"

Patrick took a seat opposite Mary Beth, happy to finally have her attention. "I've got a client who can help you get Velino."

Mary Beth looked less excited than he thought she'd be. Probably reluctance to endanger another witness, which was something Patrick and Goforth talked a good bit about. The deputy said he was willing to take his chances. He was guilt-ridden over Father Gonzalez and wanted to make amends.

"My client knows the risks."

"So who is this client?" Mary Beth asked.

"I can't tell you that. All I can tell you at this point is that my client can tie Velino into a plethora of corruption charges. Paying off public officials. Stuff that goes way back."

Mary Beth took another sip of water. Patrick waited patiently for an answer. After a moment Mary Beth stood and said, "Okay, fine. Tell Jeannie I said it was cool."

She walked past Patrick, out of the kitchen, down the hall toward the bathroom, unzipping the back of her dress as she went.

"Where are you going?"

Mary Beth opened the bathroom door. "I just spent the last couple of hours with my family. I need to take a shower and scrub away all the grime."

With that, Mary Beth was apparently done with his visit. She disappeared into the bathroom, shutting the door behind her. Patrick sat at the kitchen table, unsure whether he should leave or wait till she was done.

While he was pondering what to do, Mary Beth stepped back into the hallway, as naked as the day she was born, her red, curly hair down over her shoulders, and said, "Jesus, Connelly, are you coming or not?"

27

FOR MOST OF THE DAY Alexander Pomfried had strutted around the well of the courtroom while interrogating Mary Beth. Their back-and-forth had been freewheeling. Two adversaries mixing it up. But as the afternoon wore on, the prosecutor started spending more time seated at counsel's table, sticking to his notes, asking a lot of questions about exactly where Mary Beth was and what she was doing on specific dates and times.

Mary Beth knew he was establishing a timeline to box her into some kind of trap, but for most of his questions there was little she could do other than agree.

"On March 13 of this year, Leonard Velino's case was dismissed, correct?"

"That date sounds right."

"Velino was released from your custody that same day, correct?"

"Yes." Mary Beth was thankful that Pomfried appeared to know nothing about the prison assault she'd orchestrated or the fact that Sam had been kidnapped by Velino's men. Two facts that could seal her fate with the grand jury.

"At the time of Velino's release, Father Gonzalez's whereabouts were still unknown, correct?"

"Yes," Mary Beth said. "That's *why* Velino was released. Father Gonzalez had been abducted and couldn't testify."

"Would you say that finding Father Gonzalez was your number-one law enforcement priority at that time?"

There was nothing Mary Beth had wanted more than to find Father Gonzalez, but her department honestly had little involvement in that effort. "We engaged the FBI as a result of the kidnapping," she said. "They took the lead in the investigation."

"But certainly finding Father Gonzalez was important to you, right?"

"It was."

"Two days after Leonard Velino's release, multiple witnesses have indicated you received a visitor at the sheriff's department, on March 15, is that right?"

"I get a lot of visitors, Mr. Pomfried. You'll have to be more specific."

"A gentleman named Thomas Wiggins came to see you, right?"

Oh shit. Mary Beth thought. *Here we go.*

"*Miss* Cain?"

"Yes," Mary Beth said. "Tommy is a relative. He came to tell me that my Uncle Jimmy had died and that the family was making funeral arrangements."

"I didn't ask what you talked about. Right now, I am just asking you to confirm that you had a closed-door meeting with this Thomas Wiggins gentleman, in your office, two days after Leonard Velino was released, correct?"

"Yes," Mary Beth said. "I saw my Cousin Tommy."

"Any reason *Cousin Tommy* couldn't have called you on the phone?"

Mary Beth didn't see why that mattered. "I guess he thought it was news that was better delivered in person." There was also the business of letting Mamie back into the state, but that was too deep a rabbit hole to go down in front of the grand jury.

"Were you and Cousin Tommy especially close?"

"Not really," Mary Beth said.

"Then why was he the one to share this family news with you, as opposed to, say, your mother?"

Mary Beth wasn't entirely sure what point Pomfried was trying to make.

"My mother and I have always had a difficult relationship. For obvious reasons. Some of which you've already highlighted for this jury. But she and Tommy are close, and I assume she asked Tommy to give me the news about my uncle passing."

Pomfried opened a folder and held up a stapled series of papers that he read from. "Your Cousin Tommy is the same Thomas Wiggins who has prior charges for assault, robbery, pandering, possession of narcotics, and possession with intent to distribute."

Mary Beth hadn't studied Tommy's rap sheet but all of that sounded plausible.

"I know Tommy's had prior arrests. I don't know what all of them are or how many resulted in a conviction."

"Very well," Pomfried said, "but you are aware that at the time he came to see you, in the sheriff's office, there was an active warrant for his arrest."

Mary Beth wanted to palm her forehead. This was not going to look good to the jury. Mary Beth had promised her mother months earlier she'd take care of Tommy's warrant, but then Velino surprisingly surrendered so quickly she had forgotten all about it until Tommy showed up at her office that day.

"I was aware that there had been a warrant, issued a couple of years earlier," she said, trying to maintain a poker face.

"And after you had this closed-door meeting with Mr. Wiggins, discussing whatever it was you discussed, you saw to it that the arrest warrant against Mr. Wiggins was canceled that same day, didn't you, *Miss* Cain?"

"I can explain—"

"I didn't ask for an explanation, Ms. Cain. It's a simple factual question. Prior to your meeting with Mr. Wiggins, there was a warrant for his arrest, and after you all met, you put the kybosh on the warrant that same day, right?"

Pomfried was making it sound like there'd been some quid pro quo in her meeting with Tommy that prompted her to cancel the warrant. That of course wasn't true, but without a judge or her own lawyer present to ask follow-up questions, she had no ability to control the narrative. This was exactly why she'd been advised not to testify before the grand jury.

Mary Beth tried to tell the truth as much a she could but didn't find the sound of her own voice very convincing. "I'd been meaning to cancel that warrant for some time–as I was the complaining witness, but hadn't gotten around to it."

"Ms. Cain, it is a simple yes or no question: you had the warrant canceled later that same day, after your closed door meeting with Cousin Tommy, right?"

"Mr. Pomfried, it's not how it sounds—"

Pomfried slammed his paper down on counsel's table so hard it made everyone in the courtroom jump, including Mary Beth. "Ms. Cain, if the truthful answer to a question is yes, would you say yes?"

Mary Beth was confused by the question. "Yes?" she said, as though guessing at the answer to a riddle.

"You had the warrant canceled later that same day, right?"

"Yes."

"Thank you," Pomfried said, exasperated. "Now, I want to jump ahead about two and a half weeks to the morning of March 31, Easter Sunday. You received a call telling you about the discovery of Father Gonzalez's body, correct?"

"Yes." Mary Beth would never forget that moment. It was

Sid Cain who called and told her Father Gonzalez's body had been discovered at St. Michaels after he and others arrived at the church early that morning to prepare for the Easter service. Sid was nearly unintelligible on the phone. "Just come, please, come" was about all she was able to understand. When Mary Beth got to the church, she found the burly former sheriff weeping with such ferocity they weren't even able to interview him. It shocked Mary Beth. She'd seen the big man bury both his son and his wife without shedding a tear, but the horror of what he'd found that morning had shaken Sid so much that she asked Izzy to take him home to rest before they took his statement. She'd never forget the sight of Sid, a bear of a man, standing probably six four and over three hundred pounds, being supported by little Izzy as they walked away.

Alexander Pomfried again confronted her with photos of the gruesome scene she'd encountered that grim morning and this time displayed them for the jury as well. "This is what became of Father Gonzalez, the man you swore to protect, correct?"

The photo showed the charred remains of Father Gonzalez bolted to the burnt embers of a thick slab he'd been crucified against. God only knew how long he'd been tortured before being placed in the church parking lot, doused with gasoline or some other accelerant, and set on fire.

Most of the jurors turned, unable to stomach the image. Mary Beth said, "We were later able to conclusively determine that the remains were those of Father Gonzalez."

"On the morning the body was discovered, did you have a working suspicion of who the victim was?"

"I didn't know for sure."

"Not what I asked *Miss* Cain. I said, 'Did you have a working suspicion?' Let's tell the truth now."

Mary Beth faced the jury as she said, "I suspected it was Father Gonzalez. The body was placed essentially in the same location where both he and Brad Mayhew had been abducted. Thus, it seemed like a calling card."

"I assume you also believed that Leonard Velino was responsible for this heinous act?"

"I strongly suspected it."

"Understandable," Pomfried said. "Did it make you angry at Mr. Velino?"

Mary Beth snorted at the understatement. "Mr. Pomfried, I crossed that bridge with Mr. Velino a long time ago."

"I bet you did." Pomfried paused to read over his remaining questions, then closed his three-ring binder. Whatever was coming next, Pomfried was planning to handle it without notes.

"Later that day, Easter Sunday, after Father Gonzalez's remains were discovered, your cousin, Mr. Thomas Wiggins, met with Leonard Velino and several of his associates, didn't he?"

"I have no personal knowledge of that," Mary Beth said.

"Oh no?"

"No."

"That's fine," Pomfried said. "We can establish that through other evidence. You can't avoid this one, though."

Pomfried waddled from side to side to extricate himself from the chair that pushed in on his sides. The prosecutor approached Mary Beth with a new sheet of paper. "Ms. Cain, I have here the DMV record for a 2021 Jeep Cherokee registered to a Mr. Thomas Wiggins. Do you see that?" he asked, pointing a pudgy finger at the name.

"Yes," Mary Beth said.

"I thought so." Pomfried walked around to the side of the witness stand and turned so that both he and Mary Beth were facing the jury. "And would you please tell these fine people, isn't it true that on this day, Easter Sunday, hours after you found Father Gonzalez's remains, less than three weeks after you had this closed-door meeting with your cousin Tommy and put the kibosh on the arrest warrant against him, Leonard Velino was shot dead inside of Mr. Wiggins's Jeep Cherokee?"

There was so much about that Mary Beth wanted to explain. Things she needed the jury to know. But for the time being, Pomfried was right. It was a fact she could not deny.

"Yes, Mr. Pomfried," she said. "Leonard Velino was shot and killed while inside my cousin Tommy's car."

28

ON EASTER SUNDAY, Tommy was as nervous as a man who was about to double-cross a vicious crime boss should be. Fortunately, that was exactly how he wanted to appear to Leonard Velino, who thought he was there to help them rob Mountain Mamie. So Tommy made little effort to conceal his unease. He had met up with Velino and his guys in the gravel parking lot outside of the Loretta #4 mine and was visibly jittery, fidgeting and tapping his foot as Velino took his time inspecting the two shipping crates in the back of Tommy's Jeep Cherokee. They were filled with enough drugs to get each of them twenty to life in the federal pen.

"Nice," Velino said, eyeing the merch. "Very nice."

It seemed like even the weather was warning Tommy not to go through with Mamie's plan, as an ominous evening storm brewed beyond the mountains. Dark clouds were moving in with a low rumble of thunder off in the distance and an occasional flash of light. On top of the atmospherics, Tommy was on edge over the number of guys Velino had there with him, his whole crew of eight men, all of whom were decked out in body armor, like a SWAT team prepared for a raid.

"I've only got room for two or three guys, plus you, Mr. Velino," Tommy said.

Velino closed the crates. "I know. Jimmy and Tony will ride with us. The rest of the guys will follow in another car."

That was not the plan and would jam Tommy up, big-time. He was already going to have his hands full trying to cap three guys before getting shot himself, especially now that they were all wearing bulletproof vests. He'd have to shoot each one in the head.

Mamie's theory was that they'd all be looking the other way as Tommy reversed toward the stash house garage, thinking they were about to bum-rush her two inept guards. Thus, Tommy should easily be able to get the drop on them. As soon as he shot one—preferably Velino—the other two would likely pile out the back, right into a buzzsaw of McCray County Mafia boys waiting to cut them to pieces. If they didn't, however—if the men instead turned toward Tommy ready for a fight—he'd have to get both of them with a headshot apiece before either could return fire. And all Tommy had to work with was the little .38 he had tucked in his waistband at the small of his back. It had him feeling pretty inadequate when Velino's men started passing out AR-15s rigged to be fully automatic.

"Mine's bigger than yours, huh?" Velino said, laughing. He was holding two identical rifles that he handed to the twins, which was how Tommy had started secretly referring to Velino's main bodyguards, Jimmy and Tony. They'd each be wielding one of those choppers while lying in the back of Tommy's Jeep. Just inches away when Tommy capped Velino.

This was no easy task Mamie had set him up for, and it had only become worse. Even if Tommy managed to pull it off and popped all three guys, he would still have to contend with another car full of Velino's guys who could pin him in. Once they heard shooting, they'd probably block off the driveway, preventing Tommy from getting to safety. He'd be right in the middle of some serious crossfire between them and the McCray County Mafia positioned inside the stash house.

"This is not going to work," Tommy said.

Velino's dead stare intensified. "What's that? I don't think I heard you right."

Tommy tried to explain. "If Mamie's guys see another vehicle, it could ruin everything. They might suspect something's up."

Velino put a slender arm around Tommy's shoulder and slapped him playfully on the cheek. "Don't worry about it. My guys know what they're doing. They'll hang back so as not to cause any alarm. But in case we need back up, we'll have it."

Tommy could feel his insides flipping around like a dying fish. He needed to find a way out of this. He hated that Mamie had moved up the timetable. The plan had been to do the raid on a Monday, but he'd got the call earlier that day saying it had to happen now. Tommy didn't know why. But pulling a job like this on Easter Sunday just didn't feel right. Another rumble of thunder echoed through the valley, sounding like God himself was pissed.

Meanwhile, Velino looked delighted, rubbing his hands together. It was one aspect of mobster psychology that Mamie had pegged. When Tommy asked what would happen if Velino just sent his guys on this job, while he stayed home, Mamie had said there was no way. "He'll be there," she assured him. "From what I'm told, Velino loves this stuff. Adrenaline is the drug he covets most."

Now the mobster was slapping Tommy on the back, saying, "Let's go."

The twins climbed into the back of Tommy's Jeep, where they had laid the seats down to make room. Velino took up the shotgun, before realizing that Tommy wasn't moving.

"Is there a problem?"

"I just have a bad feeling about this, Mr. Velino," Tommy said. "Bringing another car full of guys could really mess things up. It's overkill, you know?"

Velino was visibly frustrated. "I told you not to worry about it."

"Yeah, it's just—"

"Look," Velino said. "You can either get in the car and take us to this stash house, or I'll have Jimmy beat the ever-loving shit out of you, and then you can get in the car and take us to the stash house. Now which one's it gonna be?"

That didn't leave Tommy much choice. It was what it was. Or rather, it was going to be whatever it was going to be.

"Okay, I'm coming," Tommy said. "It's no problem. I was just saying."

"No more saying. Let's get moving," Velino said.

Tommy got into the driver seat of his Jeep Cherokee with Leonard Velino seated next to him and the twins in the back, while six other men piled into a black Chevy Suburban, ready to follow behind. Everyone other than Tommy was adorned with a bulletproof vest and armed with an assault rifle.

It was a seriously fucked-up situation. Bad enough that as they rode through town, Tommy started thinking maybe he should pull a triple-cross and just legitimately help Velino's guys rob Mamie. Maybe he could act surprised when all the McCray County Mafia guys she had stuffed in that garage revealed themselves. He could hit the gas and drive Velino to safety. Give him a chance to regroup with his other car full of guys, negate the advantage of ambush, and then help them lay siege to the stash house. Or maybe he should just go ahead and come clean to Velino about what he'd been set up for.

But then Tommy thought about the way they had mercilessly tortured poor Father Gonzalez just for having the temerity to tell the cops the truth. If Velino had the slightest inkling of Tommy's betrayal, his fate would be much worse.

All Tommy could do was stick to the plan and hope for the best. Maybe once he shot Velino and the twins were dealt with, he'd be able to drive himself to safety before Velino's car full of reinforcements arrived. Or, more likely, he could just duck and cover and hope for the best, while Velino's backups and the McCray County Mafia shot it out.

The rain started to pour as Tommy considered his options. They were driving past the Methodist church, where an Easter egg hunt was cut short by the downpour and people started running for cover. It struck Tommy like a scene from an old Western, where the townspeople cleared the streets when they knew a shootout was coming.

Beyond the church was a one-room post office where Tommy turned on Piperwood Lane, the steep mountain road that led to the entrance of Audubon Park, the stash house's neighborhood.

It was an aborted subdivision that broke ground in the eighties and only completed two streets worth of homes before the builder went belly-up. There were only twenty homes, accessible from opposite sides of the mountain. Tommy had come up the south side and parked in the grass next to a pylon sign for the neighborhood that was badly in need of power washing.

"What are we doing?" Velino asked.

"Call your guys," Tommy said. "Tell them to wait here. They go any farther and they might be spotted."

"Which house is it?"

"It's 1513," Tommy said. "About eight houses down on the right. Brown house with wood shakes and gold shutters."

Velino squinted, staring off in the distance. The way the street curved, he couldn't see the stash house from where they were, which was a good thing because it was actually twelve houses down, but Tommy wanted to put as much distance as possible between them and Velino's backup.

"All right," Velino said.

Tommy thought Velino would call his guys, but instead the

gaunt mobster got out and walked back to the Suburban, where he had a whispered conversation with the driver face-to-face. In his rearview mirror, Tommy watched as Velino returned to the Cherokee, only this time he was coming to the driver's side. Velino tapped on the window. Tommy lowered it.

"What's up?" he asked.

Velino smiled, showing his pointy yellow teeth.

"I was just thinking. We look a little bit alike, you and me. Must go to the same barber," Velino said, rubbing the top of Tommy's bald head.

"Okay."

Tommy didn't understand what Velino was getting at until the mafioso said, "Move over."

"What?"

"You heard me. I said move over."

"This is a bad idea, Mr. Velino. They're expecting to see me."

"They're expecting to see the back of a bald white head as we reverse into the driveway. You just duck down over there and stay out of sight."

"I really—"

"Now," Velino snapped.

Tommy didn't like this at all but didn't know how he could refuse. He reluctantly moved to the passenger seat, where he did his best to cower between the seat and glovebox, but at six feet tall he was having difficulty. "Maybe I should just get out and wait here," he offered.

"Oh, no," Velino said. "You're staying with me. And why don't you go ahead and hand me that .38 you're carrying. Maybe you'll fit better."

Tommy froze, trying to think of something.

"I'm getting awfully tired of having to repeat myself with you," Velino said. "Gun. Now."

Velino held out his palm. Tommy's heart was banging away

like a kettle drum inside his chest as he handed it over. What else could he do, surrounded by Velino's men?

"No offense," Velino said when taking the weapon, "but this is our first date. Best to use protection."

Velino stowed the pistol in the driver-side door well out of Tommy's reach. Then he placed his right hand on Tommy's head and pushed him down until he was wedged between the seat and dashboard and lying face down on the passenger seat.

"Okay," Velino said. "I think we're ready."

He drove slow. Tommy couldn't see where they were. Velino said, "1513, right."

"Yes," Tommy answered.

"Okay, then. You boys ready?"

"Yeah," and "Fuck, yeah," were the twins responses from the back.

Tommy started saying a silent prayer.

"Just keep your head down," Velino told him. "This will all be over in a minute."

29

LIKE THE OLD Native American parable, there were two wolves battling inside Mary Beth. One was a crushing sense of grief over Father Gonzalez. The other, the dominant wolf, the one that was currently kicking grief's ass, was a burning desire for revenge. That wild dog would get her through Easter Sunday, but she needed to deal with Velino immediately, before the crippling depression over Father Gonzalez had a chance to sink its teeth in. So she'd called her mother to move up the timetable and was about to go meet the criminal matriarch when she got a return call, in which Mamie declared that she no longer felt comfortable driving and would thus be asking her boy toy, Geoffrey, aka "G Money," to bring her.

"Not only no. But hell no," Mary Beth said.

"I don't understand what the big deal is, dear. Geoffrey is very reliable behind the wheel. He's quite reliable at a lot of things, if you get my meaning."

Mary Beth was too disgusted to respond.

"You know, he can really *take* me there."

"Yes, I know, Mother. And ew. Just ew."

"Well, like I said, at my age, I just don't feel all that comfortable behind the wheel."

Here the woman was running a massive criminal enterprise in two states and had personally engineered the takedown of a major drug trafficker and his crew, and she didn't feel up to a thirty-minute drive from her home in Dulcimer, Kentucky, to the meet-up point on Canebrake Mountain.

"Mom, get your ass in the car and drive."

"You are risking my life?"

"For God's sake, Mom, we're going to a shootout. I'd think the drive over there would be the least of your concerns."

"Well," Mamie harrumphed, "I just don't feel comfortable. Geoffrey's going to have to drive me, unless you want to come all of the way out here and pick me up yourself. That's all there is to it."

They were supposed to meet at six o'clock, and it was already five.

"I can't believe you are waiting until now to spring this on me," Mary Beth said. "It would take me an hour just to get over there."

"I didn't think you'd have an objection to Geoffrey tagging along. After all—"

"You didn't think I'd have an objection? What part of 'this is just between you and me' didn't you understand?"

"But Geoffrey's practically—"

"Don't say it. I'm on my way. Just tell Tommy to drag his feet a little. Give us more time to get in position to watch it all go down."

Mamie sighed. "Very well. But you better hurry."

Hurry. Now Mamie was worried about hurrying. Mary Beth drove with lights and sirens until she crossed the state line into Kentucky. So much for keeping a low profile. Then, of course, when she got to the house, Mamie wasn't ready. The security guard at the front door said she'd be down in a minute. Mary

Beth waited in her Camaro, parked in the circular cobblestone driveway, until Mamie finally appeared beneath the columned portico. She was wearing a purple sweater with pink bunnies, like maybe she had an Easter-themed orgy planned for later that evening.

"Take your time," Mary Beth said. "It's not like we have anything important to do."

Mamie seemed to move even slower just to spite her. "I'm not as spry as I used to be." She was really milking the whole age thing. Then, when she finally got in the car and Mary Beth thought they were finally ready to go, her boy toy, G Money, came running out, shirtless as usual, showing off his washboard abs and thick gold chain.

"Yo, Maimes. You forgot your pills."

He was carrying a massive pill box with separate containers for each day of the week and a bottle of water.

"Thank you, Geoffrey, dear." He insisted on watching Mamie take them and got a goodbye kiss—with tongue.

Mary Beth felt sick to her stomach.

"Sweetheart," Mamie said, once she'd finished playing tonsil hockey with G Money. "We need to hurry. Please let's get a move on."

Mary Beth shifted the car into drive and mashed the pedal to the floor, kicking up a cloud of dust as she ripped out of there.

They rode mostly in silence after that until Mamie asked her what was with the attitude. Mary Beth didn't even know where to begin.

"I think it's kind of nice, us doing something together," Mamie said, as though they were headed to the mall or something, rather than a planned ambush and massacre.

"Are you high?"

She had never known Mamie to sample her own supply, but she had been acting so strange lately.

"It's the blood pressure medication," Mamie said. "Makes me a little loopy."

"More than a little."

Mary Beth leaned over to sniff at her mother's tacky sweater. "Oh, my God, mom, you smell like skunk weed."

Mamie giggled like a little girl. "It's Geoffrey, dear. He likes to smoke. Might just have a little contact buzz is all."

"Are you kidding me right now?"

"Oh, don't be so dramatic, dear. I'm fine. You just watch the road."

Mary Beth was already going fast but sped up even more. When she fishtailed through the next curve, Mamie told her, "Slow down. You've got precious cargo in here."

"Don't tell me how to drive."

"I didn't sign up to go on some throw-up ride."

"Then you should have been ready on time," Mary Beth shot back.

"You either slow down or you pull over and let me out. I'm serious." Mamie started undoing her seatbelt.

"Okay!" Mary Beth dropped her speed but still maintained a fairly brisk pace until they made it to the lookout point atop Canebrake Mountain, where Mary Beth spun to a stop next to the water tower, facing south, and quickly got out her binoculars. They had an unobstructed view of the stash house. "Amazingly, it looks like we're in time," Mary Beth said. "I don't see any sign of Tommy yet."

"Told you we didn't have anything to worry about. Now let me see."

Mary Beth handed her mother the binoculars. Mamie focused and refocused for a while before giving up. "I can't see anything," she said. "These new contacts are no good."

"When did you start wearing contacts?"

"Years ago, dear. Hold on."

Mamie stuck a finger in her eye and removed the tiny lens.

She had a soft leather old-lady purse that was filled with an ungodly amount of junk. After much rustling about, she finally got her contacts stowed in a container with some solution and produced a pair of the thickest glasses Mary Beth had ever seen. The whole time she'd refused to pass the binoculars back to Mary Beth, until Mamie was finally able to zoom in with the help of her Coke-bottle specs.

"Looks like we're early, thanks to all that race-car driving."

"Give me those." Mary Beth snatched back the binoculars and scanned down the mountainside. She was able to follow the entire road Tommy would have to travel and would be able to track him for about a minute before he reached the stash house.

"They're running late," Mary Beth said. "Guess we'll have to wait."

Mamie let maybe thirty seconds pass before saying, "Well, what should we talk about?"

"I don't suppose just sitting in silence is an option."

Mamie swatted Mary Beth on the shoulder. "Come on, dear. How often do we get a chance to do this? Surely there's something we can discuss."

Mary Beth swiveled around to face her mother directly. "Look," she said, "maybe this is fun for you, having finally sucked me all the way into your blackhole of murderous schemes, but in case you haven't noticed, I'm not exactly happy to be here."

"Well, why are you, then?"

"Justice," Mary Beth said. "I'm making sure justice is done. The only way I know how, thanks to—" Mary Beth waved back-handedly to her mother, referencing the perverse way she'd been raised.

Mamie huffed. She fanned herself with a ring-laden hand. "I'd think you'd have a little gratitude. After all, everything I've ever done has been to support my family."

"Bull. Shit."

"Mary Elizabeth. Language."

"Fuck you."

Mamie crossed her arms. "I don't want to talk to you anymore."

That suited Mary Beth just fine. She was able to enjoy about five minutes of silence before she caught the first sight of Tommy, turning onto the mountain road, just beginning to wind his way up toward Audubon Park. She kept quiet about it and the fact that Tommy was being followed by a black SUV. It had occurred to her that Velino might bring backup. She wondered whether Mamie had planned for that possibility as well.

"You know, Mom, there is something I've been meaning to ask you," Mary Beth said.

"I hope it's not with that potty mouth."

Mary Beth briefly removed the binoculars so her mother could see that she was rolling her eyes. "No," she said. "It's kind of like a personality test someone gave me recently. Like a Rorschach test, I guess. I'm curious how you would answer."

"I think those things are so stupid," Mamie said.

Most sociopaths would, Mary Beth thought. "Just, play along," she said. Mary Beth watched Tommy's Cherokee making the long ascent up the mountain with the black SUV in tow. Watched, but didn't say anything about it to her mother.

"Very well," Mamie said. "Go on."

Keeping her eyes trained through the binoculars, Mary Beth said, "You remember the *Challenger* disaster? Back in the eighties."

"That space shuttle that blew up?"

"Right, the one with the teacher on it."

"Of course, I remember. Those poor astronauts. At least they didn't suffer."

"Well, that's just it," Mary Beth said. "Everyone always assumed that the astronauts died in the explosion. But the capsule they were in was heat resistant and was actually jettisoned away from the rocket boosters, so they would have survived the blast."

"Well, surely they would have been unconscious at least," Mamie said.

Mary Beth watched as Tommy's vehicle came to a stop just outside the neighborhood.

"Maybe, maybe not," she said. "There would have been some serious g-forces. But they were survivable. And when they retrieved the capsule from the ocean, they didn't find any evidence it had ever depressurized. It actually looked like several of the astronauts had switched on their oxygen tanks and tried to restore power so they could pilot the thing."

Mary Beth saw Velino get out the passenger side. He walked back to the other vehicle for a moment, then returned to the Cherokee and switched seats with Tommy. *Interesting*, she thought. Looked like Velino was going to be the one to drive the last leg to the stash house.

"I don't understand the point of this story," Mamie said.

"The point is: What would you rather? Most people hear this story and think it sounds awful. It took the astronauts two full minutes to plummet to their death, and the ones that were awake would have known the whole time it was coming, but at least they were able to try and do something about it."

"Except they weren't able to. They all died, right?"

"Yes. That's the question," Mary Beth said. "Would you rather be one of the astronauts who maintained consciousness or one of the ones who didn't?"

With Velino now in the driver seat, the Cherokee was on the move again, traveling slowly toward the stash house while the black SUV stayed at the neighborhood entrance.

"I think I'd just prefer it be over in a flash," Mamie said.

A wicked smile creased Mary Beth's face. She handed the binoculars to Mamie and told her, "I was hoping you would say that."

30

TOMMY SAID A SILENT PRAYER as they reversed into the driveway. He was wedged beneath the dashboard with his head lying in the passenger seat. There was no way he could get to his gun or Velino's rifle. No way he could get the drop on him and his men. No way to complete his mission in the way Mamie had planned. All Tommy could do was keep his head down and hope the McCray County Mafia had enough men and firepower inside that garage to handle the situation.

Velino hit the horn twice. Everyone inside the vehicle waited in silence. It was quiet enough that Tommy could hear the twins' heavy breathing in the back as they gripped their rifles with sweaty palms, ready to kill.

Velino, however, was totally cool, strumming the top of the steering wheel. After a moment passed, he said, "Let's go, cheese dicks."

Then Tommy heard the gears of the garage door engage. A squeaky wheel on one of the tracks whined as the door started to climb. It would be any second now, as soon as the door lifted high enough for Velino to see he'd been set up.

Tommy felt Velino come off the brakes. They started to drift slowly backward.

Then Velino said, "What the—"

He slammed on the brakes hard enough to rock the vehicle.

Tommy closed his eyes, ready for the shooting to start.

There was a rumble of automatic gunfire and shouts, but they didn't come from the direction Tommy had been expecting. The shots weren't from the garage. The bursts of fire and yelling came from off in the distance, near the entrance to the neighborhood. Tommy heard squealing tires and sirens. And a booming voice over a megaphone yelling for people to freeze.

"Federal agents!"

Even without the benefit of sight, Tommy was aware of vehicles rushing toward them from the opposite side of the mountain they had entered from. Small cars, big cars. Trucks. Heavy machinery. Then the buzz of drones flying low. A couple of pop shots were fired at them from inside the garage.

The idiot twins, not appreciating the reality that they were now facing a bigger threat from the front than the back, jumped up in unison and started firing, shattering the rear window into a million pieces. At the same time, Velino put the Jeep in drive and gassed it. The twins lurched forward, hanging halfway out the rear window, where they were cut to pieces by shotgun blasts from inside the garage.

Tommy tried to swivel around, to sit up and see what was happening. He got halfway up in the seat just in time to see Velino wedge his way between two sedans that had tried to block them in. There were men in tactical gear everywhere coming out of hiding places and racing from between homes, swarming like angry bees protecting the hive.

Velino floored it. He scraped his way free from the blocking vehicles. Then he made a sharp left turn back toward where they'd entered the neighborhood. One of the twins fell out the back window. The other slumped down in between the crates, covered in blood.

Velino's backup car, the black Suburban, was right where they left it, parked behind the sign at the neighborhood entrance. Only his men were all outside the vehicle now. Three of them had surrendered and had their hands on the roof while two lay dead in the grass.

Agents with automatic rifles were using the SUV as cover, crouching on one knee while they filled the grille of the Cherokee with bullets. Tommy ducked down. He heard the windshield shatter. Shards of glass rained down.

The vehicle traveled over something that instantly flattened the tires, putting them into a half spin. That's when Tommy saw the side of Velino's head blown open by a burst of fire. He slumped over onto Tommy and took the Jeep with him. It turned on its side and began to roll.

• • •

Mary Beth saw her mother's hands shake as she peered through the binoculars, watching federal agents take down her men, along with Velino's crew. She wondered whether the trembling was from frailty or rage. The old woman answered that question by flinging the binoculars, striking Mary Beth in the head. Then she pounced on her daughter with the ferocity of a mountain cat. Press-on fingernails popped off as Mamie raked her claws across Mary Beth's face. Mamie knocked the sheriff's hat off as she seized a wad of red curly hair.

Mary Beth was caught by surprise, but by the time it registered that she was in a fight, her youth and superior strength took the upper hand. Instinctively she went for Mamie's hair, too, forgetting that her mother wore a wig, which she promptly dislodged, pulling it down over Mamie's eyes. Mary Beth palmed her mother's face and slammed it back against the passenger seat, pinning it there. Mamie bit into her hand and tried to go for Mary Beth's sidearm and nearly got it free of the leather safety strap before the sheriff was able to shove her mother away. Mary Beth moved on top of her mom. She was trying to turn her onto her stomach when Mamie managed to get a hold of the backup gun Mary Beth kept strapped to her ankle. Mamie pulled it free of the holster and was ready to shoot her own daughter before Mary Beth realized what was happening. She slammed her mother's gun hand against the dashboard. The gun went off, firing a bullet through the windshield. Now Mary Beth was really pissed. She slammed her mother's hand against the dashboard two more times before Mamie dropped the gun. Mary Beth had a hold of both her mother's wrists at that point, and the old woman's vision was obscured by the drooping wig. Mary Beth bent at the waist, rearing back then coming down with a massive headbutt, smashing into her mother's nose like an axe splitting a log.

Blood squirted. Mamie screamed. Mary Beth had staggered the old woman enough that she was finally able to get her flipped over and cuff her hands behind her back.

Mamie yelled into the leather seat. "You double-crossing bitch." Blood continued to pour out of Mamie's nose as she struggled and flopped like a dying fish.

"I come by it honestly," Mary Beth said. "You are under arrest, Mom. For drug trafficking and conspiracy to commit murder."

"Fuck you," Mamie yelled, apparently no longer troubled by profanity.

"You're under arrest for killing my husband."

Mamie froze. The thrashing stopped.

"What's the matter?" Mary Beth asked. "Nothing to say now?"

Mamie tried to swivel around and peer beneath her dislodged wig to face Mary Beth.

"You listen to me, child," she said between gasps for breath.

"You listen good. I've always worried you might think that, but I swear to you. I swear on the life and soul of my grandson that I had absolutely nothing to do with Bill's death."

"Really? I've been through the old arrest records. It was your operation Randy Law kept hitting. I don't know why I didn't put it together sooner. Bill was killed in a drug bust. He must have been working with his buddy Randy when it happened. The chances that it was your guys they were busting are about as good as falling out of a boat and hitting water. So whether you called down the hit or it was just something that happened while they were arresting your guys doesn't matter. Either way, you're responsible."

"I'm telling you I'm not."

"Bullshit. Patrick told me how he came to see you last year after Randy Law died. He confronted you with his suspicion that you were behind Bill's death, and you didn't deny it. All you said was he should let sleeping dogs lie."

"And he should have. Because I knew you'd get the wrong idea."

Patrick had told Mary Beth everything, however. He'd posed the same question to her about the *Challenger* disaster that Mary Beth had asked her mother. Only the sheriff answered differently. Even if she were destined to die, she'd much rather know what was going on and spend her final moments doing whatever she could to confront her situation. So Patrick had told her the truth.

"You've got to believe me," Mamie said. "I interrogated everyone, made sure we had no part in it, when I heard. I don't know who your Bill was busting, but it wasn't my guys. Check the records."

Mary Beth had done just that after Patrick shared his suspicions with her. She had them pulled out of storage and read the brief narrative Randy Law had prepared.

SHERIFF CAIN AND I HAD JUST FINISHED GETTING

A BITE TO EAT AT THE PONDEROSA ON FAIRBANKS AVENUE. SHERIFF CAIN WAS OFF DUTY AND THUS NOT IN UNIFORM BUT WOULD OFTEN MEET ME DURING MY MEAL BREAKS SO WE COULD CATCH UP. WE HAD EXITED THE RESTAURANT WHEN WE OBSERVED TWO CAUCASIAN MALES DOWN THE ROAD QUICKLY ENTERING THE CITY PARK ON FOOT. THE WAY THEY LOOKED AT US AND THEN CHANGED COURSE MADE IT SEEM LIKE THEY WERE TRYING TO GO TO A PLACE WHERE WE COULD NOT OBSERVE THEM. SHERIFF CAIN AND I GOT INTO MY VEHICLE AND DROVE INTO THE PARK. WE DID NOT SEE THE MEN UPON FIRST ENTERING BUT DROVE AROUND FOR SEVERAL MINUTES. ON OUR WAY BACK OUT WE OBSERVED THE TWO MEN AGAIN. THEY WERE ENGAGING IN WHAT APPEARED TO BE A DRUG TRANSACTION. SHERIFF CAIN AND I BOTH EXITED THE VEHICLE AND COMMANDED THE MEN TO FREEZE. THE MEN TURNED AND FIRED AT US. I TOOK COVER, BUT SHERIFF CAIN WAS HIT TWICE. THE TWO MEN RAN. I IMMEDIATELY CALLED FOR ASSISTANCE, BUT SHERIFF CAIN HAD EXPIRED BY THE TIME HELP ARRIVED.

At the time Mary Beth first learned Bill was dead, she was a civilian. She had no idea what questions to ask and simply accepted the narrative she'd been given. In all her subsequent years on the force, it had never occurred to her to go back over them. Bill's death had simply become an accepted part of her life. In a weird, masochistic way, she always kind of thought it had been her fault. A cosmic punishment for never having loved Bill the way she'd thought he deserved.

Now, however, she was determined to learn the truth. "All your guys will be in federal custody soon. We'll see if they tell the same story."

"They will," Mamie assured her.

"Move over," Mary Beth commanded. "We need to go."

"Where?" Mamie demanded.

"To jail, dumbass. I told you you're under arrest. You have the right to remain silent and all that."

Mamie struggled to get herself upright in her seat. Mary Beth didn't try to assist, worried the old woman might attack her again. If they'd been in a regular squad car, she'd have put her mother in the back, but Mary Beth's Camaro didn't have a protective barrier. She preferred to keep her mother where she could see her.

"You're wrong about Bill," Mamie said. She actually sounded scared. Something Mary Beth couldn't remember ever having heard in her mother's voice before. Not scared of going to jail, necessarily, but of what Mary Beth might do. The truth was, Mary Beth was a little scared of that herself. She knew she needed to confirm whether or not it was true but still didn't know for sure what she would do if it was.

ALEXANDER POMFRIED HAD a new sheet of paper in his hand as he approached the witness stand.

"*Miss* Cain, would you look at the top of this page and confirm that is your cell phone number highlighted at the top?"

Mary Beth took a moment to study what were obviously her cell phone records.

"Yes, it is."

"We subpoenaed your call records covering this past Easter. You made two calls that morning shortly after 9:00 a.m. And if you'll look over here to the second page, the cell tower data shows that you were in the vicinity of St. Michael's when you placed those calls."

Mary Beth looked where Pomfried was pointing. "Yes, I see that."

"Remind us, Ms. Cain, approximately what time did you arrive at St. Michael's that morning in response to Father Gonzalez's charred body being discovered?"

Mary Beth took a moment to think. She didn't have a police

report in front of her but thought she could make a pretty good guess as to the time.

"I'd say it was around 8:15, maybe 8:30."

"So you'd been at the church for at least thirty minutes before making these two calls. Is that fair to say?"

"That appears to be correct."

"My point, *Miss* Cain, is simply that these calls were placed after you observed what had become of Father Gonzalez, correct?"

"Yes … that's probably true." Mary Beth didn't see any reason to argue the point. The cell phone tower data had already more or less established that.

"And what you saw there was a gruesome sight, was it not? Father Gonzalez had been tortured and burned."

"Yes."

"Let's take a look at this first call you made after seeing what had become of this witness you were supposed to protect. This one here with the 202 area code. Who was that call to?"

It wasn't a number Mary Beth knew by heart, but she had no doubt as to who it was.

"I believe that was to Agent Clarke with the FBI."

"And what was the purpose of that call?"

"Well," Mary Beth said, glad she was finally getting to lay out this part of the story. "After the failed prosecution of Lenny Velino, I was finally persuaded that I needed help from federal authorities in dealing with him. And this is part of what I was trying to tell you when you kept asking about my cousin Tommy coming to see me, but you kept cutting me off."

Mary Beth looked to the jury for sympathy. Without a judge present during the grand jury proceedings, whatever sentiment could be gleaned from the jury members was the only referees she could appeal to.

"By all means," Pomfried said with a grand gesture. "Take all the time you need."

"Thank you. Well, my cousin Tommy invited me to attend

my uncle Jimmy's funeral. Which I did. While I was there, my mother approached me with a plan to ambush Velino." Mary Beth laid out for the jury the scheme Mamie had put together, then stated, "All of this was detailed in the arrest warrant I prepared for my mother. It would also be in the records of the joint FBI-DEA task force that had already been investigating Velino for some time. I played along with my mother and served as their undercover informant. They were the ones who conducted the raid to apprehend Velino's crew and what remained of the McCray County Mafia."

Pomfried interrupted with a question. "To be clear, the plan was to murder Leonard Velino, correct?"

"That was my mother's plan. My hope was that he could be arrested with as little bloodshed as possible. But all of that was ultimately up to the feds. It was their operation. As I understood it, they intended to announce their presence as soon as the stash house garage door started to open. At that point Velino would have committed an overt act in furtherance of a criminal conspiracy, and they could have charged him as well as the McCray County Mafia guys with the whole boatload. The timing was tight, but it was possible to make the arrests before any shots were fired."

"Possible," Pomfried said with derision. "But certainly you knew there was a high likelihood that Velino and possibly others could be killed as a result of this operation."

Mary Beth shrugged. "You can't make an omelet without breaking a few eggs."

A juror in the front row laughed until Pomfried shot him a look.

"Kind of callous, wouldn't you agree, *Miss* Cain?"

"Hey, look," she said. "These are criminals. They were planning to go shoot each other up whether I played along or not. I figured I might as well help the feds bust as many of them as I could. You know, protect and serve and all that."

Mary Beth glanced at the jury members who were nodding as though they agreed that Velino got what was coming to him.

"It probably would have gone off without a hitch," Mary Beth said, "but Velino had that extra car full of guys hanging back at the neighborhood entrance, and the feds decided they needed to neutralize them first before the agents down the street revealed their position."

"Very well," the prosecutor said. "It may have been federal officers who shot and killed your Mr. Velino. But I can't help seeing a pattern."

"I don't know what you mean."

"Oh, really? Let me lay it out for you, *Miss* Cane." Pomfried ticked off names, counting them on his chubby fingers. "Sawyer Thompson. Randy Law. Leonard Velino. Everyone who's ever crossed you, dead."

Mary Beth gave Pomfried a cold stare and something she knew she'd regret but couldn't help. "You've crossed me, Mr. Pomfried. And you're not dead."

Yet. Mary Beth thought, but had just enough self-control not to say it. Regardless, Pomfried took her statement as a provocation.

"Is that a threat, Ms. Cain?"

"No, sir. It's just an observation," Mary Beth said, regaining some composure. "You're suggesting that everyone I've ever had a personal beef with has died, and that's simply not true. Not even close. There's all kinds of people who have pissed me off and are still kicking."

"Well, we'll let the jury draw their own conclusions about that." Pomfried held up the phone records again. "Getting back to my point, however. This raid was originally supposed to take place the day after Easter, correct?"

Mary Beth knew where he was going but didn't see any way to get around it. There were other witnesses who could verify what Pomfried was asserting. She'd just have to concede some ground.

"Yes," she said.

"But on Easter morning, after seeing what had become of Father Gonzalez, you were so enraged that you called the agent in charge and insisted the raid happen later that same day, correct?"

Mary Beth tried to sound as dispassionate as possible. "I called to inquire as to whether it was possible that the raid be moved up to Sunday evening."

"Because you wanted revenge, right? You wanted Leonard Velino dead?"

"I wanted Leonard Velino off the streets as soon as possible. So he couldn't hurt anyone else."

"You wanted him dead or alive, as the saying goes, right?"

Mary Beth probably should have obfuscated, but it exceeded her ability to bullshit. "That's the way law enforcement used to handle its business."

"It's the method you prefer, right? That's why you placed this second phone call after you hung up with Agent Clarke."

Pomfried charged at the witness stand like a bow-legged hippo, pointing to another highlighted number on the phone record. "This 304 number. Who's that?" he demanded.

Mary Beth thought about pretending as though she didn't recognize it but decided there would be no point.

"It's my mother's cell phone number," she said.

"Your mother. The infamous Mountain Mamie, head of the McCray County Mafia."

"That's right."

"Why did you call her, *Miss* Cain?"

"For the reasons you've already indicated. I told her to move up the timetable. To have Tommy call Velino and tell him it needed to happen earlier than anticipated. I wanted the Velino operation to happen as soon as possible."

"I bet you did. This Velino operation where you knew it was at least highly likely that Leonard Velino would be killed."

That's the one, Mary Beth thought, but what she said was, "Mr. Pomfried, Leonard Velino was killed by federal agents in the course of a legitimate drug bust. You can't seriously be trying to hold me responsible for it."

Pomfried backed up a step. His shoulders sagged, and at first Mary Beth thought maybe she'd actually gotten to him. Like maybe he was giving up. But then he raised his eyebrows and licked at his lips, as though finally eyeing the meal he'd been waiting so long to devour.

"Oh, Ms. Cain," he said. "I know I can't hold you legally responsible for Mr. Velino's death. I think you set his assassination up too cleverly for that. But"—Pomfried wagged a short, stout finger at her—"as you know, you are not being investigated for murdering Leonard Velino. This has all been the lead-up, setting the scene for the real crime. I think you know what I'm talking about."

Mary Beth did her best not to show any reaction. She readied herself for what she knew would be the final assault of questions.

Pomfried kicked them off with one last reference to her call records. "Drawing your attention to the records from that evening. After the raid was over and you were on your way back to the station, you received this incoming call that I want to ask you about."

He showed her another sheet with a list of numbers and call times.

"That was another call with Agent Clarke," Mary Beth said. "He debriefed me on the results of the raid. He told me Velino and three of his men were killed. That the McCray County Mafia boys and the rest of Velino's men had surrendered. And that my cousin Tommy was badly injured in a car crash and was being taken to the hospital."

Pomfried looked confused. He peered down at the page and

realized he'd been pointing at the wrong phone call. "I'm sorry, it's the other number here with the 202 area code. What about this one?" he asked, sliding his finger down to another incoming call she'd received shortly after speaking with Agent Clarke.

This second one was a number Mary Beth instantly recognized since it had been both the source and recipient of umpteen booty calls over the prior year or so. Patrick Connelly. Since he was now representing her with regards to the grand jury investigation and potential murder charge, she could have claimed attorney-client privilege and refused to tell Pomfried what they'd discussed that day. The call was not actually privileged, as Patrick was not representing her at the time, but still, the evocation might be enough to get Pomfried to back off.

Ultimately, however, Mary Beth decided there'd be no point in throwing up that roadblock. She couldn't deny where that phone call had prompted her to go and what it had led her to do. If Mary Beth was to be judged fairly, she decided she might as well tell Pomfried the truth.

32

THEY WERE COMING BACK down the north side of the Old River Mountains, Mary Beth having finally gotten Mamie to shut her yapper by threatening to lock the old bird in the trunk if she didn't zip it, when Patrick Connelly interrupted the silence with yet another phone call. Mary Beth thought about letting it go to voicemail, but something about the timing told her it might be important.

Patrick quickly confirmed that instinct when he said, "I got a tip from an old friend from my U.S. Attorney days that there's some kind of raid going down. Is that true?"

"No comment," Mary Beth said.

"Shit. That means it is true. Mary, we need to talk before you make any moves against Velino."

Too late for that, Mary Beth thought. "I thought you weren't representing him anymore?"

"I'm not. It's not him I'm worried about."

Up until that point in the conversation, the call had been broadcast over the speakers of Mary Beth's Camaro, via the Bluetooth link to her phone, which meant Mamie could hear what was said. The sheriff picked her cell phone up from where she'd rested it near the gear shift and switched the call back to the device so she and Patrick could carry on in private.

"Look," she said, with the phone to her ear, "no one needs to worry about Lenny Velino, ever again."

"What's that mean?"

"Let's just say, he didn't go quietly. My info from the feds is that he was shot and killed while trying to escape."

"Jesus."

Mary Beth was a little disappointed in Patrick's reaction. His tone went beyond a simple respect for human life—even if that life was a scum-sucking shitbag like Velino—to something sounding like genuine regret.

"I'd think you'd be a little bit relieved," she said. "He can never bother you again."

"It's not him that I'm worried about," Patrick told her. "Mary, there's things you don't know. This could put Sam at risk."

Mary Beth had thought long and hard about what kind of reprisals she could be inviting by taking Velino down and was fairly confident they'd be okay. Mamie's intel was that Velino had become a black sheep within his own operation and the bosses in Detroit might actually be grateful to have him gone. Part of their motivation in sending him down to West-*by God*-Virginia had been to get him out of their hair. On the off chance they were looking for revenge against law enforcement—which was always bad for their business and thus rarely pursued— they'd likely be targeting the feds who had actually carried out the raid. Mary Beth couldn't say she had zero concern, but on balance she thought that she, her family, and every decent, God-fearing citizen of Jasper County was a whole hell of a lot safer than they'd been an hour earlier.

"Sam will be just fine," she said, confidently.

"What about Sam?" Mamie asked.

"Keep quiet," Mary Beth shot back.

"Is that your mother?" Patrick asked.

"Yeah," Mary Beth said. "I arrested her. Figured it was about time."

"Arrested her for what?"

"Still working on that part," Mary Beth said. "Taking her back to the station as we speak."

Patrick seemed really on edge. "Dammit. Everyone's going to know about this soon. Mary, this is bad. I wish you could have just waited until I'd worked out an immunity deal for that client I was telling you about."

"Your client can shove it," Mary Beth said. "I won't need your mystery man's help to get Velino now. Not after today."

"Yes, but there's things you don't know that could put Sam at risk."

Mary Beth wasn't sure whether Patrick was really concerned about Sam or just saying that to needle her because he was upset that he'd lost a chance to help whatever client he was currently representing.

"I'm listening if there's anything you want to tell me now," she said.

"I can't without breaching confidentiality. Although ..." Patrick paused and mumbled to himself, something about whether there might be an exception if it was to prevent harm to another. "Oh, fuck it," he said, finally. "They can disbar me if they want. Mary, I know who the mole is in your department."

Now Patrick had her attention. So much so that Mary Beth nearly missed the turn off of 52 onto Highway 460 and had to swerve across two lanes of traffic to catch her exit.

"Slow down," Mamie yelled.

"Don't tell me how to drive, Mom. I'm trying to concentrate. Go ahead, Patrick."

"Listen," he said. "I won't tell you who my client is. But it's someone in your department who has come to realize that he has inadvertently let some information slip, on occasion, to an acquaintance who was apparently in league with Velino."

It didn't take much for Mary Beth to guess. "Goddammit, it's Goforth, isn't it?"

"I didn't say that."

"You didn't have to. That stupid, loose-lipped son of a bitch. Who's he been talking to?"

Patrick sighed. "Okay, well, I'm not confirming nor denying that it was Goforth. But the person I believe is in league with Velino is Sid Cain."

Mary Beth laughed. "Yeah, right."

"I'm serious."

"I don't believe it." She was still having a hard time processing what Patrick had told her the other night about Bill Cain being the father of Maria's baby. Now it felt like Patrick was piling on to his effort to tarnish Bill's memory by smearing Daddy Cain as well.

"It's true," Patrick said. "Goforth has told me a lot of things that—"

"Hah, I knew it was Goforth."

"Shit."

"Ha ha."

"Who is Goforth?" Mamie asked.

"Mom, be quiet! I'm working."

"Oh, screw it," Patrick said. "Yes, it's Goforth. And there's a lot of shit he could testify to. Stuff that could put Sid away for the rest of his life. And it would make it crystal clear that Sid is the one who has been pumping him for information that he's been passing on to Velino. Also, I can't prove it yet, but I think Sid was the one who let Velino know that Brad Mayhew was threatening to expose the money they were laundering through the St. Michael's construction project."

An ice-cold chill ran through Mary Beth's body as she thought about how instrumental Sid had been in raising the money for

St. Michael's new cathedral. How proud he had been to show it off the day Mayhew and Father Gonzalez were abducted. And how he'd been the one to discover Father Gonzalez's body earlier that very morning. It had struck her as odd how emotional he'd been. Not that the experience wasn't gut-wrenching, it was just that Sid was such a stoic man's man that for him to go on blubbering the way he did and insist that he was too emotional to be interviewed was strange.

Mary Beth became so enraptured in thought that she eased off the gas and a line of cars behind her began to pass in what was supposed to be the slow lane.

"Sid had been on the take for years," Patrick said. "Velino used to give them tips to bust rival drug dealers, and they'd pocket some of the money and give some of the drugs they seized to Velino."

That accusation did seem plausible. For one, Mary Beth herself had often received tips from her mother on rival drug operations that she took full advantage of, but she never accepted bribes or skimmed any cash or drugs. But now she was thinking about her very first bust. The one she had done with Goforth when he started talking about how tempting and easy it would be to hang on to some of the spoils. And she thought about how Sid Cain later told her he'd put Goforth up to it to test her. Sid's claim was that he wanted to make sure she wasn't dirty. But what if the reverse was true? What if what he'd really done was ask Goforth to test whether she was corruptible?

"It wasn't just Sid," Patrick said. "Goforth says several guys were in on it."

"Like who?"

"Some of this isn't definitive," Patrick cautioned. "I honestly think Goforth was more of a useful idiot than a co-conspirator. But from what he's told me, I'd say Randy Law at a minimum. Probably your beloved, Bill, too."

Mary Beth's instinct was to call bullshit, but she couldn't.

For so long she'd instinctively defended Bill's memory, but now she didn't know how to feel. To that point the emotions his name evoked were mostly ones of guilt. Even when learning of his infidelity, her first thought was that their mostly sexless marriage had driven him to it. It was almost understandable. Although the fact that it had been with Maria Ruiz, whom Mary Beth had viewed like a little sister, was enough to make her want to puke her guts out. Still, she refused to believe that Bill had anything to do with Maria's death. He seemed too desperate to find Maria. Had worked her case too hard.

Mary Beth was still wanting to lay the blame for Maria's murder at Randy Law's feet. It was confirmed that he had commissioned the hit. His motive was still a mystery, but maybe he had been banging her, too, and thought the baby could have been his. It also seemed likely that Randy could have been complicit with Sid Cain and Velino, since he was the one who kept busting Mamie's rival operation. She really didn't want to think Bill could have been in on that too. He was so earnest and righteous about being a cop, like it was the world's greatest calling. Plus Bill was a pretty simple black and white kind of guy. But was it possible that Bill's father and best friend could have both been dirty without him knowing about it?

Mary Beth didn't think so. As much as it killed her to admit it, it was starting to seem a lot more likely that Randy had Maria killed either for Bill's benefit or at his behest. She thought about Randy Law's final words. What he said right before turning his gun on himself.

"The things you do for your friends, huh?"

Oh, my God, Mary Beth thought. *What if Bill's obsession with Maria's disappearance was all an act? A mixture of guilt and self-preservation that drove him to put on such a show.* Could her husband, her Bill, really have been a killer? Could he and the seemingly pious Sid Cain really be just as corrupt and ruthless as her own fucked up mother, Mamie? Maybe even worse.

"Don't you see?" Patrick asked. "Sam is in a lot of danger if Sid hears about what happened to Velino. Sam is staying at his house, for God's sake."

"Yeah, but Sid's not gonna hurt his grandson." As soon as Mary Beth said it, she knew how stupid it was. She was still adjusting to her new reality, part of which was that Velino had known that Sam wasn't really Sid's grandson. And if Velino and Sid had been in cahoots, then maybe Sid knew that, too.

"Yes, but—" Patrick started before Mary Beth cut him off.

"Wait, don't say it. I get it. Just give me a second to think."

Mary Beth pulled to the side of the road and slowed to a stop on the narrow highway shoulder. If Sid knew Sam wasn't his grandson, what could that mean? How long had Sid known? He'd always acted as though he adored Sam. But maybe now he saw him as a symbol of how Mary Beth had betrayed Bill. What would that knowledge allow him to do?

Shit, what if Sid was the one who told Velino's men where Sam lived so they could abduct him earlier and hold him hostage to leverage Velino's release from jail? If that was the case, then it confirmed that Sid really had no concern for Sam's well-being at all and was willing to use his life as a bargaining chip. *Oh my God.* That was probably why Sid was housing Sam now. Keeping him close. His final bargaining chip in case he was exposed and the walls started closing in. And here Mary Beth had actually felt a sense of security with Sam staying in Sid's home that was stocked with more weapons than a gun expo. She'd left her baby inside the lion's den.

"Perhaps there's something I could do to help," Mamie said.

Mary Beth shushed her.

"If Sam is involved, then I—"

"Quiet, mom." Mary Beth closed her eyes, and tried to will the formulation of a plan.

Mary Beth's first instinct was to call Sam and tell him to get the hell out of Sid's house immediately when another thought stopped her. If Sid was keeping tabs on Sam as potential collateral, then after finding Father Gonzalez that morning he'd be on high alert and watching Sam like a hawk. Especially if he'd already caught wind of the Velino raid. Any move she made to get Sam to leave suddenly would alert Sid that he'd come under suspicion. It could actually put Sam at much greater risk. What Mary Beth really needed to do wasn't to get Sam away from Sid, it was to get Sid away from Sam before he started feeling the heat that his Velino connection had been revealed. That was the safest play. But how?

"What are we going to do, Mary?" Patrick asked.

Mary Beth took another deep breath, allowing herself to feel all the motherly fear coursing throughout her body, then blew it out and switched back into sheriff mode. "Patrick, get your client and whatever evidence you have against Sid and meet me at the station ASAP."

"But what about Sam?"

"Just do it."

"Okay, fine. But what are you going to do?"

"I've got to get off and make another call."

"To who?"

"I don't have time to explain," Mary Beth said. "But don't worry. I have an idea."

33

CHIEF DEPUTY IZZY BAKER didn't want to raise any undue alarm as he pulled up to the home of former sheriff Sid Cain, but it was hard not to draw attention driving a jacked-up Chevy Blazer with monster-truck-sized tires and a nitrous-boosted engine. He parked down the street where a neighbor was mowing a lawn that wasn't really big enough to justify a riding lawnmower, but he was using one all the same. A big, pot-bellied man with his shirt off, who nodded to Izzy as he turned his mower in a tight circle. Izzy nodded back, smelling the freshly cut grass and tried to let it settle his nerves as he walked down the block.

Sam Cain's silver Honda Civic parked in the driveway. The deputy knew that Sid's car was probably still back at St. Michael's since he'd been so distraught after finding Father Gonzalez that Izzy had driven him home earlier that morning. Izzy walked down the drive, up onto the front porch, and knocked on the door.

It was Sam who answered. "Hey, Izzy," he said, removing a pair of earbuds. "What's up?"

"Just need to speak with your granddad a minute. Is he around?"

"Yeah, sure. Come on in."

Izzy stepped inside the foyer of the home and stood between a coat rack and table with an old family photo of Sid with his wife and son, who were both now deceased. Bill had died years ago, during Izzy's first year on the force. He'd heard that Dorothy passed from ovarian cancer not all that long ago.

Sam yelled down the hall. "Hey, Gramps, Izzy's here to see you."

Sid Cain was a big man who made the hallway look small as he appeared around the corner, carrying a cup of coffee, though it was late in the day. "Hey, Iz," he said. "I know I owe you guys a statement, but do you think this could wait until tomorrow? I'm just not feeling up to it yet."

'I understand," Izzy said. "But this isn't about Father Gonzalez."

"Oh?"

"Yeah, there's something else that's come up that we could really use your help with."

Sid's slumped shoulders straightened. He started looking around for a place to set his coffee cup, like he wanted his hands free. Izzy saw that Sid was armed. A pistol holstered to his hip. But that was nothing unusual. Sid always carried a gun. Even on Sundays when he was worshiping. *Praise the Lord, and pass the ammunition*, Izzy thought.

"Here," Sid said, handing his coffee mug to Sam. "Can you go stick this in the sink for me?"

"Sure." Sam was already putting his earbuds back in after having answered the door and was cueing up something on his phone to tune out the world as he went down the hall.

"What's up?" Sid asked.

Izzy sighed and shook his head. He wanted to create the impression that he was really there seeking Sid's help. That they were on the same side. The last thing he wanted was for Sid to get defensive. He was an old man with a heart condition, but he was still a former cop who was the size of a grizzly bear, and he was armed. Izzy suspected that Sid could be plenty dangerous if cornered.

The deputy cocked his head, trying to see past Sid, who filled the hallway, like he was checking to make sure Sam was out of earshot. "It's Goforth," he whispered. "Mary Beth took another run at him. She still thinks he may have been the one who gave up Father Gonzalez to Velino."

Sid was shaking his head. "Benny? No way."

"I didn't want to believe it, either," Izzy said. "But he was acting real squirmy about it. Then he wanted a lawyer. Then he started making all kinds of crazy allegations about stuff from back in the day."

This was the play that Mary Beth came up with. Izzy still wasn't sure it was the best plan but Mary Beth figured that Sid had been so reluctant to give them a statement about Father Gonzalez that the best way to get him out of his house and down to the station would be if he thought Goforth was pointing the finger at him but Mary Beth and Izzy didn't believe it and wanted his help to expose Goforth's lies. That way, she figured, Sid would want to rush down there to either shut Goforth up or make sure he took the full blame for whatever culpability remained.

Izzy watched as Sid uncrossed his arms and let them hang at his side, his right hand just inches from his gun.

"What kind of allegations?" he asked.

Izzy rolled his eyes. "It's all bullshit," he said. "We know it is, but he's trying to make it sound like the whole force used to be on the take from Velino and it could have been anybody from that era who gave him the info that allowed him to grab Father Gonzalez from witness protection."

Sid remained silent. As he stared Izzy down on that Easter

Sunday, the diminutive deputy, who stood just below five feet tall, thought he knew how David must have felt squaring off with Goliath. Izzy did his best to maintain an air of camaraderie. "The stuff he's talking about with the department all predates me and Mary Beth and everybody else we've got now. That's why we need you to come in and call bullshit on him. Goforth respects you. If he sees you, Mary Beth is sure he's going to crack. We just need you to come stand in the interrogation room with us, while we take a final run at him."

Sid rubbed at his mostly bald head. "If he's making allegations about time as sheriff, it kind of sounds like maybe I'm the one who needs a lawyer?" he said, forcing a chuckle.

Izzy forced a chuckle of his own. "Come on," he said, bopping Sid on the elbow. "We just need you to be a prop. Come give Goforth that patented mean Cain stare while Mary Beth asks her questions, and we may finally get some answers."

Sid rolled his head around, stretching his neck. "I don't know, Iz. I'd like to help you all, but I'm retired, you know, it's—"

"You'll be back here in an hour or two," Izzy said. "We owe this to Father Gonzalez, don't you think?"

The reference to the priest was enough of a prod to get Sid moving. "Okay." He nodded, sighed, and turned and yelled down the hall for Sam, who didn't answer until Sid yelled louder. The gawky, redheaded kid came around the corner hurriedly taking out his earbuds, like he was used to being called out for not responding.

"Sorry, I didn't hear you," Sam said.

"Listen," Sid told him. "I'm headed down to the station with Izzy. Probably be back in a couple of hours."

Sam looked alarmed. "Is everything okay?"

"Yeah, yeah. Everything's fine. Just helping your mom with a case."

"Can I come?" Sam asked.

Before Izzy could say Hell No, Sid answered, "Sure."

"I don't think that's a good idea," Izzy said. His main purpose in being there was to get those two away from each other. But now Sid had his arm wrapped around his grandson's shoulder in a way that could have been read just as easily as a threat as a gesture of endearment.

"Come on," Sid said. "What can it hurt if he waits around until we're done? I'm sure the sheriff would love to see her boy."

"I really don't—"

"Did you bring your truck?" Sam asked, unwittingly making matters worse. Izzy'd been promising him a ride in Beulah ever since he got the nitrous booster installed.

"Of course he did," Sid said. "Izzy doesn't go anywhere without that monster. I know Sam would love to go for a ride in it."

"Absolutely," Sam said, excited. He rushed to the window and drew back the curtains to look for the vehicle. "Why'd you park so far away?" he asked.

"I, uh …"

"Let him come along, Iz," Sid said. "Maybe we can all go grab a bite afterward."

Mary Beth was probably more likely to bite Izzy's head off for bringing Sam, but Izzy didn't think he could avoid that now without arousing suspicion. Plus, he was a little worried about driving with Sid alone. Afraid the former sheriff might try something while Izzy had his hands on the wheel and eyes on the road. Having Sam there made that seem a lot less likely. And if they could all make it to the station together, Sam would be safe at that point. They'd leave him in the lobby while handling their police business with Goforth.

"I guess…it would be okay," Izzy said, reluctantly.

"Awesome," Sam said.

Soon they were all headed for the driveway and down the block to where Izzy had parked. Sid was tall enough that it wasn't difficult for him to climb up into the passenger seat of

Izzy's jacked-up Blazer. He didn't need the rope ladder Izzy relied upon.

Unfortunately, Sid opted for the back seat.

"Why don't you ride shotgun, Sid?" Izzy said just halfway up the rope ladder at that point. He didn't like the idea of having Sid behind him on the drive over. But Sid insisted.

"No. No," he said. "Sam wants to see how everything works. Let him sit up front."

Sam was just finishing his climb up and jumped in the front seat. Again Izzy didn't think there was much else he could say about it without seeming suspicious.

He climbed up on the driver seat and fired up the engine, gassing it a few times with the extended pedals to really let the engine roar.

"Wow," Sam said. "It sounds like a jet plane."

Izzy pulled away from the curb. He tried to keep the mood light on the way to the station, mostly talking to Sam about his vehicle. Sid kept unusually quiet, but the drive was otherwise uneventful.

When they filed into the station, Izzy immediately caught Mary Beth's evil eye when she saw that Sam was with him. Fortunately, she chose not to ream him out in front of everyone. "You decided to come, too, huh?" she said, while giving Sam a hug and staring daggers into Izzy.

"Yeah," Sam said. "Granddad thought maybe we could all eat dinner together after."

"Is that right?" she asked.

Izzy shrugged, meekly.

Mary Beth was forced to play along. "Good idea," she said, smiling at Sid. She released her son and shook hands with her father-in-law. "Thanks for coming."

"Sure," Sid said, sounding anything but sure. "Don't know that I can help, but I'm happy to try."

Mary Beth looked back to her son. "Sammy, baby, why don't

you have a seat out here, while the cops go and discuss our game plan. I don't think this is going to take too long."

Sam plopped down on a chair in the waiting area and pulled out his phone. Mary Beth led Sid and Izzy down the hall toward the interrogation room. She stopped outside the door. There she put one arm low around Izzy and the other high around Sid, making for an extremely awkward huddle, given the extreme contrast in their heights.

"I'm assuming Izzy got you up to speed?" Mary Beth said.

Sid responded, "A little. I know Goforth's been making allegations about stuff he says happened here in the past."

Mary Beth was nodding. "Yeah. We know it's bullshit. He's obviously deflecting. Real easy to cast aspersions on whoever's not in the room. That's why we wanted to bring you in."

"I feel a little funny about questioning somebody, given my status," Sid said.

"You won't have to," Mary Beth assured him. "In fact I don't know that there will be any more actual questioning today at all. After Izzy left, Goforth invoked again. He's got his attorney in there with him now." Mary Beth led them a few more steps down the hall to where they could look through the two-way mirror into the interrogation room. Inside was Goforth seated at the table next to Patrick Connelly.

Sid visibly relaxed at the sight. "Guess we came out here for nothing, then" he said.

"Maybe," Mary Beth said. "Still, I want him to see your face. Let him know that he can't just start defaming fellow cops and think that's going to get him out of Dutch. See if it makes him decide to go ahead and come clean. I'm going to let him know this will be his one and only chance to make a deal."

Sid understood the maneuver Mary Beth was suggesting, and though he didn't appear happy about participating in it, he was no longer showing the kind of hesitancy he'd had up until then. Goforth having an attorney present was likely putting him at ease. It meant Goforth was unlikely to do any more talking and any heat he might send Sid's way would be a matter for another day.

"It's your show," Sid said.

"All right." Mary Beth pointed at the men in turn. "You two just stand on either side of me, looking pissed, and I'll do the talking, okay?'

"Got it," Izzy said. Sid nodded.

Mary Beth started to open the door, then stopped. "Oh," she said, as though it was an afterthought. "Protocol."

She pointed to the lockbox mounted on the wall where officers were to deposit their weapons before entering the interrogation room. She punched in a code and the door swung open. She unholstered her sidearm and placed it in the metal locker toward the back. Izzy noticed she didn't remove the little backup gun she always kept strapped to her ankle, but he didn't say anything, assuming this was intentional. Instead he was quick to hand over his ridiculously large .44 Magnum handgun, with its extended barrel, which invited a smirk from Mary Beth. "Compensate much?" she said as she put the gun into storage.

"Whatever," Izzy said.

They both looked at Sid, who'd made no move to disarm himself.

"Let's go, Daddy-o," Mary Beth said with a smile.

"Oh, right," Sid said, embarrassed. He unholstered his pistol and surrendered it to Mary Beth, who locked it away along with the other two weapons.

"Okay," she said. "Everybody ready?"

Both men nodded.

Mary Beth opened the door to the interrogation room. They walked inside, and she shut the door behind them. Goforth stood.

"Sid?" he said. "What are you doing here?"

"You tell me," Sid said. Goforth walked around the table,

offering his hand to his old friend. Sid reached out to shake it, and that's when they pounced.

Goforth grabbed Sid's right arm while Mary Beth seized his left. Izzy lowered his head and drove his shoulder into the back of Sid's legs like a battering ram, dropping the big man to his knees. The former sheriff was strong but too surprised to put up much of a fight before the three officers had him down on the ground, face smashed against the floor and both hands cuffed behind his back.

34

IT TURNED OUT THAT getting Sid Cain down on the ground was a lot easier than getting him back up. He had a bad knee and wasn't helping much as he demanded to know what in the hell was going on. It took all three officers plus Patrick to get him up and into a chair.

"I demand to know what's going on," Sid shouted.

"You're about to find out," Mary Beth told him. Then to Izzy, she said, "Bring the other one in."

"Other what?" Sid asked.

"You'll see," Mary Beth said.

Izzy and Goforth left and returned a few moments later with Mary Beth's mother, who still had her hands cuffed, although they'd moved them to the front to make her more comfortable while she waited.

"Get your hands off me," Mamie bristled.

"Just relax," Izzy told her.

He and Goforth helped her into a chair opposite Sid, who was leaning forward, his chest against the table, hands cuffed behind his back.

"What in the hell is this?" Sid demanded.

"Think of this as a little family meeting," Mary Beth said. "I've got questions, and one of you two has got the answers."

Everyone stood for a moment like they were waiting for her to say something else.

"That will be all, gentlemen," Mary Beth said.

Patrick and her deputies looked confused.

"Family meeting," she said. "The rest of you out."

"Mary—" Patrick started before she shut him down.

"You too. Everybody get lost."

Izzy and Goforth moved reluctantly toward the door.

"Oh, and Iz," Mary Beth called after him.

"Yeah?"

"No recordings."

"But—"

"No recordings," Mary Beth repeated. She didn't know what was about to happen in that interrogation room, other than the fact that she wasn't leaving the room without the truth. No matter what it took. That might involve methods she wouldn't want memorialized. And she really wasn't too worried about preserving any confessions she might elicit, because prosecutions had become almost beside the point. This was personal. She was ready to take the law into her own hands if necessary.

Izzy gave her one last look of warning to let her know he still didn't approve. "You just say the word, and we'll come rushing in."

"I know," she said.

As they exited, Patrick opened his briefcase and took out a file folder that he handed to Mary Beth. "The written statement's on top. There's seventeen distinct criminal events detailed, and there's probably more we'll eventually be able to put together. It was all Goforth could get down on paper with the time we had."

Mary Beth tried to take the file, but Patrick wouldn't release it before asking, "Full immunity, right? We're agreed?"

Mary Beth frowned. "Yeah, full immunity," she said reluctantly. "The DA will go along with whatever I recommend. But Goforth retires now," she said. "Today's his last day."

Patrick nodded and let go of the file. Mary Beth tucked it under her arm.

"Sam's out in the waiting room," she told him. "Why don't you two go take a walk? You've got a lot to talk about."

Patrick raised an eyebrow. "You mean … ?"

"No more secrets," Mary Beth said. "Not after today."

He stammered. "Oh, uh … well, don't you want to be there for *that* talk?"

"Of course I do. But if I'm there, Sam will get angry and defensive and push away. If it comes from you, he'll take it a lot better. I'll follow up with him later once the shock's worn off."

"But—"

"Look, I need your help, Connelly. Now, can you handle it or not?"

Patrick looked like he wanted to debate some more but stopped himself. He straightened up like a grunt coming to attention.

"I'll take care of it," he said.

"Good. Now get. I've got some business to attend to. Go talk to your son."

Hearing Mary Beth publicly declare that Sam was his son was all the motivation the attorney needed. He gave her a knowing smile and left to confront Sam with the long hidden truth.

Once he was out of the room, she closed the door behind him before taking a seat across from her two prisoners.

"Okay," she said. "No recording devices. No witnesses, other than me, and we all know my word only goes so far. I'm not telling you that nothing you say here will be used against you. I'm not making any promises at all other than this: I will know the truth before anybody leaves this room."

Mamie and Sid both stared back at her stoically.

Mary Beth absorbed their silence for a moment then shattered it with a clap of her hands. "So," she said, "who wants to go first?"

Neither prisoner volunteered.

"Okay," Mary Beth said. "Then I'll start. Let's go ahead and finish getting the Maury Povich moment out of the way. Bill wasn't Sam's father."

Mamie's eyes doubled in size, but Sid didn't flinch. His eyes were smoldering. "You've been nothing but a damn curse to my family." He spat on the ground. "Cursed redheads."

There it was, that stupid old miner's myth. And that's when Mary Beth put it together. She'd grown up in coal country and had never heard anyone say anything about red-haired women being bad luck. Not until Sid shared that piece of folklore with her months earlier. Yet somehow Leonard Velino seemed to know about the superstition when she confronted him inside the jail. He had to have heard it from Sid. Just as Sid must have already known about Sam from Velino's surveillance.

"You already knew about Sam, didn't you?" she said, confronting her father-in-law. "You know because Velino bugged Patrick's house."

She gave her nothing in return. No acknowledgment. No denial. So she hit him where it hurt. "Did you also tell Velino's guys where Sam lived so they could kidnap him? Huh, Granddad?"

Sid recoiled. "I would never," he hissed.

Mary Beth put her hand to her ear. "Speak up, now."

"I would never hurt Sam," Sid said, louder and more emphatically.

"Oh no?"

"No."

Mary Beth stared at him another moment before Sid added. "I don't care whether Bill was his father or not. Sam is my grandson as far as I'm concerned. That's all there is to it."

Mary Beth wasn't sure whether or not to believe that. Sid had played the part of the doting grandfather for so long, that if he'd only recently learned that Bill wasn;t the father, he wouldn't have been able to just turn off all of his affections for the boy could he? Or, could he? There was obviously more to the man than Mary Beth had previously appreciated. She still didn't know what to think.

"That's real nice," she said to Sid. "Sweet. But you were passing info to Velino. I know it and you know it. Goforth was supposed to have lunch with you the day the trial started. He called and told you he had to cancel because I was sending him on an errand out of state. You guessed that he was going to retrieve Father Gonzalez, and you told Velino's guys to follow Goforth."

Sid started breathing really heavily. Little beads of sweat popped up on his forehead that reminded Mary Beth the man did have a heart condition.

"Look, Sid. The jig is up. I'll get your goddamn phone records. Your bank records. Have forensic accountants go through all the fund-raising and construction projects at St. Michael's with a fine-tooth comb. I'll scour the files of every case you ever worked. Talk to everyone you ever worked with. Crawl up your ass like a pissed off proctologist. And I'm sure I can drum up more witnesses like Goforth who will confirm you were on the take."

She held up a legal pad filled with Ben Goforth's handwritten statement. "You know I will, Sid. I'm a hunting dog and I've got your scent. Got you up in the tree. Just a matter of time before you come down and accept your fate."

Sid closed his eyes and squirmed in his chair. "I would never hurt Sam," he repeated, as though trying to convince himself.

"Maybe," Mary Beth said. "Maybe Velino grabbed him without your help. But you did give up Father Gonzalez and Brad Mayhew, right?"

Sid shook his head, No. Mary Beth didn't take it as a denial so much as a refusal to answer.

"Come on, Sid," she said. "Your son's gone. Your wife's gone. There's nobody left to protect."

Sid opened his eyes, revealing tears where Mary Beth had expected rage. "There's still my name," he said. "The Cain name. The same name you carry."

Now we're getting somewhere, Mary Beth thought. She could work with this. "Fortunately for you, I'm worried about that, too," she said. "I did Bill wrong from the start. I'll admit that. From the time Sam started talking, I more or less knew that Patrick was the father, but I kept it from Bill. And maybe you had your suspicions too, but I know Bill never did, did he?"

She was looking to Sid for an answer. After a pause, he said, "No. If he did, he never said anything about it to me."

"No," Mary Beth said. "Bill was oblivious, when it came to Sam. But what I haven't been able to reconcile is whether and to what extent he was mixed up with the drug stuff–whatever you had going on with Velino. I'm damn sure his buddy Randy Law was dirty as hell. He was smart and crafty. But Bill was no mastermind. I've got a feeling that if his hands were dirty, it was mainly from doing what he'd done his whole life, which was whatever you told him to do."

Sid closed his eyes again but couldn't keep the tears from running down his cheeks.

"What about Bill's reputation?" Mary Beth prodded. "What's to be left of his name? What's Sam to think of him? I'm not keeping any of this secret from him. I know Bill cheated on me with Maria. Got her knocked up. That's bad. As bad as what I did to him. But what I need to know. What Sam needs to know is, was Bill a killer?"

Sid refused to answer.

"I don't want to believe it, Sid. But unless there's more you can tell me to exculpate your son, then I've got to admit that

Bill was the only one with a motive for killing Maria, to hide the affair. I know Randy Law commissioned the hit, but before he died, Randy said something that made it sound like he'd done it just to help his friend."

Mary Beth paused to see if Sid would fill the silence. If he would rush to his son's defense. But he refused to look at her. She noticed the sweat along his brow had intensified and was now pouring down, mixing with the tears that managed to escape his scrunched eyelids.

The sheriff tried one more time to prod him into admitting what she hoped was the truth.

"As pissed as I am at Bill for cheating on me with Maria. I still can't believe he had it in him to kill her. No. What I think is, he got in trouble and did the same thing he always did, when he had a problem. He went to Big Daddy to fix it. I think maybe you were the one who worked it out for him with a plan that was way too grand for Bill to have come up with. I think you had your stooge Randy Law take care of the dirty work. Got those cartel guys to grab Maria, kill her, and hide her in that abandoned school. I figure that's why Bill worked the case so hard at first. He didn't know why she disappeared. He was really trying to find her, wasn't he?"

Sid's head dropped toward the table to the point Mary Beth thought for a second he was passing out. But he shot back up and stared at the ceiling as though asking God to intervene.

"If you know, Sid that Bill is innocent of Maria's death and you don't say something, then you will be responsible for Sam spending the rest of his life never knowing whether the man he's hero-worshipped his whole life was nothing but a shitbag murderer."

Sid swooned again, slightly then steadied himself. "Jesus," Sid muttered. "Never had a chance."

Mary Beth wasn't sure whether he was referring to Bill or Sam. Or maybe both.

She leaned in. "Give him a chance now, Sid. Just tell me the truth?"

Sid opened his eyes and stared at her in desperation. "I need my pills," he said. "My heart pills. I've got a case in my pocket. I need to take them."

"Okay," Mary Beth said. "First, answer my question, though."

"Just let me take my pills and I will."

"Uh-uh. Answer first."

Sid took a deep breath. Mary Beth could see his pulse vibrating in his throat. His heart was really racing.

"Think about Sam," Mary Beth said. "You say you love him regardless, and I want to believe that. Now prove it. Tell me what Bill did or didn't have to do with Maria's death and your involvement with Velino. Give Sam a chance to remember Bill as something other than a murderer and a crooked cop."

Finally, Sid relented. "Okay, okay."

"Okay, what?"

"It's basically like you said," he began, struggling to get the words out. "Bill was always a good boy. Did what he was told. Mostly looked the other way, when it came to me or Randy, who was a lot more corruptible. Bill never knew half the stuff that was going on with Velino, and most of the stuff he did know about he thought was harmless. Just cops pocketing a little extra they stole from drug dealers. Who cares?"

"But what about Maria?" that was the question Mary Beth most needed an answer to.

Sid grunted in frustration. "Dammit Mary, I need the pills."

"First, I need to know about Maria," she demanded.

Sid leaned back, squirmed, and slouched forward against the table. "You've already guessed at it," he said, quickly. "Bill came to me for help when he found out she was pregnant. Said you'd kill him. Divorce him. Sam would never speak to him again. It would be a big scandal that would ruin him. Ruin our family name. He didn't know what to do. Right about the same time, an opportunity presented itself when that attorney, Pomfried, reached out to Randy wanting to see if he could get some back channel communication to the cartel for some snitch client he was representing. He knew Randy had sources in the drug world and wanted to know what kind of retribution his current client was looking at if he ratted on the guys he'd been working for."

"You're talking about Raul Kowalski. The guy who killed Maria."

"I forget his name," Sid said. "But yeah. Whatever it was, when Randy told me about it, I saw a way to work things out. I had Randy approach this Raul or whoever and tell him he'd worked out a deal with the cartel that there'd be no reprisals if he made Maria disappear. Randy was always game for whatever as long as there was money in it. I told him I'd make it worth his while and he'd be doing his best buddy Bill a solid. Bill would never have to know. Could just chalk it up as serendipity that his Maria problem magically worked itself out."

Mary Beth felt an enormous weight lift off her shoulders at that notion. She wanted so badly to believe that was true but needed to confirm. "So Bill really didn't know what happened to Maria?" she asked.

"Not at first. But after he looked into it he got suspicious. The timing was just too convenient. He confronted me about it. Threatened to expose what bits he'd seen about our relationship with Velino. Said he'd even come clean about the little involvement he'd had in it. He wanted out of the whole arrangement. Insisted I step down as sheriff and let him clean house."

That sounded more like the Bill, Mary Beth knew.

"So what happened?" she asked, doing her best to control her tone, because this was starting to sound a whole lot like Sid would have had a motive to make Bill disappear. That piece still wasn't fitting with her emotionally. The idea that Sid could have had something to do with Bill's death. But she'd had her mind blown so many times up to that point she couldn't dismiss the possibility.

"Mary, please," Sid said, sounding almost like a child. "I need my pills."

"I need to know what happened first. You come clean, and you'll get your medicine."

"I could die."

"Don't threaten me with a good time, Sid."

The former sheriff got his back up at that, switching from pleading to defensiveness. "Don't get sanctimonious with me," he spat. "Not you, of all people."

"What's that supposed to mean?"

"It means you know how it works. Don't don't to me like I'm some arch criminal. It's not like I woke up one day and decided I wanted things to end up the way they did. It starts with something small, when you're trying to do the right thing. Cut a little corner here and there. Plant a little evidence. Doctor a record. Coerce a confession. Sound familiar?"

Mary Beth wasn't tolerating any false equivalencies. "Pushing the envelope to catch bad guys is a lot different than doing a drug dealer's dirty work."

"Is it?" Sid asked. "It starts the same way—with the best of intentions. Just taking a stupid little campaign contribution, playing along with the scheme they've got to get around the fund-raising laws by spreading the money through different strawmen and dummy corporations. All the time, telling yourself it will just be this once. That it's a means to an end. All for the greater good. But then they come back for another favor and threaten to expose the last one they did for you if you don't go along with it. You can't have that, so you go along again. Just one more, you tell yourself. But then they come back again, and now they've got two things they can blackmail you with if you don't play ball. And it just escalates and escalates. The deeper you get, the more leverage they've got, until they own you completely."

Mary Beth mimed playing the world's tiniest violin for Sid. Then, for the first time in the conversation, she looked to her mother for help. "Randy Law was busting your operation all the time. And you're telling me you made absolutely one hundred percent sure that none of your guys were involved in the bust where Bill got killed."

"One hundred percent," Mamie said.

The sheriff turned back to Sid. "Bill was killed right after the time he told you he wanted out? Right after he threatened to expose the corruption. Who killed him? Velino? Randy? You?"

"God, No. How could you ever think that?"

"I don't know what in the hell to think," Mary Beth shot back. "That's why I need you to tell me."

Sid's eyes scanned the room as though searching for help. "Please, Mary," he said. "My pills."

"Fine." Mary Beth stood and came around the table. Sid straightened his leg enough for her to get the pill case out of his right pocket. It was oval shaped. White plastic. She dangled it in front of Sid like a carrot.

"Come clean right now and you can have these. I want to know who killed my husband."

"Please Mar—"

"Now!"

"It was them!" Sid shouted, his voice hoarse and mournful. "We met at the park."

"Who?"

"Randy, Bill, and me. We met with Velino and his men. And they killed him. Bill tried to put an end to it all, and they killed him. They killed my own son right in front of me, goddammit, and there was nothing I could do about it, because they owned me, Mary. All I could do was protect my wife and what was left of my family name. So I just took it. Like a sap. And I had Randy cover it up. There you've got your answers now give me my pills."

Mary Beth couldn't believe it. Big bad Sid Cain. Just accepting that. Velino killing his son and Sid just eating that shit sandwich and staying quiet to save his reputation.

"If you were willing to give into Velino on that, then I've got no doubt you were willing sacrifice Mayhew and Father Gonzalez too."

Sid didn't respond.

Mary Beth held the pills in front of his face, taunting him. "Right?"

"Give me my pills?"

"Give me my answer."

"GIVE. ME. MY. PILLS."

"Not until you admit what you did. You helped Velino launder money through the church. When Mayhew grew a guilty conscience and was going to confess it, you dimed him out to Velino who took him out. Then, when you found out Goforth was going to get Father Gonzalez, the witness who saw Velino kill Mayhew, you gave him up to, so Velino could silence him as well, right?"

"Mary, please. I need my–".

Mary Beth slammed her fist down on the table. "RIGHT?" she screamed.

"Yes!" Sid yelled back. "Yes. Goddammit, yes! Now give me my fucking pills!"

35

MARY BETH WAS SO STUNNED by Sid's confession that it froze her for a moment. Normally breaking down a witness and getting a confession like that brought on a sense of joy, a high of righteous indignation, or the ick of pure disgust. But in that moment Mary Beth felt more a sense of relief. It buoyed her soul to know that Bill hadn't been quite the monster she feared he might have been. But with that thought also came a sudden and heavy sadness, realizing that the career her dead husband inherited, the one he'd been so proud of, was damn near as corrupt as her own family's business.

"I guess I need to get you a glass of water," she said to Sid, now concerned the man could have a heart attack any second if he didn;t take the pills she'd been withholding.

"Thank you," Sid, sounding breathless, and maybe a little relieved himself at having finally unburdened such long-held and horrible secrets.

Mary Beth was turning to the door to go get something Sid could use to wash down his medication when Mamie said, "I have a question."

At that point Mary Beth really was worried she'd pushed things too long without letting Sid address his heart condition, but still couldn't resist asking, "What?"

Mamie, who had the benefit of hands cuffed in the front, used them to gesture to Sid. "You mentioned campaign contributions was how this all got started with Velino. But your daddy had been sheriff before you. You were a shoo-in to win. If I remember correctly, seems like you always ran unopposed. Why would you have been so desperate for campaign contributions you'd take them from someone like Leonard Velino?"

Sid glanced half-heartedly at Mamie but appeared to be in too much distress to respond.

"What are you getting at?" Mary Beth asked.

"Take a look at your legal pad there," Mamie said. "The list of things your Deputy Goforth says he did with old Sid—how far back does it go?"

Mary Beth scanned down through the list Goforth had put together.

Sid leaned forward like he might throw up. "Please," he whispered.

"Does it go back to the nineties?" Mamie asked.

Mary Beth didn't want to take too long reading through for an answer; she really did need to get Sid his medicine. But as she scanned quickly though the narrative, she saw a reference to Goforth working with Sid when they were both deputies. That would probably have been in that era.

"Yeah, looks like it," she said, still not registering what Mamie was getting at.

"It was your daddy who first got mixed up with Velino, wasn't it?" Mamie asked Sid.

He didn't answer.

The possibility that the Velino corruption started with Sid's predecessor, his father Gus Cain, was interesting. It could possibly explain why Sid felt so trapped by the family legacy and determined to protect it. Maybe when he'd said, "Never had a chance," he'd actually been referring to himself. But nothing was going to excuse the things he'd just admitted to.

"Why does that matter?" Mary Beth asked her mother.

"Because," Mamie said as though it should be obvious. "It means they were already dirty back in '97."

It took Mary Beth another second to catch on.

"Nineteen ninety-seven," Mamie said. "Hello?"

Now Mary Beth understood. Her body seemed to get the message before her mind. Filling her with an ice cold tremor that made her arms shake. That was the year the DEA raided their family farm and killed Mary Beth's father.

No. No. That would be too much. There'd been so many skeletons unearthed in this interrogation, Mary Beth's skepticism told her there was no way that could be tied in too.

"Mom, that was the feds," she said.

"Yeah, but why?" Mamie asked. "We were small-time back then. It never made any sense the feds would target us. I bet they put them on to us. You know, take out the upstart competition."

Mary Beth looked back at Sid who appeared to be choking back bile. Visible spittle had formed at the corners of his mouth. There may not be time to fetch Sid some water.

"Well," Mamie said, "ask the son of a bitch before he keels over and dies of a heart attack."

Mary Beth popped open the pill box. Inside were two capsules she dropped into the palm of her hand. "How 'bout it?" she asked. "The sooner you fess up, the sooner you get these."

Sid closed his eyes and nodded. Mary Beth and Mamie looked at each other. Mamie nodded for her to keep going.

"I'm going to need a little more than that," Mary Beth said.

Rivulets of sweat framed Sid's eyes as he opened them and said, "The DEA." He paused, panting, then continued. "They were putting pressure on Velino. We had to give them someone else to go after."

Suddenly Mary Beth felt like she was the one about to have a heart attack. Her head started spinning with the implications. That raid had been *the* pivotal event in her whole family's life. The moment that would always divide everything into before or after. And among her lists of regrets, which were legion, it ruled supreme. As a teenager she'd been placed in charge of Sawyer. It was her he got loose from, and when he ran after their father, who was trying to surrender, a DEA sniper fired the shot that had echoed in her nightmares ever since.

How many times in the decades since had she woken up in a cold sweat, wondering what if. What if she'd just managed to keep a hold of Sawyer like she was supposed to? Her father would still be alive. Sawyer, who was turned into a right psycho from the experience, would probably still be alive, too.

"You were behind that raid?" she asked.

"Please," Sid said, pleading with his eyes as much as his mouth. "No more." He closed his eyes again and laid his forehead down on the table.

"Wake up," Mamie scolded. It took Mary Beth a second to realize her mother was talking to her. "It wasn't a raid," Mamie said. "It was a goddamned hit."

Mary Beth looked at her mother, barely able to grasp the implications if that was true. For one, it would mean that maybe Mary Beth wasn't responsible at all for her father being shot. *If* that had been the plan all along. Though, if she had to guess, killing her dad was more likely a welcome by-product of the raid than its express purpose. A high probability of collateral damage, just as it was with Velino. Mary Beth never insisted that the Motor City Mafioso be killed, but she sure as shit didn't lose any sleep over the possibility.

"What do you have to say about that, Sid?" she asked.

"Please," he mouthed.

"Last question," Mary Beth insisted.

"You promise?"

"Promise."

Sid took three gasps to try and slow his breathing. She could see him doing his best to will his heart into submission, but he had about as much control over that faulty ticker as a bull rider holding on for dear life.

"The truth is, I don't know," Sid said. "My dad's the one who had a contact in the DEA. I know he tried to steer them away from Velino by putting them onto the McCray operation. Did Velino want your dad killed as part of the raid? Maybe. Did he get to somebody inside the DEA to make it happen? I suppose it's possible. I just don't know. That's the God's honest truth, Mary. I just don't know."

Mary Beth stared down into her palm at those two capsules. She no longer saw the pills. What she was holding now was a life. A life of a man who she now believed bore significant responsibility not only for the death of her husband, Bill; for Maria, her once cherished family friend; for Father Gonzalez, the witness she'd sworn to protect; and Brad Mayhew, who certainly didn't deserve to die; but also was at least somewhat complicit in the death of her father, and, by extension, her brother, Sawyer, as well.

"Please," Sid said.

That's right. Beg, she thought. Beg like Father Gonzalez must have while those monsters savaged his body. *Plead for your life the way Brad Mayhew did when Velino put the gun to his head. Beg the way I begged all those nights for God to bring my daddy back to me. To make it not all my fault.*

"Okay," Mamie said. "That's enough. Go on and give the son of a bitch his pills. You found out what you needed to know."

Mary Beth looked over to her mother, then back at Sid. She thought about how Bill had been assassinated right there in front of his father and best friend, both armed, sworn officers of the law, who just stood by and watched, then covered it up. She allowed her mind to travel back to that fateful day a sniper's bullet blew open her dad's head, right there in front of his family.

"Sweetheart, he's gonna die on you if you don't give him those pills," Mamie said.

Mary Beth focused in on Sid's narrowing eyes, then looked back down at the pills one last time. Thinking about how easy it would be to crush them in her fist.

"Please," Sid said, again.

Mamie piled on, too. "Sweetheart, if this man dies because you denied him his pills, you'll be in a whole heap of trouble."

"I don't know," Mary Beth said. "No cameras. No witnesses. If the man responsible for so much misery were to succumb to natural causes …" Mary Beth shrugged indifferently.

"Please," Sid begged.

"I'm the last person you should be asking for help, don't you think?"

There wasn't much Sid could say to that. Mary Beth took another move toward the door.

"You're just going to get water?" Sid asked, desperately. "You'll be right back?"

Mary Beth glared down at her father-in-law. "Gee, Sid. I just don't know."

Sid hung his head in defeat.

Mary Beth looked to her mother. "Come on, Mom. I won't make you wait in here with this piece of shit."

Mamie nodded, started to rise, then dropped back into her chair. "I think I'm going to need you to help me up, dear. I've been sitting too long."

Mamie was looking a little peaked. She started fanning herself with her cuffed hands. "I'm feeling a little lightheaded myself. This has all been so overwhelming."

"Mary, please," Sid said meekly as Mary Beth approached the table.

She ignored him and reached down to help her mother stand.

Mamie fell into her, spilling out of the chair, almost collapsing to the floor. She caught hold of Mary Beth's lower leg to steady herself.

"Mom!"

Mary Beth reached down to try and help her mother up, but just as she did, Mamie sprung to her feet, the crown of the old woman's head catching Mary Beth under the chin with enough force to send the sheriff flying onto her back.

Starry-eyed, Mary Beth looked up and saw that Mamie had got hold of her hummingbird, the little compact Beretta the sheriff kept holstered to her ankle. The gun Mary Beth neglected to lock up when she and Izzy were stowing their other guns in the police locker so Sid would as well and thus be unarmed when they went to detain him.

"Gun!" Mary Beth shouted. Her first thought was that Mamie was going to fire at her. That his was an escape attempt. She was calling for Izzy and Goforth to come intervene. But the old woman swiveled around to point the weapon at Sid just as the deputies stormed into the room. Izzy got to her first, but not before Mamie pumped enough bullets into Sid Cain to leave him a heaving, bleeding mass of humanity on the floor.

Even after Izzy tackled Mamie and all the bullets had been expelled, she continued to pull the trigger.

Mary Beth laid on the ground listening to the sound. *Click. Click. Click.*

MARY BETH WAS REMINDED of the sound her emptied gun had made that day, as Alexander Pomfried clicked his ink pen while seated at counsel's table, reading over the coroner's report.

"Says here that Sid Cain was unresponsive by the time the EMTs arrived. He was lying prone on the ground, hands cuffed behind his back. Multiple gunshot wounds to his chest and abdomen. They were unable to detect any pulse. CPR was attempted en route to the hospital, but no pulse was ever detected. The ER doctors at Jasper County Hospital called for the crash cart and made multiple attempts to revive the patient, all of which were unsuccessful. Sid Cain was officially declared dead twenty minutes after he arrived."

Pomfried put down the paper he'd been looking at and picked up another. "Lists here on the death certificate that the cause of death was cardiac arrest."

Mary Beth was ready for this. "Almost everyone dies of cardiac arrest," she said. "You get shot in the chest six times, eventually your heart stops and you die. Read the rest of it to the jury," she insisted. "It says 'cause of death: cardiac arrest, *secondary* to gunshot wounds.'"

Mary Beth had read that document so many times since being informed she was a potential target of the grand jury's investigation into the death of Sid Cain, that she could almost recite it verbatim.

"The jury is going to have access to the whole thing," Pomfried said, waiving the death certificate. "I've certainly got nothing to hide."

Pomfried wiggled free from his chair, where the armrest had pressed in on his sizable girth. He struggled to get up on his stubby legs and waddled over to the jury box, where he passed out copies of the death certificate and coroner's report.

"Here," he said to Mary Beth. "You can have one, too."

"No need," Mary Beth replied. "I'm familiar with it."

"Very well. Then you should know that just below Cause of Death is a line for Related or Contributing Factors, which lists underlying hypertension and a history of arrhythmia. In other words, the man had a heart condition, he was suffering from some type of cardiac event, and you were denying him his medication, correct?"

Mary Beth didn't try to duck the question. "Yes," she said.

"The report also says that none of the bullets damaged any vital organs, right?"

"But the blood loss was—"

"Ms. Cain, let's cut to the chase. Isn't it true that Sid Cain, your father-in-law, very well may have died even if he wasn't shot, because you denied him his medication for such a prolonged period of time?"

Mary Beth had discussed this very question with the county coroner, Bashid Patel, extensively. The cantankerous, chain-smoking man, who worked with impressive flourishes of profanity as much as he did dead bodies, had accurately answered that question by saying, "How the fuck should I know? You see any goddamned crystal balls in here?"

To paraphrase, Mary Beth responded, "My understanding is that it's impossible to know. Is it possible he would have died anyway if he wan't shot? Yes. It's possible. Just as all things are possible. But most likely it was the gunshots that killed him. We'll never know what would have happened otherwise."

"Were you going to give him those pills?" Pomfried asked.

"Of course," Mary Beth said. "I just needed a moment to calm down, but my plan was to take my mother out of there and then send Izzy back in with the pills and a glass of water so I didn't have to look at Sid again."

"Awfully convenient to claim that now."

"I don't find any of this very convenient," Mary Beth said, gesturing to her position on the witness stand.

"Oh no? I think the whole situation was extremely convenient. When Sid Cain died, he was in your custody, correct?"

"Yes."

Pomfried clicked his pen one more time and looked up. "Your gun was the murder weapon. You would agree with that, wouldn't you, *Miss* Cain?"

Mary Beth had already said as much. "It was my gun," she agreed.

"Your gun that you keep concealed around your ankle?"

Mary Beth wanted to quibble as to whether or not the ankle gun was really concealed but didn't think it would go over well.

"Yes," she said.

"Your gun that procedure dictates you should have locked away before entering the interrogation room, right?"

"That was an oversight, Mr. Pomfried. I was focused on making sure Sid Cain surrendered his weapon before we tried to arrest him. Once he did, my mind shifted to the task at hand."

"We'll have to agree to disagree on that point, *Miss* Cain. I think you kept it in case you might decide to use it. But putting that aside, you'd agree that you violated policy by taking that gun into the interrogation room, right?"

"Yes."

"And this occurred as you were preparing to interrogate two people, at least one of whom you believed may have been responsible for your husband's murder, right?"

"Yes."

"In an interrogation you conducted without any other officers present?"

"Given the family nature of the issues involved, I thought I was more likely to obtain information if the other officers left the room."

"You also asked them to turn off the recording devices, right?"

"Again, because I thought—"

"Yes or no, *Miss* Cain?"

"Yes."

"And your testimony is that it was a complete oversight that you smuggled a gun into this interrogation?"

"I didn't smuggle it. I just forgot it was there."

"*Right.* You're telling the jury that is the God's honest truth?"

"Yes. That is the truth."

"And during the course of this interrogation, you discovered that the man sitting across from you was responsible for Brad Mayhew's death correct?"

"He bore some responsibility, yes."

"He was responsible for Father Gonzalez, the man you swore to protect, being tortured to death, correct?"

"Yes."

"You found out he was the one who had your family friend Maria Ruiz killed?"

"Yes."

"You found out Sid Cain, or at least his family, played a role not only in the death of your husband but also the raid that resulted in the death of your very own father?"

"It's a lot, I know."

"Meanwhile, your mother was handcuffed, right?"

"Yes."

"An old woman who's dying of cancer, right?"

"I didn't know about her diagnosis at the time. She didn't tell me about the cancer until later."

"Another *convenient* fact. Regardless of whether or not that's true, she was taking cancer treatments at the time of this back-room interrogation, correct?"

"I know that now. I did not know that at the time."

That was true. Mary Beth knew her mother wore a wig but assumed that was just the result of age and vanity. She also knew Mamie had seemed doped up and "off" the last couple of times she saw her but thought it was from partying with G Money. But now that Mamie was in custody and receiving her medical treatment through the state, Mary Beth knew that her mother had stage four liver cancer.

"You expect this jury to believe that this sick old woman overpowered you, head-bustin' sheriff Mary Beth Cain, and is the one who killed Sid Cain?"

"It's what happened. Others saw it. Izzy. Goforth. She was still holding the gun when they came into the room. They saw her shoot."

"I've seen their statements. Ben Goforth, who was begging you for an immunity deal and to keep his retirement money, and Isaiah Baker, who's been your BFF and partner in crime since high school, right?"

Mary Beth was honestly shocked. She thought Pomfried's case would be based on the argument that Sid's heart condition killed him before the bullets could. She didn't think that could hold up and thought she might be able to head it off at this early investigatory stage and avoid an indictment. That was why she chose to testify in front of the grand jury. But this was a whole different angle. Pomfried thought Mary Beth was actually the shooter.

"My mother confessed," she said, indignantly.

"Oh sure, she did. She's dying anyway. What does she care?"

Mary Beth actually snorted, finding comical the idea that her sociopathic mother would take the rap for her.

"Mr. Pomfried, if you are suggesting that my mother is covering for me—"

"Why would she need to shoot him?" Pomfried asked. "Even if she could overpower you in her weakened condition, why would she need to shoot Sid Cain? You're the one with the weapon. You're the one with the motive."

"She had a motive, too. She held him responsible for my father's death."

"Maybe," Pomfried said. "But why did she need to be the one to do it? You were already taking care of getting your family's revenge by denying Sid Cain his medicine."

"I was going to give him his damn medicine," Mary Beth insisted. "I just wanted Sid to think maybe I wouldn't. To play it out a little longer."

"Your mother didn't know that?"

"Sure she did. She knows I'm not a killer."

But Mary Beth was unconvinced by her own statement. She didn't honestly know what she would have done if her mother hadn't intervened. Mary Beth was so shaken and enraged, she certainly wasn't thinking clearly. She told Pomfried she would likely have sent Izzy back in with the pills and some water. And maybe she would have once she calmed down and didn't have to look Sid in the face. She liked to think so. But the real, whole, honest-to-God-truth was, at the moment Mamie took her gun and ended it, Mary Beth didn't really know what she was going to do.

"Why, Ms. Cain?" Pomfired asked. "Why would your mother take it upon herself to overpower you and kill a man who was in custody, near death, who'd just admitted to charges that would put him away for the rest of his life?"

Mary Beth paused longer than she should have before responding, but it was a question she still wrestled with herself.

"Well, Ms. Cain?"

Mary Beth reached up to her forehead, wanting out of habit to adjust her hat the way she did when she was contemplating. Only she wasn't wearing her floppy-brimmed Stetson in court. She'd left it with Izzy when she accepted suspension and turned in her badge and gun.

"Answer the question, please."

Mary Beth couldn't stall any longer. She shared with him and the jury the only conclusion she'd been able to reach.

"Mr. Pomfried," she said, "The only thing I've been able to figure, is that Mamie took it upon herself to kill Sid Cain, in order to protect me from myself."

AFTER MARY BETH'S grand jury testimony finally concluded she went by the hospital to visit her mother, still not knowing whether or not she was about to be indicted. It was late August, four months since everything with Velino had gone down, and the temperatures were climbing into the nineties which was unusually hot for such a high elevation town. Thankfully the hospital had excellent air conditioning that was more or less contained by the rotating door entry. Mary Beth made her way through the ground floor, around an el-bend into the cancer ward where she'd visited frequently enough that the charge nurse recognized her on sight and buzzed her through the electronically locked double doors without asking any questions. Mary Beth knocked lightly on the door to her mother's room as she entered. Inside was Mamie, lying in the hospital bed, looking like a decaying corpse of her former self without the benefit of wig and makeup and designer clothes.

She'd grown weak enough that they no longer bothered to cuff her wrist to the bed, but Mary Beth still kept a deputy on duty. Thus, Skipwith was there in the corner, playing cards with G Money. Both men nodded hello.

Mamie's crew were all in jail or prison, either having pled guilty or still awaiting trial, and most of her other employees and hangers-on had abandoned her since she'd been forced to sell the big house in Kentucky. G-Money had stuck by her side, though. Mary Beth suspected he was still hoping for an inheritance when Mamie finally kicked. And maybe that did factor in, but she couldn't deny that G had been awfully sweet and dutiful, tending to Mamie during whatever time she had left.

Mary Beth said her greetings and was about to ask what game the guys were playing when G Money snatched a card off the discard pile and said, "Ha. Rummy, motherfucker."

"Damn," Skipwith said. "I should have seen that."

Mary Beth looked down at Mamie, who looked doped up and only half awake. She squeezed her mother's shoulder. "How you doing, Mom?"

Mamie looked up, recognized her daughter, and smiled. "I'm dying, dear."

Mary Beth sat at the edge of the bed. "Aren't we all."

"Yes," Mamie said. "But the doctors are telling me it could be any time now. No point in trying to treat it anymore. They're just focused on keeping me comfortable."

Mary Beth sniffed, determined to keep a stiff upper lip. "I'm sorry to hear that," she said.

"I told them not to count me out, though. I'm too mean for any old tumors to get me."

Mary Beth smiled. She reached her hand out, and Mamie took it. Her mother's hand felt bony and weak, yet warm.

"How's Sam?" Mamie asked.

Mary Beth was afraid that might come up. "Sam's grandmother killed his grandfather. He's a little freaked out. By that, and a whole lot of things. He's had quite a lot laid on him these last few months."

"I'd love for him to come see me."

"I know, Mom. He's just not ready for that yet."

"You could make him. He'd come if you told him to."

Mary Beth shook her head. "I'm done telling Sam what to do. He's grown up now. Gets to make his own decisions."

Mamie obviously didn't like that answer but didn't argue the point. "Is he still planning on leaving?"

"Yeah," Mary Beth said. "He's all packed up. Patrick and I are taking him up to DC tomorrow. We'll stay the weekend and make sure he's settled in at Georgetown before we head back."

Mamie held up Mary Beth's hand and studied it. "Why, Mary Elizabeth, if I didn't know better, I'd say that's an engagement ring on your finger."

Mary Beth smiled. "Yeah. Now that we've told Sam the truth about me and Patrick, and Bill, it felt like it was time."

Mamie smiled. "Well, congratulations. You two have certainly taken your time finding your way back to each other. I hope you'll be very happy."

Mary Beth patted Mamie's hand. "Thanks, Mom. Right now, I'm just waiting to find out whether it will be a prison wedding. Grand jury is deliberating as we speak."

Mamie scoffed and started coughing. When she finally cleared the dry-sounding-mucus, she said, "I can't believe they're bothering you with that nonsense."

Some beeps from the monitoring equipment alerted them to the fact that Mamie's blood pressure was rising and her O2 sats were a little low.

G Money left his card game to come to look at the monitor above Mamie's bed.

"This may be too much excitement for Maimes right now," he said. " I think she needs her rest."

Mary Beth nodded appreciatively. "Okay, I'll go. There's just something I need to ask you real quick though, first."

Mamie looked up at G as though asking for permission. When he nodded his consent., she said, "Go ahead, dear."

Mary Beth fumbled with ways of broaching the subject. It seemed like something they should have discussed before then, and now that they hadn't, it felt awkward to bring it up. Ultimately, Mary Beth decided to just spit it out.

"Why did you do it, Mom?"

Before Mamie could ask what, Mary Beth explained. "With Sid, I mean. Pomfried thinks you're covering for me. Taking the fall by lying and saying you were the shooter."

"Oh well, you and I both know that's nonsense." Mamie had to pause to let loose another phlegm-filled cough.

"You know what I told him?" Mary Beth said.

"What's that?"

"I told him you were protecting me. I know you had plenty of reasons to want Sid dead. But I was close to taking care of that myself. I think the reason you shot him was so the responsibility would fall on you instead of me."

Mamie smiled and started to speak before launching into another coughing fit. G Money had her sit up to take a sip of water. When she was finally able to speak again, she spoke the refrain that had so often grated Mary Beth's nerves, but this time she repeated it along with her.

"I have *always* supported my family."

There was a lot Mary Beth could say about that, but she no longer saw the point. It was probably more or less true in Mamie's mind. and, at least in that one instant, had rung true to Mary Beth as well. She kissed her mom on the forehead and said, "I'll see you on Monday."

Mamie and Skipwith waved their goodbyes. G Money offered Mary Beth a fist bump and she obliged.

"Take care of our girl," she said.

"Will do, sheriff."

"It's not sheriff anymore," she told him. "You can just call me Mary."

• • •

Izzy's wife, Princess, was a minor celebrity around town. A former runway model who stood a foot taller than her husband, Princess was naturally a head turner but garnered even more attention due to her status as a local news reporter. She'd been doing her best to cover the grand jury's secretive investigation into Mary Beth and was the first to get the scoop on their decision. Putting her professional interests aside, when she left the courthouse, she went straight to the station and told Izzy.

"Oh, my God," Izzy said. "I've got to find Mary Beth."

Princess rolled her eyes. She and Mary Beth had never cared much for each other. Both were jealous over how much of Izzy's attention the other received.

"You better hurry," Princess said. "I'm about to go on air. This is big enough to break into daytime TV."

Izzy didn't want Mary Beth finding out that way. This was news that needed to be delivered in person. He knew that she and Patrick were taking Sam by the cemetery that afternoon to give him a chance to pay his respects to Bill before leaving for school. If he hurried, he could probably still catch them there.

"Can you hold the story for me, baby? Just for a little bit?"

Princess looked down at her watch and sighed.

"I'll give you thirty minutes."

That wasn't much time, but Izzy knew not to push his luck by asking for more. He scrambled to gather his things, then started to leave before realizing he hadn't even said goodbye to his wife. He went back to her and stood on his tiptoes to kiss her. "Thank you, baby. You're the best."

"Mmm-hmm," she said, unimpressed, but stooped down enough for her husband to kiss her.

After that, Izzy dashed out into the parking lot, climbed the rope ladder into his big Blazer, and went roaring down the city streets and out onto Highway 19, down to Briar Bush Cemetery. He saw Patrick's BMW in the parking lot and breathed a sigh of relief that he'd caught them in time. The deputy climbed back down the rope ladder and headed up the hill, on a paved path lined with oak trees. He found his friends about halfway up the hillside. They were on their way down, and Sam looked like he'd been crying. He was hugging his mother. Patrick was the first to notice Izzy and waved. Izzy approached quietly, realizing he was interrupting a solemn moment. He heard Sam tell his mother, "I just don't feel like I even know who he was anymore."

Mary Beth said, "All of us are all different kinds of things, Sammy. You know who he was to you. That's all that matters."

Sam was nodding as Mary Beth caught sight of Izzy too. "Well, look who's creeping up on us," she said.

"I came with good news," Izzy told her. He was holding Mary Beth's beloved floppy-brimmed Stetson with its wine-colored band and little sheriff's star behind his back, ready to present it to her as a prize of redemption. "Dismissed," he said, beaming. "Jury declined to indict."

Patrick clapped his hands. "Yes! See, I told you it was a good idea to testify."

"Bullshit," Mary Beth said, rolling her eyes. "You did your best to talk me out of it."

Sam hugged his mother again. "That's great, Mom. Congratulations."

"Sooooooo," Izzy said. "I think you'll be needing this."

He revealed the gift he'd been hiding and handed the hat over to Mary Beth. She smiled and held it in her hands at her waist, looking down at it but making no move to put it on.

"Hey, guys," she said to Patrick and Sam, "why don't you all go on to the car and give me and Izzy a minute to talk."

Izzy couldn't understand why she wasn't more excited. "What's the deal?" he asked as soon as they were alone.

Mary Beth put her hand on his shoulder. "I'm not coming back, Iz."

He was waiting for her to crack a smile and tell him she was just kidding, but her face didn't change. She seemed both determined and oddly peaceful, which was unnerving coming from Mary Beth.

"What are you talking about? Of course you are."

"No," Mary Beth said. "Too much has happened. It just wouldn't be right."

Izzy couldn't believe this. It had killed her to go on leave. He knew it had. When she first left Izzy in charge of the office, she couldn't wait to clear her name and get back to work. Now she was quitting?

"But it's all over," he argued. "You're in the clear—innocent."

"You and I both know I'm not innocent," Mary Beth said. "I didn't murder Sid Cain, but I'm far from innocent."

This was not the Mary Beth Izzy knew. She saw shades of gray where others couldn't and had never, ever accepted defeat before.

"Come on now, MB. I mean you and I, we've had our disagreements over the years, and I know you've bent the rules a time or two."

"I've done more than bend them, Izzy. And people have been hurt because of the things I've done."

Izzy knew she was talking about Father Gonzalez, and Sam, and even Izzy himself. "Yeah," he said, "but how many people have been saved? I mean, this is a tough job. You've done what you had to do. Who else could have dealt with Velino and the McCray County Mafia like you did? Who else could have kept the feds from slaughtering everybody up at Old Wengo, kids and all?"

Mary Beth smiled. "I'd like to think that I did some good there. Maybe I was the right person at the right time for some of that stuff. But that time's over, Iz. Sawyer's dead, Velino's dead, my mother doesn't have much time left. Hell, Pomfried's a prosecutor now. Times have changed."

Izzy felt an enormous sense of dread over the idea of Mary Beth quitting. "There will be people to take their place," he argued. "New bad guys. New challenges. New—"

Mary Beth put a slender finger to his lips to silence him. "It's okay," she said. "It's not all up to me, remember?"

It felt to Izzy like a jab. "I didn't mean it like that. I was just—"

"Right," Mary Beth said. "You were just right, Izzy. You were right about everything. In fact, I think the county will actually be a lot better off in your hands."

Izzy was still waiting for the punchline. He felt sick thinking about what could happen to Jasper County without Mary Beth around to protect it.

"Hey, buck up," Mary Beth said. She placed her hat on Izzy's head, pushing it down to the point it almost covered his eyes. "There's a new sheriff in town."

Never in their multi-decade relationship had Mary Beth given Izzy such a vote of confidence. "You're really serious?" he asked.

Mary Beth didn;t have to say Yes. Instead she bent over and hugged Izzy. "Thank you for always being there," she whispered and kissed him on the cheek.

Izzy was stunned and sad. It felt like someone had died. Like he was losing Mary Beth forever as she took a step back and saluted him before walking away to rejoin her men.

Patrick and Sam were waiting for her about twenty yards down the cement path, below where a beam of late-afternoon sun filtered through the canopy of leaves.

"I'm going to be calling you for advice all the time," Izzy shouted after her.

Mary Beth waved and shouted back, "Anytime."

Izzy watched as she turned and linked arms with her family. Sam on one side, Patrick on the other. Then, like the cowboy Izzy had so often accused her of being, Mary Beth walked off into the sunset.

ACKNOWLEDGMENTS

I'd like to thank my writer friends who helped me workshop this book: Scott Blackburn, Steve Daugherty, Bill Floyd, Grant Hetherton, Philip Kimbrough, John Rasinske, and Casey Stegman. Also, a special thanks to those who blurbed the book and to my agent, Mark Falkin. Finally, thank you to Ron Earl Phillips and Shotgun Honey for providing the perfect home for this series.

RUSSELL W. JOHNSON is an attorney who got so sick of billable hours he started writing crime fiction. His first story was published in *Ellery Queen Mystery Magazine* and won the Edgar Awards' Robert L. Fish prize in 2015. Since then, he's had stories published in a number of outlets and recently won the West Virginia Writers Association's Pearl S. Buck Award as well as First Place for Book Length Fiction. More information on his writing is available at www.russellwjohnson.com.

ABOUT
SHOTGUN HONEY

Thank you for reading *The Miner's Myth* by Russell W. Johnson.

Shotgun Honey began as a crime genre flash fiction webzine in 2011 created as a venue for new and established writers to experiment in the confines of a mere 700 words. More than a decade later, Shotgun Honey still challenges writers with that storytelling task, but also provides opportunities to expand beyond through our book imprint and has since published anthologies, collections, novellas and novels by new and emerging authors.

We hope you have enjoyed this book. That you will share your experience, review and rate this title positively on your favorite book review sites and with your social media family and friends.

Visit ShotgunHoneyBooks.com

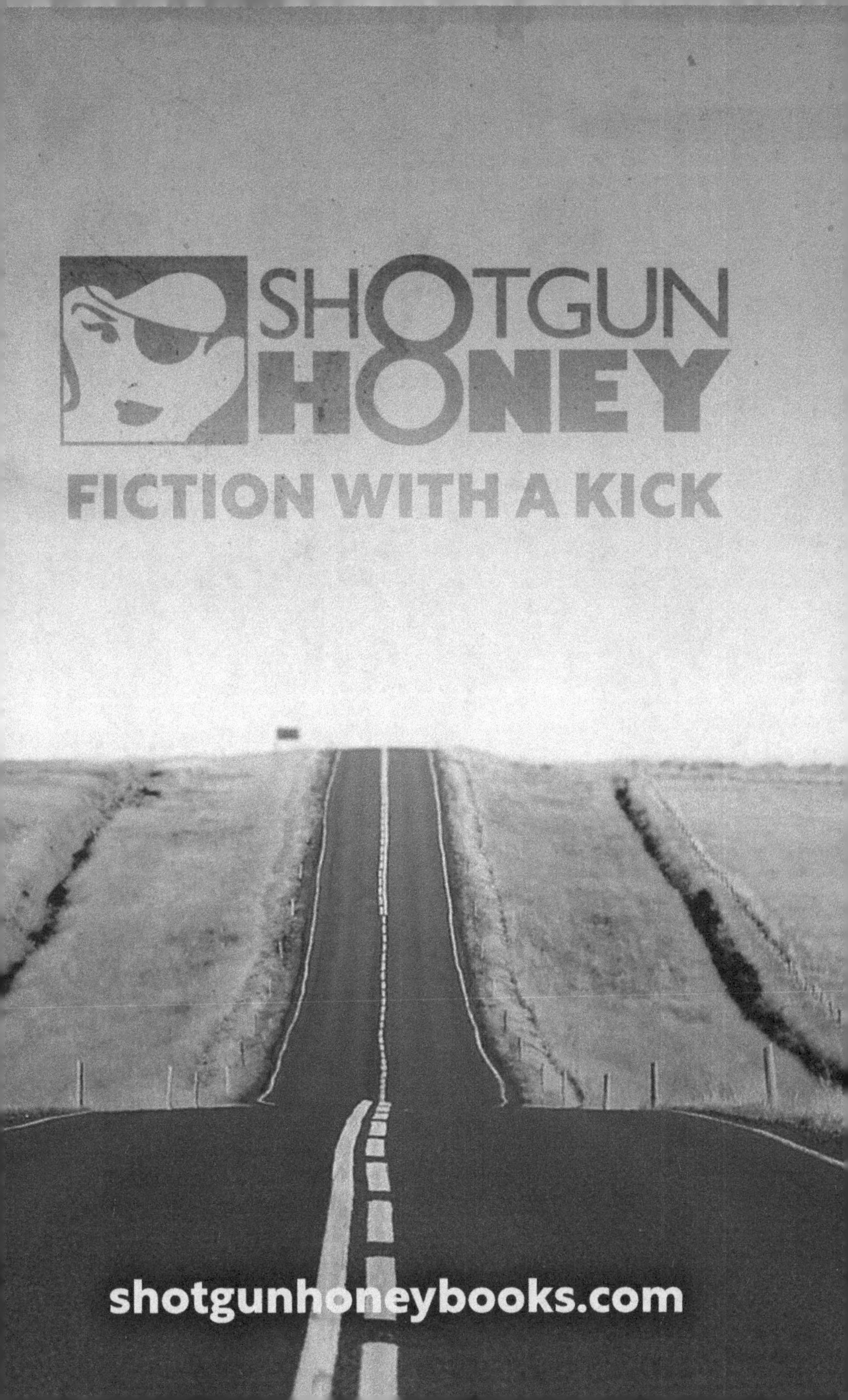
SHOTGUN HONEY
FICTION WITH A KICK
shotgunhoneybooks.com

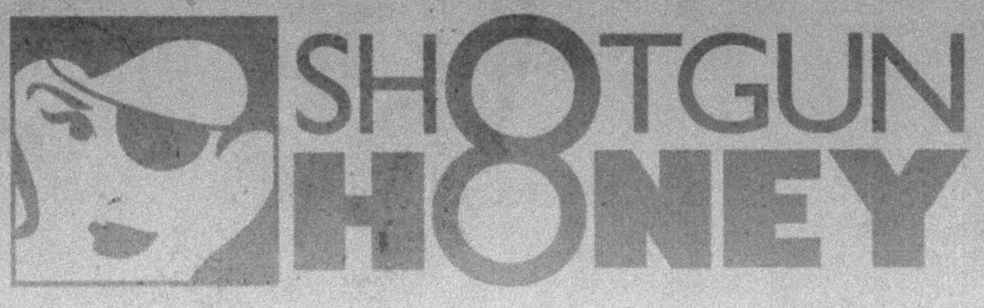

9 781956 957846